The Road to Mercy

Melissa McGovern Taylor

www.melissamcgoverntaylor.com

To my husband, Jerry.

Prologue

Lillian Denwood sighed in frustration. She stood in her solid red kitchen paneled with apple-dotted border that in no way matched her mood. The whole room was themed around Lillian's affection for apples, a fancy that befitted a fourth grade teacher. A dark, cold cave would've been a more suitable setting in a moment such as this.

Pensively staring at the bulky answering machine, Lillian watched the flashing red button. She was no stranger to this feeling. The anxiety had haunted her for not only most of the year but most of her marriage. She closed her eyes and punched the button.

"Raymond, where are you? Your shift started an hour ago. Call me when you get this." Her fears were realized once again. The unhappy, aging voice belonged to her husband's boss and the owner of the Aldridge General Store, Frank Aldridge.

Lillian plopped down at the table, taking a moment to massage her temples. Her fingers passed over the worry lines that crawled across her brow. The struggles of a twenty-year marriage to an alcoholic had taken their toll on her.

He was at the bar again. There was no doubt in her mind. Since the welding company layoff, that dingy joint had become a second home.

The familiar sounds of the front door opening and footsteps padding across the hardwood floor parted Lillian's thoughts like the Red Sea.

"Where's Dad?" She looked up to meet eyes with the thirteen-year-old spitting image of herself. Her daughter, Karen, stooped before her under the weight of an overloaded purple backpack. She pulled at a stray lock of blonde hair, curling it around her forefinger. Lillian remembered fighting the same sign of anxiety in her younger years. Much to her displeasure, she had caught Karen pulling at her hair more and more lately.

"He's out at the bar again," Lillian said.

"He left a note?"

Lillian could see a spark of hope in her daughter's eyes. She had to fight the urge to scoop Karen up in her arms. Her constant faith in Daddy seemed to be the only reason Ray ever tried to get on the wagon. Still, Lillian didn't need to answer the question because Karen knew the answer.

She sighed like her mother had only a minute before. "I guess it's just you and me again tonight."

Memories of nights without Ray filled Lillian with sorrow. When her husband was at home with them, a sense of completeness settled in the house. Karen never failed to express how much she missed quiet evenings with both of her parents. Clearly, Ray and Karen's relationship suffered just as much as Lillian's marriage. His weakness for beer had erected a wall between him and the sober world. Oddly enough, in the midst of his struggle, Lillian and Karen drew closer.

Lillian looked up at her daughter in a desperate attempt to offer some reassurance. In the process, she noticed a sheet of paper in Karen's hand.

"What's that?"

Karen looked down at the paper and shrugged. "It's nothing."

Her mother cocked her head, unconvinced. Karen didn't get bad grades or even the smallest complaints from her teachers.

Suspicion overwhelmed Lillian, and she reached for the paper. Karen gripped it tightly, finally speaking up.

"I won first place." She said this as if she were reporting the weather.

Lillian gasped. The annual school art competition was Karen's Super Bowl or Olympics.

"I knew you would win!" She rose from the table and embraced her daughter with all of her strength, perhaps too tightly. "I'm so proud of you, Karen."

Karen beamed, surrendering the first place certificate. "They're going to frame my painting and hang it in the school library."

She recalled her daughter's detailed picture of a moon over rolling hills of forest. "God gave you a special gift."

Karen shifted her glance to the kitchen floor, her smile fading. "I wish Dad was here."

She gently placed the certificate on the table. "I'm going to get him."

"I'll go with you."

Lillian shook her head. "I don't want you anywhere near that awful bar. Go over to Aunt Val's and do your homework."

Guilt burdened Lillian over the fact that Karen had spent more and more time at her aunt's house. But she couldn't allow her to see her father drunk. It was no image for a young girl to have of the man she looked up to. Lillian thanked God everyday that this was the only thing she needed to shelter her daughter from. Ray was not a violent man, not even when intoxicated. After several beers, he only became more depressed and nearly incomprehensible.

"Mom, don't be too hard on him. He was three weeks clean. We can get him back on track."

Lillian nodded, but she honestly felt like giving up. "I know, Karen, but sometimes I lose patience with him."

She led her daughter out of the house and under a foreboding sky. The warm, August air threatened a powerful storm with groans of thunder.

"Be a good girl." Lillian kissed Karen on the forehead without much thought in doing so.

3

"Mom, I'm a teenager now," she said, her cheeks growing rosy.

Lillian rolled her eyes. "I'm so sorry, *Ms. Denwood*."

Her daughter hurried across the yard. "I love you, Mom."

Her words caught Lillian off guard, and she almost forgot to respond.

"I love you too," she finally called back as a fat raindrop soaked her scalp.

Hopping into her blue Toyota, she couldn't shake an overwhelming feeling of dread permeating the air around her.

"Father, please give me strength," she said in a whisper, cutting on the engine. More prayers built up in her heart and poured from her lips. Tears burned her eyes as she said the last one. "Please do what you need to do to help my husband recognize Your gift of salvation."

Memories swirled through her mind as she followed Main Street out of the tiny town of Mercy, North Carolina. This place had been her home since childhood. On any given day, Mercy looked like a little slice of Eden, residents bustling along the short streets with smiling faces. On this day, it stood empty, the handful of residents already home with their families.

Envy stung Lillian at the thought. This wasn't the way things were supposed to be. Her family was supposed to be at home, preparing a meal together and talking about the ups and downs of the day. It wasn't fair. She had become a Christian; Karen had become a Christian. Why did Ray resist? She firmly believed Jesus could free him from the alcoholism and heal their family. What was holding him back?

About ten miles outside of Mercy, Lillian pulled the car up to the door of Wiley's Bar, parking beside her husband's red Chevy truck. She stared at the building's old stucco exterior and tacky neon green sign. Much to her relief, Mercy had no bars, and the only grocer in town, the Aldridge General Store, carried nothing more potent than a small variety of wines.

Taking in a deep breath, Lillian mustered up the strength to push open the car door. She jogged clumsily in her pumps on the gravel lot. As she pushed through the bar door, a fog of stale cigarette smoke hit her nostrils, a shock compared to the clean, wet air outside. Old beer advertisements and more neon signs covered the walls of the dimly lit bar. The large room contained two grimy pool tables that took up much of the space. A wide mirror lined the wall behind the long counter, reflecting images of bottles of alcoholic cocktails.

As soon as Lillian's vision adjusted to the smoke, she met eyes with the bartender. He nodded with a grim expression, his thick, grey mustache twitching.

"I've been trying to keep him at bay here, Mrs. Denwood," he said in his hoarse voice, directing her attention to several hooks on the wall behind him. Her husband's keys dangled from a rusty hook in the middle.

She nodded at the bartender. "Thanks."

Surrounded by peanut shells and several empty beer bottles, Ray stared at his reflection in the bar mirror. His heavy eyes were as unfocused as a dead man's gaze. His normally well-groomed appearance was wrecked with self-pity and disorder, his brown hair untamed and clothes wrinkled and dirty. He was the only customer at five o'clock on a Tuesday. The tall, broad-shouldered man never looked smaller and weaker to her than he did in that moment.

"Ray?" she said.

Her voice snapped the life back into him. He met eyes with her reflection before him.

"I'm not going back to that job, Lilly," he said.

She approached the bar. "We'll talk about it later."

Working at the Aldridge General Store wasn't the worst job in town, but Lillian understood why her husband hated it. It was discouraging for a professional welder to find himself making minimum wage stocking groceries. He had worked his way up as one of the highest paid welders locally at a company outside of Mercy. But when the company went bankrupt and had closed two months earlier, Ray was left with nothing but a small severance package. Unemployment was disastrous for him, dragging him like a vicious tide into depression. Depression then led him to drinking.

Lillian took her husband gently by the arm. "Let's go home, honey."

"What home? We'll be foreclosed on any day now. Then there won't be a home to go to."

"Ray, I need you. Karen needs you. Let's go." She pulled his arm now with more force, clutching his bicep.

"Karen, my little girl." His eyes burned with tears. "I'm so pathetic."

"It's okay, honey. She's with Valerie. She won't see you," Lillian said as he stood up on wobbly legs.

He straightened up. "I'm okay. I can walk."

Lillian released him from her grasp and followed his uneven path to the door.

Outside, the rain fell harder now, pounding on the gravel into scattered, little puddles. The fresh air seemed to snap Ray into yet another mood.

"Give me the keys," he said, turning back to her.

Lillian clutched the key set behind her back. "You're not driving, Raymond."

Raindrops drenched her blouse. It clung to her form in lukewarm bunches. Her blonde hair now felt like a hood around her head and face. The thunder echoed through the pines as lightning lit up the sky.

"Give me the keys!" he yelled through gritted teeth. His green eyes flashed an amount of frustration she rarely saw in them.

Lillian could smell the alcohol floating heavily on his breath. She longed to be somewhere else with the Raymond Denwood she loved. He was so gentle and calm as a sober man. It was his charm and wit that captured her heart those years ago. She remembered how he used to make her laugh, tickling her at unexpected moments. They shared a goofy sense of humor— even during the serious struggle with his drinking. The carefree times felt so far away now. She missed those times. She missed her husband.

Lillian shook her head. "You're too drunk! Get in the car!"

Raymond's face tightened, and he thrust an open hand out at Lillian's shoulder. The shove was painless in itself, but it was enough to throw his wife off balance. She lost her grip on the keys, trying to catch herself as she fell back on the wet gravel. Ray snatched the keys from the ground and made his way to the driver's door, stumbling a little.

Shaken, Lillian could only stare at Ray in shock. He had never turned on her like that before. She pushed herself up on stinging hands. As she rose, her muddy palms stung.

She hurried after him. "Ray, you'll get us both killed!"

It was too late. Her husband was behind the wheel and closing the car door.

"Open the door!" Her voice grew shrill as she desperately yanked at the handle. It was locked.

"Come on, Lilly. You're soaked. Get in the car." His voice muffled as he started the engine.

Lillian felt weary from fighting with him, weary from her fall. *It's only a few miles,* she thought. *I'll grab the wheel if he starts to veer.*

She hurried around the car and hopped into the passenger seat.

Raymond threw it into Reverse and backed out before she could even get the door closed.

"Hold on, Ray!" She pulled the door shut and grabbed for her seatbelt. The belt slipped across her torso with unexpected ease.

He ignored her pleas and pulled on to the highway to head for Mercy.

She couldn't grip the seatbelt tightly enough. "Slow down!"

Rain drummed on the windshield, making the road a gray blur. Lillian reached over and switched on the windshield wipers. The back of an eighteen wheeler came into view, and Raymond slammed on the brakes. Lillian gasped. The huge truck turned off of the road, clearing their path. Ray pulled his foot from the brake and resumed a steady pace.

"You're starting A.A. again tomorrow," she said between heavy breaths. "I've had enough of this."

Raymond said nothing.

She waited for him to accuse her of spending too much time at work and neglecting their family, as always. When he was drunk, everything was her fault. Then everything was his fault. The blame changed with his mood, flipping back and forth like the windshield wipers.

Suddenly, two lights ahead of them broke through the rain and through Lillian's bitter thoughts.

7

She dived for the wheel. "Ray, look out!"
The light grew brighter and brighter.

Chapter One

Karen sat in front of Principal Howard's desk beside her temporarily sober father. Her eyes remained fixed on the plastic pencil cup on the finely polished oak desk as she pretended to ignore the principal and her father's exchange.

The principal leaned forward in her high-back chair. "I understand the circumstances your family is facing at this time, Mr. Denwood." She looked more the part of a grandmother than the head of a middle school. "But I can't ignore Karen's truancy, her lower grades, or the fact that her attention is wavering in classes."

Her father shifted uncomfortably in his seat. "We'll have a long talk about this when we get home."

"I feel compelled to let Karen slide. I've contacted Pastor Bell, and he's agreed to meet with Karen for counseling."

"That won't be necessary." He cleared his throat. "I can handle this."

Mrs. Howard frowned. "With all due respect, Mr. Denwood, it's been three months now since your wife passed away. Your daughter is crying out for help."

Karen continued to examine the items on the desk, successfully avoiding the principal's glances.

"Karen, would you be willing to meet with Pastor Bell?"

With a sigh, Karen finally met eyes with Principal Howard. "I guess so."

Karen's father rose from his seat. "We're done here."

The principal narrowed her eyes at him as she stood up. "I don't think we are."

"I can take care of my family. I don't need you or Pastor Bell to do it for me."

Karen met eyes with her father. His brown hair was disheveled, green eyes heavy with weariness and dripping shadows. His face was bearded now, making him look ten years older. He was pale and thinner, a ghost of himself.

Karen rose from the chair and followed her father out of the office but not before looking at Mrs. Howard. The concern on her face made the weight of Karen's backpack heavier. She knew Jesus could carry her burdens, but what about her father's? When would he stop giving in to the bottle and start being her hero again?

The two-lane road back to Mercy from Kipling Middle School was the stretch of highway on which her mother took her last breath on, a path lined with pine trees guarded by draping power lines. They held back the trees like police tape at a crime scene. Between lengths of woods along the way, Karen's eyes met barren rows that once occupied ripe tobacco plants stretching for acres. She soon saw the small, unmemorable sign that read *Mercy* in white capital letters. Just a few yards after it, her father carefully pulled left onto Mercy Road and followed it into the sleepy town.

They rode past the businesses on Main Street. Her father showed little interest in the locals who waved as they passed. The townspeople had been more caring than usual since her mother's funeral. Their tenderness had given Karen reason to hope for better times. Perhaps someday, when she made a home of her own in Mercy, she would be able to return such kindness.

After passing Mercy Church, Karen's father pulled the truck onto Blooming Avenue, one of only two neighborhood streets. If they had followed Main Street any further, they would have passed Mercy Pond and then met an obscure state route. On Blooming Avenue, however, oak trees, pines, and weeping willows continued to thrive. The trees formed a canopy over the road, bowing away from charming, old Victorian and Cape Cod style homes. Some were single-story, others were two or three, but all were well-maintained. The third house on the left, a blue Cape Cod, was the one the Denwoods called home.

Karen followed her father inside of the unusually dark and quiet house in heavy silence. She missed the echo of her mother's laughter across the living room and the sound of her digging through pots and pans in the kitchen. After only a few months, Lillian Denwood's gentle scent of cucumber body wash and Wind Song perfume disappeared, leaving behind the unpleasant smell of empty beer cans and dust. Although it sheltered two people, the house didn't feel like a home any longer.

Karen wanted the silence to end in that still house. She ached for her father to say something, anything, but he didn't. Although it didn't surprise her, it hurt just the same. She missed their conversations, even his lectures. Silence had dominated their relationship since her mother's passing, leaving her alone with her thoughts, worries, and desperate prayers.

Not long after the funeral, Karen could no longer allow the rage to fester. His drinking had only worsened, and she couldn't take it anymore. After trying to encourage her father and hold together what remained of their family, she finally snapped. One night she had screamed out every awful thought that had crossed her mind since the accident. It was his fault. How could he be so selfish? How could he let his alcohol abuse kill her mother? And why did he keep drinking? Did he not care? His response was a quick retreat to Wiley's Bar.

Her angry accusations only pushed her father further away and deeper into his habit. Almost every evening, he would go to the bar and not return until the dark hours of the morning. By dawn, Karen had to beg him to get up for work. It was only through the efforts of family and friends that they managed to stay afloat financially. Every night Karen feared she would awake as an orphan. All she could do was lie in bed and pray until she fell asleep.

Karen watched her father set his work keys on the coffee table. "Are you going out?"

He finally shared her gaze but only for a second before lowering his eyes to the floor. "Yeah."

"What about that talk?"

"There's nothing to talk about."

"You said you would handle it!" She hardly meant to be so loud or passionate, but all she wanted was an evening with him, a conversation, even simply his presence in the house—anything.

Her father shook his head and left the room. Karen knew he was going to change out of his work clothes, his usual routine. She dropped on the couch heavily, still wearing her coat and backpack, and awaited his return to the living room.

He headed for the door without looking at her. "I'll be back tonight."

She looked away as he walked out of the house. He closed the door, and she heard the engine to his Chevy roar to life. As the sound of the truck faded away, her blue eyes filled with tears. She drew her knees up to her chest and started to cry all over her blue jeans. Heat filled her belly as she thought of her father's drinking. She wiped the tears away. Slipping off her full backpack and letting it fall where it may, she hurried out of the house and into the brisk, November air.

The street grew darker by the minute under a star-speckled, fall sky. Karen walked at a determined pace that gradually built up to a sprint toward Main Street. Her heart seemed ready to burst from her chest. The dry, frigid air stung her face. Her lips felt chapped. Yet, no physical pain or discomfort could compare to her emotional turmoil. No relief was to be found, especially not in Mercy. Everywhere she looked, Karen was reminded of her mother. On Main Street, they used to spend Saturdays frequenting the little shops.

Karen didn't want to remember how they would always head for Main Street first thing in the morning. She didn't want to think about the first stop at Bailey's Coffee Shop and then browsing Aunt Maggie's Book Store together. Over cocoa and muffins, they would talk about Karen's paintings, the boys she liked, and the ones she couldn't stand. Her mother would share giggles with her and give her advice. At the Mercy Variety

Store, they would try on old hats. No matter how many times they had been in the antique shop, Karen always managed to discover something new with her mother. Then it was time to gather the groceries for the week at the Mercy Town Bakery and Deli and the Aldridge General Store. Her father's face would always light up when they entered the general store. She hadn't seen that look on his face in so long.

After what felt like an eternity of running, Karen arrived at Mercy Church on the corner of Blooming and Main. In the fresh light of the moon and the sliver of sunlight left on the horizon, she could make out the cross and steeple towering above her. She climbed the front steps and ran around to the back of the building. In the shadow of the church, she met darkness dotted with gray and white shapes, the only visible remnants of Mercy's dead. She opened the iron gate to the cemetery. It creaked as she expected, comforting her in her routine.

Among the old and fresh headstones, she easily found her mother's. She just had to look for the angel. It was a dominant figure in the cemetery, second only to the statue of the town founder, Henry Abraham Aldridge. The angel stood on a two-foot, marble block, all totaling six feet tall. The entire town had contributed money to purchase the carefully carved piece.

Even in the moonlight, Karen recognized the gentle face that looked so much like her mother's, tender and soft with a dimple in one cheek. The angel held a book in one hand as it gazed ahead. The wings were slightly curled over its shoulders like a cloak. The hair flowed out. Karen bent down and touched the angel's feet as she approached the cold, solid slab of granite.

Her eyes filled with tears again as Karen dropped to her knees, hands clasped together. A cool breeze kicked up locks of her blonde hair and sent dead oak leaves dancing around her feet. They shifted and spun about like so many of her emotions.

"Lord," she said, "please stop Dad from going to the bar. Please let him stay home with me. I need him, God. I don't want to be mad at him anymore. Please make him stop drinking."

She repeated this prayer over and over again as she cried.

A wind whipped across the cemetery, sending her words across the graves and tossing her hair in the air full force this time. She stopped for a moment to look up at the angel with her wet eyes. Suddenly, she heard the familiar creak from the iron gate. A figure she couldn't recognize in the moonlight walked toward her. She jumped to her feet, her heart pounding hard and fast.

An aging voice broke through the night air. "Karen Denwood?"

The old man stopped a few feet from her, and now she could see clearly that it was her father's boss, Frank Aldridge. His tall, thin figure seemed ominous in the moonlight, but relief swept over Karen. Anyone in Mercy willing to give her father a job despite all of his problems was no threat to her.

Mr. Aldridge pushed his thin-rimmed glasses up his nose. "I was stopping in to visit my wife's grave. Are you okay?"

She could see the concern in his gentle, brown eyes. "Yes, just visiting my mom's grave."

"It's after dark. Where's your father?"

"At home," she lied. "He said I could come here whenever I want."

He looked thoughtful for a moment as another breeze passed through the cemetery, disturbing his carefully combed grey hair. "I'm sorry I never got to give my proper condolences to you at the funeral. Your mother was a darling lady."

She dropped her gaze to the ground. "Thank you, sir."

"I don't believe in holding grudges, Karen. It's a shame how the town can't see how guilty your father already feels. That's punishment enough for a man."

Karen said nothing, but it was true. While some locals extended great kindness to the Denwoods, still others snubbed her father for his sins.

He smiled warmly at her. "Karen, things will get better. I know you miss her, but she's with Jesus. There's no better place to be."

Karen nodded in agreement, recalling her mother's deep faith and love of Christ that was so clear in everything she did and said.

"Well, you'd better get on home, little lady. Don't keep your father up worrying about you."

"Yes, sir."

They left the cemetery together without another word. At the street, they parted, and Karen watched the old man walk, slightly stooped, toward his son's home back up Main Street. The Aldridge house was less than a quarter of a mile from the shops.

Karen turned and climbed back up the church steps. Having no desire to return to an empty house, she resumed her place in front of her mother's grave. After another ten minutes of tearful prayer, the chilly air told her it was time to go home.

In only the light of street lamps, Mercy might give a lonely traveler chills, but Karen had no fears. Mercy was the safest town in the state. The last crime committed in the little town happened some eleven years before. A local had left a stalled truck near Highway 401. When he returned the next day to charge the dead battery, the vehicle was gone, stolen during the night. This was the worst crime the little town had seen since its establishment some ninety-two years before.

In the dim light of the moon, the Denwood house came into Karen's view. To her surprise, her father's truck sat on the street in front of the house. Her heart began to thump hard in her chest. He almost never came home early. She hurried through the front door.

Before Karen could even close the door behind her, her father entered the living room with a beer in hand.

He frowned at her. "Where were you?" His voice quaked with each syllable, the result of fear or concern, or perhaps it was only a side effect from the beer. Karen couldn't tell which.

She removed her coat and hung it by the door. "The cemetery."

He sighed and took a seat on the sofa beside a six pack of beer. Their small television was on, showing a sitcom. He guzzled down the beer as he stared at it.

Karen crossed her arms. "Why aren't you at the bar?"

He shrugged. "Just didn't feel like driving that far."

She allowed her arms to fall at her sides. All of her hopes for a night with her sober father were lost.

She stared at the beer can in his hand. Her jaw tightened. Her mother would never allow such filth into their home. Yet, in her absence, it had taken up residence in nearly every room.

"I wish you wouldn't bring that stuff in the house."

Her father turned to her, narrowing his eyes. "I pay the mortgage. I can do whatever I want in this house."

The truth was he didn't pay the mortgage. The church was paying it through contributions from friends, neighbors, and even Aunt Val. Reality didn't matter to him. She could tell by the tone of his voice and slight slur of his words.

"I want you to be my dad again!"

Her father rose from his seat and approached her, dropping his empty beer can on the way. "I'm still your dad! I've always been here!"

Karen stepped back, her heart rate jumping ahead. She feared her words had pushed him too far. Her eyes searched the room until she saw a framed photo on the TV. It was her favorite picture. She reached past him.

Karen grabbed the small picture, forcing him to look at it. "Don't you remember when we were a family? I want to be a family again!"

The cherry wood frame held a picture of Karen and her parents smiling in front of Mercy Pond.

Her father snatched the frame out of her grasp. "We can't be a family without her!" In a quick motion, he slammed the framed photo to the hardwood floor, shattering glass around their feet.

Karen stepped back, struggling to breathe for a moment as she watched the glass settle. Her father was still frozen there with rage in his eyes.

A burning sensation rose in her chest, aching to escape. She couldn't hold it in any longer. "I hate you!"

Karen darted out of the living room, leaving no time to see the reaction on her father's face. She slammed her bedroom door behind her. The sound of her father's heavy footsteps immediately followed.

He fiddled with the locked doorknob. "Open this door!"

Still fully dressed, Karen curled up in her bed under the pink, cotton blanket. She lay there, listening to her father. After a few minutes, she heard him walk away and then return. It sounded as if he were sitting in front of the door. She heard a crack. He was opening another can of beer. Her eyes burning, she pulled the blanket over her head. She didn't want to hear him or speak to him. She vowed to herself never to speak to him again.

She closed her eyes and began praying in a whisper. "Jesus, please help me. I can't do this without you."

An hour later, Karen could hear snoring outside of her bedroom door. She sat up in bed and glanced out her window. She could pack her things and run away. He wouldn't know until morning, maybe not even until the afternoon. He would wake up thinking she went to school.

She wondered where she would go. Aunt Val was her only relative. She had no cousins, and both sets of grandparents had long passed away. She considered hitchhiking to the bus station, but she had only enough money saved for one or two tickets, not enough to survive on.

Karen shook her head as if the action would stir away these selfish thoughts. It couldn't be right to abandon her father in such a state. Yet, he had been given so many chances. Even after his drunkenness had killed her mother, his drinking persisted. Karen suddenly grew bitter. The thought of his words and the broken picture frame made her anger return. She had to escape, let him know somehow that she was serious. She started packing her clothes.

Chapter Two

6:48pm. Frank Aldridge sighed. *Another ten minutes,* he thought, his aging eyes looming over the tedious forms on his desk.

He rubbed his forehead as if to rub away his exhaustion. He hated having to work late, but he loved the quiet atmosphere of his upstairs office. It was perched above his small general store, which carried magazines, snacks, and necessities. His father, grandfather, and great grandfather had worked at this very desk, running the store finances. He was proud to be an Aldridge. Since Henry Abraham Aldridge first established the town of Mercy, trading and selling had been the Aldridge way of living. It was only recently that his son, Richard, had cultivated their land for corn crops.

If only Richard had wanted to keep up the tradition, he often thought.

Yet, he couldn't deny Richard his dream of being a farmer. His son loved the family home too much to go away to college or work in the general store all day. Despite their differences, Frank was proud of Richard's natural ability to care for land and livestock.

His desk telephone rang out in a shrill tone, causing Frank to nearly jump from his chair.

He fumbled with the receiver. "Hello?"

"Hey, Grandpa."

He knew that voice well. "Hey, Joe!"

"You won't believe what happened!" Joe said breathlessly. "Knappy had her calf, and I was there to watch the delivery! It was amazing!"

Frank laughed at his grandson for a moment. Joseph's fascination with animals was so unlike the typical interests of a boy his age. His little brother, Eric, played football and raced through the woods on a four-wheeler for fun. Fifteen-year-old Joe found more pleasure in reading up on dog breeds and the physics behind bird flight. He knew Joseph would make a brilliant zoologist or veterinarian one day.

Frank grinned. "I couldn't be more thrilled for you."

"Dad tried calling you earlier. Where were you?"

Frank's grin faded. "I went for a stroll to get some air."

"He wants to know if you're about ready to come home. It's getting late."

Richard was always babysitting him, nagging him over this and that. He never imagined that one day their roles of father and son would feel reversed.

"I could come over and walk home with you," his grandson offered.

A small smile curled Frank's lips. "I think your mother would prefer you stay put. I'll head home in about ten more minutes."

"Okay, Grandpa," Joe mumbled, not disguising the disappointment in his voice.

"See you soon, Joe."

He hung up the phone and sat wondering for a minute. *Maybe I could renovate this top floor and make it into a home.* This consideration had crossed his mind several times since his wife passed away a year earlier. After her death, Frank passed the family home down to his son. Yet, he still lived with Richard's family. This made him feel like a useless moocher.

"No, Frank, it's still your house. It always will be," he remembered Helen, his daughter-in-law, insisting.

"And all of my things are in the basement," he muttered, rubbing his forehead once again.

A sudden but muffled creak from below ripped Frank from his thoughts. He sat up in the old, wooden chair, listening closely. It didn't sound like any of the typical squeaks and groans he would hear from the antique building.

He rose from his chair, listening intently. He was sure he had heard something below. With the greatest of care, he slowly pulled open the bottom desk drawer. From the back, he removed an aging Colt Revolver. His father had used it in the First World War, and Frank felt odd holding it without the excuse of curiosity. In a community like Mercy, few residents saw the need for alarm systems, let alone guns. Yet, he kept the gun in its place in memory of his father who once treasured the weapon.

Another noise fell hard on his ears, making his heart pump harder. It sounded like footsteps.

* * *

Karen crept through the darkness of the Aldridge General Store. With her father's work keys in hand, she made her way through the unfamiliar storage area by the back door to the familiar cashier's counter. The quaint store looked strange in the dark. The shelves and aisles closed in on her in the shadows. She felt as if she were going to suffocate. Her footsteps could scarcely be heard over the pumping of her heart.

Despite her fears, Karen felt this was the only way she could get the money she needed to leave town for a while. As soon as her father found her and dragged her home, she would work off the debt to Mr. Aldridge.

At the register, she began to fumble through the ring of keys as she had outside the back door. One by one, she tested the keys on the register lock. Finally, a small, silver one slid in and turned with ease. The drawer came open gently, releasing the hushed ding of a bell inside. Karen scooped up every bill she saw. She lifted up the tray in the drawer and pulled out a few twenty dollar bills from underneath. As she flipped through the money, she realized that she had only gathered one hundred dollars, not nearly enough.

Since Karen had made it this far, it wouldn't hurt to go a little farther. The store safe had to be upstairs in the office, and there was a good chance the safe key was on the ring.

A pair of wooden staircases met at a platform sat right beside the register. Karen hurried to the first step but a sound made her freeze. It sounded like a door creaking open. She listened intently, her heart beginning to beat even louder in her chest. *I saw Mr. Aldridge walk home. There's no one here,* she assured herself.

Karen climbed halfway up to the landing before she froze again. Unexplained sounds pierced her ears. *It's just the wind! Go!* she silently commanded herself.

As she stepped on to the landing, a shadowy figure appeared, crashing into her. Karen cried out as she fell back toward the stairwell wall. Visibly startled, the dark figure struggled to stay balanced. Something fell heavily on the platform. A loud clatter dominated the noise in the stairwell as she saw the dark object tumble down the steps.

Suddenly, a flash of light flickered simultaneously with a sound Karen immediately recognized. It was a gunshot. She screamed and covered her head. The object, which she now realized was a gun, finally settled at the bottom of the stairs.

In the darkness, she could finally make out a person. Collapsed on the landing, he breathed heavily and groaned. Karen jumped up, feeling along the wall for a light switch. Her fingers finally found one, and a light popped on right above them. Squinting, her eyes adjusted, and she recognized Frank Aldridge. He lay groaning on his side.

"Mr. Aldridge?" Karen crouched beside him. "Are you okay?"

He looked up at her, squinting from the light. "Karen?"

She put a gentle hand on his shoulder as the old man started to roll on his back. Then Karen's eyes grew wide in shock. His plaid work shirt was covered in blood.

He gasped for air. "The gun."

Karen couldn't speak. She struggled to breathe.

"Call 911," he whispered.

Karen hopped to her feet and stumbled down the stairs into the darkness. Her legs were like rubber but heavy as if coated with cement. An eternity passed before she came across the telephone beside the cash register. She managed to dial the number, and a weight lifted from her when the operator assured her that help was on the way.

Back at Mr. Aldridge's side, Karen found the front of his shirt soaked in a pool of deep crimson. His face had grown paler, his eyes weak. Karen pulled her stuffed backpack off and grabbed several t-shirts from it. She balled them up and pressed them against Frank's wound. He winced and recoiled.

"It's gonna be okay. Help is coming," she told him, her voice trembling.

Frank slowly lifted his arm and placed his hand on Karen's. "It's okay."

Karen could see an odd look in his eyes. His expression appeared more relaxed, even peaceful.

"I'm so sorry, Mr. Aldridge," Karen whispered, tears searing her eyes. "I just needed some money. I was gonna pay it back. I didn't mean for this to happen."

He shook his head. His eyes seemed to look beyond her into something unimaginably beautiful. He cracked a small, reassuring smile.

Karen watched his eyes start to close as the sound of sirens filled her ears.

* * *

"Ms. Denwood, Frank Aldridge was your father's boss, correct?" the young, black prosecutor asked, approaching Karen.

Karen shifted in her seat. "Yes."

She gripped her hands together on her lap. The sweat had to be pooling on her skirt under them. Everyone in the courtroom stared at her, their eyes following her every move. They were dying to see her crack, to see her go down. She could see it on their faces. Only her Aunt Val's face held an expression of sympathy.

"And how did your dad feel about working for Mr. Aldridge?"

Karen's attorney, Michael Archer, rose from his seat. "Objection, Your Honor. Relevance?"

"I'm establishing motive."

The judge, a bald man with a full, grey beard, nodded. "I'll allow it. Answer the question, Ms. Denwood."

Karen thought for a moment. The attorney had prepared her for this. "He liked Mr. Aldridge a lot. He thought he was a very nice man."

The prosecutor could see this coming a mile away. "Was he happy working at the Aldridge General Store?"

She froze, not knowing what to say. They were trying to corner her. "He was a welder. He loved welding."

"Answer the question, Ms. Denwood," the judge instructed sternly.

She couldn't lie. "No."

"And your father drank when he was unhappy, didn't he?" the prosecutor asked.

"Yes."

"You didn't like his drinking, correct?"

"That's correct."

"So you were ready to do anything to stop your dad from drinking. Is that right, Karen?"

Karen met eyes with Mr. Archer, desperately trying to read his face for help, any direction at all. She saw nothing. "Not anything."

The prosecutor paced before her. "Why did you go to the Aldridge General Store that night, Ms. Denwood?"

"I was going to borrow money from Mr. Aldridge. I mean, I was going to take it, but I was planning on paying him back."

The faces around the courtroom were grim, some even smug in reaction to her response. *Breathe, Karen. You can do this.*

She remembered her attorney's careful instruction. He explained how the prosecution was going to say she intentionally shot Mr. Aldridge. They wouldn't have a leg to stand on, though. He assured her that all of the evidence proved her only crimes were breaking in and robbing the store, not murdering Frank Aldridge. Yet, she was on trial for just that.

* * *

"Ladies and gentlemen of the jury," the prosecutor said, standing before them, "we would like to believe in our hearts that the death of Frank Aldridge was, in fact, an accident, but then, we would have to ignore a number of facts.

"First, Karen Denwood herself admitted to attempted robbery. Her intent was to gain money to runaway from Mercy. Put yourself in this girl's place. You have an alcoholic for a father, your mother recently died, and you're desperate to get away from all of your troubles. The question is, just how desperate would you be? Was Karen Denwood desperate enough to kill?

"Secondly, folks, we cannot deny the facts our gun expert shared. The chances of that gun firing from a fall were very slim, and even if it did as Ms. Denwood insisted, isn't it a little too convenient that the bullet happened to hit Mr. Aldridge right in the chest? We want to believe Ms. Denwood's claims, but we cannot deny the truth. Ms. Denwood stumbled into Mr. Aldridge in the store that night. They struggled with the gun. She got a hold of it and threatened Mr. Aldridge to keep quiet. As an honest man, Mr. Aldridge refused, and she shot him. In her panic, Ms. Denwood realized she would never get away with her crimes by running. She would have to face the jury and play the victim."

Karen couldn't believe her ears. His outrageous claims made her want to scream in protest. It took every ounce of her strength not to cry out. *They have to know it was an accident,* she thought desperately.

"Ladies and gentlemen, Frank Aldridge was a leader in the town of Mercy. He was respected and loved by everyone in the community. He was a member of the Mercy Town Board and the Mercy Church. He ran his family's general store for over thirty years. Don't let this man die in vain. Our county cannot allow such deviance to go on unpunished. Because of this young lady's actions, a well-respected leader is dead, and an entire town mourns the loss. Friends, the power is in your hands. Give Frank Aldridge justice."

The prosecutor returned to his seat beside Mr. and Mrs. Richard Aldridge. They both nodded at him with stern approval.

Sitting at the opposite table, Karen felt as if she were going to suffocate. *Why does he have to make me sound so evil? It was all an accident,* she thought, wanting to scream it at the top of her lungs. She wanted to cry too, but she had cried so much in the past few months that the tears had lost all meaning.

At night, she couldn't sleep. When she closed her eyes, all she could see was that last look on Mr. Aldridge's face. *If only he were alive. He could tell them how the gun fell. He could tell them. Why did he have to die?*

Although she was surrounded by people, Karen never felt so alone in her life. Every so often, she would have to look back at her aunt and her father sitting with the crowd. Aunt Val always gave her an assuring smile, but her father avoided even making eye contact with her.

Michael Archer rose from his seat beside Karen and quietly approached the jury. He cleared his throat as his icy blue eyes met with the eyes of each juror. Every time Karen heard his voice or met eyes with him, a new hope burned in her heart. Now he stood there like an angel, her last hope, all she had. He believed her, and she believed in him.

"Ladies and gentlemen, we cannot deny that the town of Mercy has . . ."

Mr. Archer's words melted together and then floated away from Karen. She closed her eyes.

God, please hear me. I need you. You know I'm innocent of murder. Please make the jury see the truth. I'm so sorry for what I did. Please make things right again. Please.

She prayed this over and over, hoping that God would interrupt her with an affirmative answer. Instead, her mind took her far away from the courtroom. She was at home again, watching her mother cook at the stove. The gentle scent of vanilla and sugar filled the kitchen. Her father walked up and tickled his wife. She giggled and turned to embrace him. Everything was back to normal again. No drinking. No funerals. Life was perfect again.

Karen heard rustling behind her. As she opened her eyes, reality choked her once again. Whispers began to fill the courtroom. She turned in her seat to see her father hurrying out of the room.

"Order!" the judge demanded, pounding his gavel.

Karen watched her father disappear through the door. She wanted to call out for him, but she would be wasting her breath. They hadn't spoken since the night she'd attempted to run away. Her last words to him were still "I hate you." She had said them in the heat of the moment, in a fit of rage. She could only hope he didn't remember their exchange.

As she returned her attention to the front, Aunt Val reached forward and put a comforting hand on her shoulder. It did little for Karen's pain.

Mr. Archer resumed his closing argument. "Here are my facts that you must consider. Karen called 911 for Mr. Aldridge. She did not abandon him at the scene. She even remained at the scene when the authorities arrived. Secondly, Karen's testimony of that night has never varied throughout the investigation and this trial. Also, we cannot ignore the testimonies shared by Karen's school friends. She has no history of violence and no criminal record. Friends, this young girl is innocent."

Karen's attorney returned to his seat beside her as the judge sent the jury out to decide their verdict. The judge then cleared the courtroom, and a police officer escorted Karen into an empty conference room. As she took a seat at the long table, her aunt entered the room and filled the chair beside her.

"Hey, darlin'."

"Where's Dad?"

She took Karen's hands into her own. "He needed to get away from all this. He needs time."

"But I need him." Karen stared into her aunt's green eyes. They were identical to her father's.

Her usual fireball of an aunt was very quiet. Karen could tell she was holding back tears. Finally, she looked up at Karen and forced a smile. "Don't worry. I paid off half the jury. You'll only be in for twenty years."

Karen couldn't smile at her aunt's bad sense of humor, not when a group of strangers from all over the county held her fate in their hands.

She stood and walked up to the window at the front of the conference room. Aunt Val followed her and put a hand on her shoulder.

27

"No matter what happens, I'll always be there for you, kitten," her aunt promised, using that old nickname Karen loved.

Karen nodded and turned to look through the open blinds. She saw the Aldridge family crowded together down the hallway, embracing each other. For the first time, she noticed two boys among them. They looked very similar, definitely brothers, wearing white dress shirts and black slacks. She was sure that the shorter one was her age, and the taller boy was only a year or two older. They stood quietly beside each other, watching their relatives chatter in whispers. She remembered them now, Joseph and Eric Aldridge. Eric had been in her fourth grade class in elementary school, and both boys attended worship at Mercy Church with her.

"I ruined their lives."

Aunt Val followed her gaze. Then she looked at Karen intensely. "Honey, it was an accident. We all make mistakes. Death is part of life. Life is unfair, and so on and so forth. You cannot blame yourself for the ways of the world."

Karen knew what she meant to say, even though Aunt Val was never one of eloquent expression.

"God is still in control," Karen whispered.

"No matter what happens, kitten . . ." Her aunt's voice trailed off. It was then that Karen saw something frightening in Aunt Val's eyes—utter hopelessness.

*   *   *

Karen returned to her seat in the courtroom with a nagging pain in her gut. Watching the jury return to their seats, she felt a fear like she had only felt in nightmares. *Please, Lord, tell me they saw the truth.*

She and Mr. Archer rose to hear the verdict. He put a strong arm around her shoulders. He had been the father she missed so much all this time. He tightened his grip on her shoulder as the jury foreman stood to read Karen's fate.

"In the charge of murder in the first degree, we, the jury, find the defendant, Karen Denwood, not guilty."

The courtroom roared with disapproval.

Karen felt a weight drop from her. *They believed me.*

"Order!" the judge cried, hammering away. "Order in this courtroom!"

The room fell quiet. "In the charge of manslaughter, we find the defendant guilty."

The courtroom erupted in applause.

Aunt Val jumped up from her seat. "This is an outrage!"

"Order!"

A weight like a ten-ton yolk dropped on Karen. Her throat tightened, and her eyes burned. *This isn't happening,* she thought, panic crashing over her like a tsunami. *I was telling the truth.*

She turned to see Richard and Helen Aldridge, Frank's son and daughter-in-law, embracing. Helen cried tears of relief on to her husband's shoulder. Eric and Joseph sat expressionless beside their parents. Karen's eyes locked on Joseph's for a moment. The boy stiffened and shot his glance from her.

Mr. Archer gently took Karen by the arm. "We'll fight this, Karen."

She shook her head, hot tears burning paths down her pale cheeks. No words would come to her. With the death of her mother, she'd lost her joy. Now, with the loss of her freedom, she didn't even have her hope.

As the sheriff's deputy tightened handcuffs around Karen's wrists, she felt a burning inside her chest. It rose up to her throat, warming her face. The heat dried her tears and locked her jaw.

She was a good girl. She always had been. She told the truth. She followed the Lord. Yet, there she stood. *Guilty.* Did God not love her anymore? Why had He abandoned her?

Chapter Three
Nine Years Later

Karen sat on her bottom bunk bed, holding a pack of ice to her swollen bottom lip. The once lively girl had decayed like a sheltered flower. Her face was drawn, weary from the years of incarceration. Her blue eyes that once matched her mother's in luster had lost their sparkle. The long, blonde hair now hung to her ear lobes and boasted a shade darker than the one from her youth.

"Why can't she leave you alone?" Maria ranted. "If you don't want to gamble, that's your business."

"You know how Cora is." Karen winced, pain stinging her lip with each twitch. "It's her yard."

"And where were the correction officers?" her friend continued with more fervor. "Gossiping in the corner as always! They never look out for you."

"Relax. I'll be okay. It's only a few more weeks." With the thought of her approaching freedom, a wave of peace came over Karen. It was suddenly easy to forget her aching lip.

Maria huffed, shaking her head as she paced in front of their bunk bed. "Next time, you need to hit her back. You know I would have if the guards hadn't finally decided to show up!"

"Maria, be quiet! She'll hear you!" cried Karen in a hushed voice.

She glanced across the busy dormitory. Three rows of bunk beds away, she saw Cora laughing with two other inmates. The anger returned as Karen remembered the fist flying at her. Cora kept pressuring her to play Poker with her gang, and the game was always rigged. It was only a con to get whatever they wanted out of the other prisoners. Even if she had wanted to, Karen didn't have the impulsivity to return the punch. Much of that composed thirteen-year-old remained intact despite years of adapting to a harsher way of life. She learned early on that nothing between the prison walls was worth fighting for when it would only add time to her sentence.

"Maria, you're all talk," Karen finally said. The petite but tough Hispanic woman was in for robbing a department store.

"It was a dare," Karen recalled Maria telling her. "It wasn't worth six years, though. I only stole, like, eight hundred dollars, two radios, and a pair of shoes."

"A pair of shoes?" she had asked.

"What woman can resist a pair of cute sandals?"

Maria was the only other prisoner who believed Karen's story about Mr. Aldridge's death. Her trust and understanding gave Karen a warm sense of comfort in the cold prison. Their shared faith in Christ was icing on the cake. Maria and Karen weren't the only Christians in the prison. Much to Karen's surprise, most of the minimum security prisoners attended Bible study or were willing to discuss Jesus.

Maria shrugged. "I know I'm all talk, but that's not the point."

Karen sighed, trying to ignore the throbbing pain in her lip. Looking at the half completed painting lying on her bed was a healthy distraction.

Maria followed Karen's gaze. "When are you going to finish it?"

For a week now, Karen had been working on yet another piece to make her sentence more bearable. While in the juvenile detention center, Karen had honed her artistic skills by painting and illustrating during her free time. Her aunt had carried home countless paintings over the years. Karen owned at least two dozen full sketch pads. The prison psychiatrist often examined her works for meaning, but she knew what they really meant. The images she usually created were of her memories of life in Mercy.

"Landscapes take time. They have to tell you they're complete," Karen replied, still staring at the pastel sky which would fade into lines of pine trees but now only bordered the white of the canvas.

Normally, inmates weren't allowed to bring such items into the prison dormitory, but Karen had managed to get into the warden's good graces. About two years earlier, the warden had requested a painting of her granddaughter. She was so pleased with the result that Karen was guaranteed any reasonable favor. Being able to view her canvas between art classes helped Karen envision where the next stroke of paint should fall.

"So are you going to art school or what?"

Maria's question sounded foreign because it involved some place not within the confines of their lives as prisoners.

"I really hope so." A warmth filled Karen's chest at the thought. "I'm going to get a job in Mercy and save up as much money as possible over the summer."

"I bet you'll be a famous artist someday, Karen. You have a gift."

Karen blushed as she always did when she received compliments on her work. It was simply a hobby, but she held big dreams in her heart, dreams of an art degree and her own studio and gallery. Some days she feared they were pipe dreams. Other days she felt it was her calling to paint. Either way, Karen knew she loved creating images on canvas.

"Oh, you got a letter," Maria said, digging through a stack of papers on her bed above Karen's.

Karen instantly perked up. "From Ricky?"

"Nope, not Lover Boy this time." She tossed the letter on Karen's bed. "It's from your dad again."

She set the ice pack down and picked up the letter, examining her father's all too familiar handwriting.

Maria flopped down on the bed beside her. "You think he'll say he's coming?"

"Don't know." She fiddled with the envelope.

"Open it!"

Karen offered it to her. "You open it."

Maria let out an irritated groan and snatched it from her hand. She tore the edge of the envelope off. Her eyes skimmed down the page carefully.

"He just talks about where he is and Jesus again."

Maria offered her the letter. Karen sighed with relief and took the letter back. She began to read it.

Dear Karen,

I'm writing you from Florida now. It's nice here. The weather is probably the best on the coast. I'll only be here for about twelve hours. Then I'm heading up to New Hampshire for a meeting with another head honcho. Setting up welding contracts is tedious work, but soon I'll have saved up enough money to settle into a more normal job.

So now it's only about a month or so to go, right? I'm so excited for you. Please let me know if there is anything at all that you need—money, a place to stay, help getting a job.

I know that maybe you're not ready to forgive me and maybe you don't believe me, but I'm a new man. Jesus has taken away my desire to drink and made me whole again. I miss your mother and the life we used to have, but I can't change the past. I want to make a new future for us. I miss my little girl. Please write and say you forgive me.

Karen bit her lip and took in an unsteady breath. She refolded the letter and returned it to the envelope. From under the bed, she pulled out a shoebox and added the letter to nearly fifty others.

Maria frowned. "Are you still afraid he'll say he's coming?"

Karen nodded, closing the box and sliding it back under the bed. "I still don't know if I can forgive him. I know I'm supposed to, but what if when I see him, all of the anger comes right back?"

"Writing it is one thing. Saying it is another story all together," Maria concluded.

"Right. I would like to believe I'd forgive him in person, but what if I'm wrong?"

Maria nodded as Karen returned the ice pack to her lip.

"I still regret the last thing I said to him."

"I'm sure he knows you don't hate him."

"I can't express my real feelings in a letter."

Sympathy filled Maria's expression. She forced it away. "Are you going back to Bible Study on Tuesday?"

Karen shrugged. "I guess, but some of those church people can be . . ."

"Stuck up?" Maria filled in.

Karen nodded, rolling her eyes.

"I'll go with you. My mom says I need to go to the prison activities. It's good for us to get involved."

Karen considered this for a moment and then decided Maria's company would make it worthwhile. "Okay."

* * *

The Aldridge House was the oldest and most beautiful house in Mercy. It was originally a one-room home, but a fire in 1911 had left nothing but ashes. It was rebuilt as a Victorian style, two-story home. At least ten different colors had graced its wooden siding, but in its current state, it was a pale blue. Behind this well-kept, renovated home sat a horse stable, chicken coop and nearly fifty acres of corn crops. The huge, green front lawn was so big that it was often the setting for family parties or town gatherings. In its history, the Aldridge front lawn had been the scene of thirteen weddings, nineteen funerals, forty-four town meetings, and nearly one hundred birthday parties and socials.

Now, once again, the lawn was crowded with Mercy locals. Joseph Aldridge hadn't seen his boyhood home this crowded since his eighteenth birthday party. This party was laid out in the same way. Uncle Robert flipped burger patties at the grill, its chrome hood gleaming in the late spring sunshine. Long tables clothed in red and white checkered tablecloths were set up on the lawn, shaded by several towering oaks and pines. The only thing to distinguish this party from any other was the banner over the large, wrap-around front porch. Instead of reading, "Happy Birthday, Joseph," it read "Congratulations, Dr. Doolittle."

Joseph smiled as he read it. That was his comedian brother's idea, no doubt. After six years of study at the state university, he was now ready to take the state exam to officially become a veterinarian. After passing the exam, he planned to open his clinic at home in Mercy.

"It's so good to have you home again, Joe," his mother said, coming up beside him.

She looked different to him. In the last few years, he'd only made about a dozen trips home. Her short, auburn hair was beginning to gray and small wrinkles were forming at the corners of her mouth and eyes. He hadn't been home enough to see these changes come progressively so each time he saw her, the differences seemed very drastic—as if he were traveling in a time machine. She was still his same sweet mother, though, a constant that would always bring him comfort as they both aged.

"I'm glad to be back." He hugged her for what seemed like the millionth time that afternoon. Each time felt better than the last.

"I'm sorry if this was too much, dear. I know you must be tired from the drive, but—"

"Let me guess," he said, "Eric said I would love it."

She smiled. "Yes. You know your brother."

"He never passes up the chance to surprise me."

Joe scanned the packed front lawn for his mischievous little brother. He often had to remind himself that Eric wasn't so little anymore. At twenty-two, his height was now beyond even his older brother's, and he had grown rather robust from working alongside his father on the farm.

As Joseph continued to search for his brother's face, another one appeared before him.

"Hey, Joe! Missed me?" The familiar voice matched a person Joe had nearly forgotten.

He nearly spilled his soda. "Emily Bailey, it's been a long time.

Emily grinned, her short, brown hair flowing in the warm, May breeze. She looked just as he remembered: big smile, petite, hourglass figure and vibrant, hazel eyes. She wore a knee-length white dress dotted with blue flowers that matched her dress sandals, revealing to him that her sense of style was also the same.

"Satterwhite High prom king and queen. Cutest couple." She released a high-pitched giggle.

"How could I forget?" he muttered, trying hard to hide his distaste for the memory.

Joe and Emily had been quite an item in high school but only in her memory. According to his, they were forced together by popular demand because they looked "cute." He had given her a chance but found they had nothing in common. He was on the Bowling Team, president of the Biology Club, and their class valedictorian. She was a cheerleader with straight B's and no interests beyond acting and the latest fashions. This was not the full extent of their differences. Joseph had made a list on paper before he broke up with her after graduation. He hadn't looked forward to breaking her heart. In fact, he genuinely wished Emily was his type, but she wasn't.

"Have you been in Mercy all this time?" he asked with mild interest.

"No, silly! I got my degree, and I've been a missionary in Argentina for the past two years. Your uncle hired me to take over the Outreach Ministry."

Uncle Robert was the pastor of Mercy Church. About ninety percent of the town attended worship there. The other ten percent traveled out of town. His father's sister married Robert Bell five years earlier. The church had been passed down through a long line of Pastor Bells', and this tradition was vital. The church almost lost the Bell name when Robert's great grandparents had seven girls. Their mother, Elizabeth Bell, refused to bear anymore children for the hopes of a boy, so they adopted and raised a boy to pastor the church. The Bell blood was not lost, though. Their adopted son, William, married his Bell sister, Angelica. The town of Mercy happily permitted this for the sake of keeping the Bell legacy.

"That sounds nice. What do you all do?" Joe asked her.

"We make out of town trips twice a week to a women's minimum security prison to teach one-on-one Bible study," she replied, "which brings me to my favor."

"Favor?"

"Well, I heard you're going to be in town for quite some time, and I really need another volunteer to help me with this ministry."

Joe nodded. "Consider it done. I'll be there."

Her eyes widened in a dangerous combination of surprise and joy. "Really? Joseph, that would be great! I lost one of my volunteers, and you can take his place. This is wonderful!"

Emily leapt into his arms, squealing and making Joe nearly spill his soda again. He had to adjust himself to her choking embrace but was grateful to see Emily so happy. The guilt of breaking her heart in their less mature days had set in again so heavily that he couldn't bring himself to turn her down.

"We go every Tuesday and Thursday evening. We've only gone twice so you'll have no trouble catching up." She released herself from him. "We'll have a great time, and I know you'll grow closer to the Lord."

Joe tried to crack his back. "I'm sure it will be."

"So I'll see you at six o'clock on Tuesday?"

"Of course."

"Thanks again, Joe. It's great to have you back." Emily turned and disappeared into the crowd.

"Well, that was a nice gesture."

Joe didn't know his mother had been listening to them the whole time.

"It'll be good for me," he said. "I've been neglecting my own Bible study."

She put both hands on her hips. "Are you sure you want to get Emily's hopes up like this?"

"What are you talking about?"

"She's still crazy about you, Joseph."

"How would you know that?"

His mother blushed. "Her mother might have mentioned a few things."

"So you two still gossip, huh?" He remembered the two women chatting away on the front porch as he grew up.

"What are best friends for? Anyway, why wouldn't Emily be interested again? You *are* the most eligible bachelor in Mercy."

"Hey, what about me?" Eric asked, appearing through the crowd behind his mother.

"You're the most macho bachelor in Mercy," she quipped with a smirk.

Eric laughed. "Nice save, Mom. Was that Emily Bailey I just saw?"

"Yes," Joe said, "she's home and working for Uncle Robert. She asked me to be one of her volunteers."

"She didn't ask me," Eric muttered. Joseph couldn't tell if his brother's frown was genuine or fictitious.

"Well, just ask her if you can come," their mother said. "I'm sure she'd be happy to have another person."

Eric ran a hand through his messy, brown hair, a nervous habit. "I don't have time for that stuff anyway. When's the shop opening, Joe?"

"In about six weeks. That's my goal, but if the town planning committee declines my request for the building renovation, I'm not sure what I'll do."

His mother took him by the arm. "Don't worry. With your father on the committee, you'll have no trouble."

Joe scanned the crowded lawn. "Where is Dad, anyway?"

She frowned. "Feeding the horses, I think."

A sick feeling came over Joe. They were celebrating his return home, and all his father could do was hide in the stable.

Joe's mother dropped a gentle hand on his shoulder. "Why don't you go drag him out here?"

That's the thing. I have to drag him, he thought.

"Do I have to?"

She nodded, eyebrows raised. "Tell him I said to get out here *now*."

Joe decided that arguing with his mother about making his father come to the cookout was pointless. She didn't understand how Aldridge men preferred to let each other wallow in their bitterness rather than fight it out or put on a happy facade.

Along the gravel drive around the house leading to the stable, Joe couldn't help but allow the frustration inside him overwhelm his thoughts. Why couldn't his father support him in his endeavors? Just because he didn't want to be a farmhand like Eric, he's not acceptable in his father's eyes?

Inside the wooden, four-stall stable, Joe found his father brushing their old appaloosa, Starla. The horse raised her head a little and huffed through her nose at Joe.

Joe gave her a pat on the head. "Hey, old girl."

"She doesn't like to be bothered when I'm grooming her."

Joe felt his shoulders tense up as he met eyes with his father. The stinging eyes held no sign of delight to see Joe. His jaw was tight, face cold. He reminded Joe of John Wayne in his cowboy film days. He was a tall man, muscular from head to toe. Years of hard labor in the sun had added a few premature wrinkles to his face. Gray patches were beginning to spread through his brown hair.

Joe frowned and stepped back. "Sorry."

"You've been gone a while. You wouldn't remember."

The bitterness in his tone was as visible to Joe as the old, brown brush in his father's hand.

Joe cleared his throat and rubbed the back of his neck. "Mom says you have to come out for the cookout."

His father carefully examined the pattern of the hair on Starla's back. "I'll be out in a few minutes. Starla needs me. When somebody needs you, you've gotta be there for 'em."

Joe's jaw dropped. "Dad, if you have something to say to me, don't dance around it."

Once again, his father looked him straight in the eyes. Joe took another step back.

"Tell your mother I'll be out in a minute."

Joe took in a deep breath. "I really need your support before the town planning committee tomorrow."

The idea of Joe tearing apart the old Aldridge store to make way for a veterinary clinic had never sat well with his dad. He had prepared his father for it since his freshman year of college, though. After all, the store had been left to Joe in his grandfather's will upon Joe's eighteenth birthday. Legally, Joe could do what he pleased with it.

Joe had explained to his father more than once that he wasn't literally going to knock the old building down. He only wanted to renovate the interior. They had many battles, but in time, Joe won the war. The store was important to the family history and the memory of his grandfather, but Joe wasn't called to reopen it. He was called to be a veterinarian. He still wondered if his father understood this to be God's will for Joe. He only hoped that the town planning committee would be more easily persuaded than his father.

"I won't make any promises," his father said in a monotonous tone.

Joe clenched his fists. For a second, anger began to rise up inside of him, but soon an overwhelming feeling of resignation subdued it. He turned and started back out of the barn. A thought crossed his mind, and he stopped in his tracks.

"Starla has a small laceration on her right back leg. It looks deep, and it could be infected."

Joe turned to see his father's face. His dad lowered his eyes to examine the horse's leg.

He frowned and nodded. "I didn't see that before."

"I've got my medical kit and some antibiotic in the house."

His father nodded, and Joe hurried out of the barn. Pride swept over him when he realized that his father had cracked a smile.

Chapter Four

With dreamy eyes, Karen examined the picture of a handsome blonde decked out in a tuxedo. She tried to match his voice with his face, the one she had never seen in person.

"Hey, girl, how's my caged bird?" Ricky asked over the phone line.

Karen rolled her eyes and smiled. "So what does that make you? A worm?"

He laughed. "Clever."

She loved their banter and the way Ricky made her feel. After two years of letters and once-a-week phone conversations, she was beginning to fall for him. She could never openly admit this, though. Her experience with men was limited even more than her knowledge of them. *Do girls just say "I like you"? Should I ask him to be my boyfriend?* These thoughts consumed her lately. She didn't know the first thing about love, only that she wanted to feel it. Prisoners weren't immune to the romance movies of pop culture. A different one played every other Wednesday evening, and each viewing only fed Karen's fantasies.

"I'm counting down the days." She tried to mask her excitement with a calm tone.

"I know. How long is it now?"

"Only about three weeks. You're a week behind me, remember?"

"Wow. You've made the time go by faster."

Karen could feel herself melting, staring at his photo. Half of the image, his prom date, was cut away. He cradled the lucky girl's hand in his own. Karen's heart grew heavy. She never had a prom. This thought led her to think of Mercy again. "I can't wait to get back home."

"Murphy, right?"

"No." She laughed through her nose, not meaning to let a faint snort sneak out. "Mercy."

"Right. I'll come and meet you as soon as I get out."

"I can't wait." She cleared her throat. "I mean, all I have is this one photo. You know how pictures aren't the same as the real thing."

"True," he whispered in a mysterious tone. To a girl whose last kiss from a boy was in the seventh grade, merely the sound of his voice gave Karen goose bumps. "But that drawing of you looks real to me."

Karen had sent to him a self-portrait when they first became pen pals through the prison system. With no recent photos of herself, all Karen had to offer Ricky was a sketch.

"You should go sell your art in New York. It's really good."

Ricky had flattered her with comments like this many times before, but she never took them seriously. They were a form of flirtation to her.

"I'd better go," Karen said. "I still need to call my aunt."

"Okay, same time next week?"

"As always."

Watching the clock on the painted cinderblock wall, Karen dialed her aunt's number.

"Hey, kitten!" Aunt Val chimed. After nine long years, Karen was still Aunt Val's darling, little niece.

"How did you know it was me?"

She giggled. "I have super human powers."

"Caller I.D.?"

"Is that what they call it these days?"

Karen couldn't help but chuckle at her spunky aunt. At forty-three, she had the spirit of a twenty-one-year-old. It had brought Karen through many dark days.

"How are you, babe?" Her Southern twang dominated the question.

"I'm overjoyed!" Karen said, feeling more like herself. She rarely bothered subduing her feelings with Aunt Val. There was no fooling her.

"This is so exciting. I'm gettin' the attic all set up for you."

"I can't wait to see how your house has changed."

Karen remembered the miniature Victorian down the street as a dainty dollhouse. Aunt Val said she had since added on a sunroom and had her walk-up attic finished. It was a small, three-bedroom home, but for a single woman, it was a lot of house. Aunt Val had lived there for as long as Karen could remember. She missed the smell of cookies in its kitchen, her late Grandma Sue's doll collection in the master bedroom, and the cozy, leather sofa she used to curl up on to watch TV. It was so long ago and so far away now.

"Is that boy still coming by to meet you?"

"His name is Ricky, and he's a sweet guy," Karen said for the eightieth time.

"He called you Katie once!"

"It was a silly mistake and that was months ago," she countered with a shrug.

"A guy who is hung up on a girl never gets her name wrong."

Karen recoiled a little. The truth was like a punch in the gut for her. Her aunt was right. She was always right. He couldn't even remember the name of her hometown. Maybe Ricky wasn't as interested in her as she was in him.

"He's still my friend, and I want to meet him," she said, still staring at the worn prom photo.

"I don't know, kitten. This guy is in jail too. He could be trouble." Her aunt's protective nature made her a good stand-in for Karen's mother.

Ricky had been mistakenly identified as an accomplice in a gas station robbery that ended in murder. The judge had handed him a sentence of eight years when he was seventeen. At first, all Karen could find in common with him was their mutual innocence. She had decided to finally admit her faith in Christ to Ricky. To her delight, he had accepted Jesus over the phone with her not long after that.

"Aunt Val, Ricky is innocent like me."

"Honey, they all say they're innocent."

* * *

Joseph watched intently as the members of the town planning committee stared at the nervous young man before them. The aging members sat at a long table at the front of the fellowship hall in Mercy Church.

"I feel this gas station would offer more convenience to the locals of Mercy," he concluded.

The committee was quiet. Finally, one of the members, Peter Sampson, spoke up. "Sir, are you a local of Mercy?"

Even from his seat near the back of the room, Joe could see the sweat forming on the man's forehead. He swallowed. "No, I'm from Wilson."

The members exchanged glances. Eighty-year-old Mr. Sampson spoke up again in a gruff tone hardly matching his gentle grandfather demeanor. "Then you certainly wouldn't know what Mercy needs. I motion that this request be denied."

"I second," Eva Perdy chimed.

The other members nodded in agreement.

"Motion carried." Mr. Sampson smacked his gavel down as the man's head dropped.

Joseph couldn't help but pity the young entrepreneur, but few out-of-towners successfully satisfied the town planning committee. Lugging a heavy briefcase, the man hurried out of the meeting room like a dog that just felt the smack of rolled up newspaper on his bottom.

"Next on the agenda," another member announced, reading some papers, "Joseph Aldridge and the proposal for a veterinary clinic on Main Street."

Joe rose from his seat, dressed in his best navy suit and most conservative tie. He scurried to the front of the room, smoothing his brown hair back along the way. His father nodded at Joe from the member's table. Joe forced a smile and returned the nod.

"Good morning, gentlemen *and* madam," Joe greeted, taking a moment to smile at Mrs. Perdy on the end. The elderly, black woman blushed and smiled in response. "When my grandfather, Frank Aldridge, died nine years ago, he left the Aldridge General Store to my father until I turned eighteen. At that time, I would assume responsibility for the property. It was his hope that the store would be passed down through the family as it had been in the past. As you know, though, my father's interests lie in farming, not in running the store, so it was closed shortly after Grandpa's death. I would like to renovate the existing building into Mercy Veterinary Clinic."

"What type of renovations are we talking about, Joseph?" Mr. Sampson asked with one raised, white eyebrow.

Joe cleared his throat. "Interior mostly. I will only be adding a new sign to the exterior front and another beside the sidewalk for passing cars."

The members nodded at each other.

"Joseph, for what reason did you decide not to reopen the store and continue your grandfather's legacy?"

He thought carefully for a moment, caught off guard by the question. "Well, my grandfather had a passion for keeping that legacy. We have a lot of family pride. I felt the same pride, but when I helped him in the store as a kid, I never felt much satisfaction. My passion is for helping animals. My grandfather always said to go after your dreams. That's why my father was able to go into farming without much trouble. My grandfather didn't want him to do anything he didn't want to do."

Mr. Sampson turned to Joe's father. "Richard, how do you feel about this? Is your son a reliable vet?"

Joe held his breath.

"I don't doubt my son's abilities. I would trust every chicken and horse on my farm to him. He's always had a gift when it comes to animals."

A rush of relief swept over Joe and turned into a burst of excitement that remained with him all the way home.

At the house, it was like old times again. His mother prepared a celebration dinner of homemade fried chicken, mashed potatoes, peas, biscuits, and Great Grandma Betty's pecan pie. Needless to say, it took her several hours to prepare the meal. She started as soon as she'd heard the good news.

The smell of his mother's cooking brought back a lot of memories. He had missed those lingering aromas when he was microwaving pizza pockets in his college dorm room. Most of all, he had missed dinner with the family. The dining room was a little different now. His mother had painted it a buttery shade of yellow and purchased a new oak table to seat six, even though it usually had been dinner for three over the past six years.

Everything else was the same. She still used the same set of cream, pansy-dotted china plates with a matching gravy boat. The purple, cotton napkins had been in the family for years. Mom and Dad always sat at the ends of the table and Joe and his little brother would wolf down their food between them. It was good to be home.

"Mom, this is delicious," Joe said, taking another bite of his jelly-covered biscuit. "I haven't eaten like this since Christmas."

She smiled, glowing from his compliment. "Well, don't eat too much. You need room for some pie."

"To Mercy Vet Clinic," Eric said, raising his glass of tea.

Everyone followed suit.

"And to Joe," he continued. "May he never misdiagnose."

Joe grinned. "Here, here."

With the click of their glasses, they returned to their food.

"So how long are you going to be living here, son?" his father asked.

Joe's mother glared at her husband. "Rich, he'll stay as long as he needs to."

"He's a grown man. He needs his own home."

"Eric's a grown man," Joe said, sounding like a ten-year-old. "He still lives here."

Mr. Aldridge wiped his mouth with a napkin. "Eric works with me. He pays for his room and board."

His wife frowned. "Oh, for heaven's sake, Rich, he's just getting on his feet."

"Dad, it'll only be a few months. I take my state exam in a couple of weeks. After that, I'll be sitting down with a contractor to look at the store blueprints. I hope all of the renovations go smoothly," Joe said. "If you want, I can help on the farm in my spare time."

Eric laughed. "*You* work on the farm? It's not like when we were kids, Joe."

His father nodded. "All right, one month. No more than that. When mid-summer comes so do the droughts, and that's when we can't afford any extra mouths."

"We could afford him for eighteen years," Joe's mother said. "Surely, we can afford him during one more summer. After all, he worked hard to pay for his schooling. He saved us a lot of money."

Joe's father snorted. "Us? If he didn't work for school, we sure wouldn't have paid for it."

Mrs. Aldridge frowned and raised her hands in surrender. "New table topic, please."

The family became quiet except for the sound of Eric's chewing and silverware clicking on plates.

She gave her youngest son a sharp look. "Eric, chew with your mouth closed."

He rolled his eyes in response and did as he was told.

Just like I'm ten again, Joe thought with a smile.

His mother turned to Joe. "Did you meet any nice girls at the school this last semester, Joe?"

He was taken aback by this question. *Definitely not ten again.*

He hesitated. "Not really. I went on a few dates, but I only really knew other vet medicine majors and dating another vet was weird."

"You know, you ought to be looking out for a nice girl. After you start your clinic, you'll want to settle down."

A curious expression covered his father's face. "What about Emily Bailey?"

"We're just friends."

His father chuckled. "Well, she sure was eyeballin' you at the cookout yesterday. I haven't seen a woman eyeball like that since I first met your mother."

She laughed. "*You* were doing the eyeballin', mister."

"No, I remember. I'll never forget it. She was stuck on me like glue," Richard told his sons as they laughed.

Joe's mother shook her head and smiled. "Joe, maybe you should give Emily a second chance. She is very pretty and so nice."

"Emily isn't really my type, Mom."

Eric scowled. "Geez, Joe. You're so picky! Emily is great. She's the perfect girl. She's smart and funny. She's got a beautiful smile and pretty eyes and—"

By this time, Eric noticed his family staring at him inquisitively. He quickly returned to eating his food.

Mrs. Aldridge raised her hands again. "New table topic, please."

* * *

When Joe saw Emily again on Tuesday to go to the women's prison, Sunday dinner came to mind. He wondered if he really was being too picky as Eric so passionately put it. Did he really have the right to reject her even six years later? Maybe she was a little different now. Maybe she had more to offer. Maybe they even had something in common.

The ride to the women's prison answered all of his questions and proved otherwise. Emily's personality had gravitated further from Joe's during the college years. In fact, it seemed that now they were not only different but polar opposites.

"Opposites attract," he heard his mother's voice say in his head.

He frowned. *Not these opposites.*

The most stimulating part of their conversation was their discussion of a movie they had both actually seen. He liked it, and she didn't. It ended on the edge of an argument about the plot twist. Despite this, Emily seemed cheery and eager to arrive at the prison. Joe wasn't dreading their arrival, but he wasn't eager either. He had never been to a prison and didn't know what to expect.

The ten-passenger church van pulled into the prison parking lot after a forty-minute drive out of Mercy. The prison, a two-story, brick building surrounded by a barbed wire fence, was secluded in a wooded area off the highway. It was only a minimum security facility, so only one guard was posted outside at the front door.

Inside, Emily spoke briefly with the guard at the front desk, and the group was escorted by another guard to a white cinderblock room with two long, cafeteria tables. The guard left them, and they waited.

The place reminded Joe of a hospital, cold and sterile. The smell brought back memories of several different surgical rooms he'd assisted in during his college internships. He couldn't imagine calling such a place home. Looking around, though, he was reminded of God's grace. Every person belonged in a place like this. Every sinner deserved far worse even, but Jesus paid the penalty. Still, it weighed heavily on his heart that some people never saw the outside walls of these places.

"They're finishing dinner, so it will be a few minutes," Emily explained. "We're studying Philippians today. Your place in the book depends on the pris—" she cleared her throat with a smile, "student. We work at their paces."

Joe began to flip through his Bible to Philippians. The realization that he hadn't studied this book in years made his stomach tighten.

The metal door creaked open, and the guard reentered with eight women in orange attire. They were instructed to take a seat, and the guard took her position in front of the door.

Of the eight women, Joe's eyes were drawn to the one with short, dirty blonde hair. She looked very out of place with kind, blue eyes and an innocent face. *She belongs in a spring dress at a picnic,* he thought. What surprised him was not the thought but the image in his mind. She also felt familiar to him, but he couldn't place her in his memory.

Emily stood before the group. "Welcome, ladies. We're going to continue our one-on-one study of Philippians today, but I would like to introduce a new volunteer. His name is Joe. Joe will be taking Ryan's place, so he will be working with you, Karen." She motioned to the blonde-haired woman who nodded with no sign of pleasure or distaste. Joe himself was relieved. The other women didn't look as tame as Karen.

Emily took a seat across from two inmates as the other five volunteers paired up with the remaining women.

Joe took his seat across from Karen. "Okay, where are you in Philippians?"

She was silent for a moment, jaw stiff. Then she raised her eyes to his. "Aren't you going to ask?"

Joe paused. "Ask what?"

"What I'm in for. You people always want to know."

"You people?" *Maybe she does fit in here.*

She frowned. "You church people with your perfect ideas and all of your answers to life's problems."

He was bewildered, but a sudden thought came to mind. "Isn't this Bible study optional for you?"

She narrowed her eyes at him. "I want to learn the Bible whether it's from a know-it-all or not."

He sighed. "Well, I don't care about your past. I'm here for your future."

She looked impressed and cracked a small smile. "The second chapter, verse nineteen."

They opened their Bibles together, reading and discussing for an hour. By the end of their session, Joe really wanted to know what she was in prison for. She still seemed out of place—gentle, cunning, and even witty. She challenged him with her questions and impressed him with her Biblical insight. It didn't make sense to him that she was locked away.

"Two more minutes, guys and gals," Emily said.

Karen leaned across the table. "You're a lot better at teaching than that Ryan guy."

Joe's heart skipped a beat. "Really?"

"He was slow-paced and talked too much."

"Everyone has their own approach. Thanks, though."

She leaned back and lowered her glance. "I'm sorry about what I said earlier. I've had some bad experiences in the past."

He shrugged. "No problem. Will you stick to our studies then?" The hope in his tone surprised him.

"Just a few more times." She bit her bottom lip. Joe thought he saw a twinkle in her eye. "Then I'll be free."

"Oh." He wasn't sure how to reply. "Congratulations."

She laughed lightly. It sounded nothing like Emily's laugh, and he loved it.

Joe offered his hand across the table. "It was great meeting you, Karen."

"You too."

She had a firm grip, a handshake his father would be proud of. Her delicate hand was rougher than he expected, especially around her finger tips. He noticed colorful stains like dried paint around her nails.

Emily rose from her seat. "We'll see you gals on Thursday."

Joe and the other volunteers made their way to the door. He offered Karen an awkward wave. She smiled and returned it.

* * *

Karen followed her fellow inmates in single file down the long hall way outside the classroom. Her new Bible study partner was so unlike any previous one she had met before. Joe seemed kind and easy to talk to. It was as if they had been friends for years.

"Karen's gotta boyfriend," one of the inmates taunted.

Maria laughed. "I know! They were flirting the whole time!"

Karen rolled her eyes. "We were not."

"He was cute, Karen. You shoulda got his number!" another inmate said.

The other women continued joking, but Karen was silent, now ignoring their comments. She felt good after talking to Joe. He treated her like a human being, not some weirdo or menace. With the mention of flirting, she realized she had stared at him when he read aloud, and she often wasn't paying attention to the Scripture he was reading.

How could I ever deserve a guy like him? she wondered. *What free man wants a jailbird?*

Without much hope in her heart, she went to bed trying not to think of Joe, only freedom. That would be hers sooner than any man.

Chapter Five

Joe found it hard to concentrate on his studies to prepare for the state veterinary exam. The woman from the prison, Karen, kept interrupting his thoughts. They seemed to click somehow like two fitting puzzle pieces. If they had no time limit on the Bible study, he was sure they would spend forever in that little cinderblock room, reading, and chatting away about God's Word.

After meeting with Karen a couple more times, Joe had grown more and more curious about her past. He had so many questions to ask and a longing to know everything about her—all of the bad and good. He hoped these thoughts were merely curiosity and not infatuation. After all, what would she see in a nerdy veterinarian from Mercy? Nevertheless, he was actually happy to see the prison each Tuesday and Thursday.

Joe took his usual seat across from Karen on their second Thursday together. "Hey, Karen. How are you?"

She smiled. "Good. I'm feeling better and better as the days go by. Only one week left."

Joe flipped open his Bible. "Where are you going home to?"

They were both surprised by the sudden question. He had been holding back for too long, though. He was grateful she wouldn't be locked up anymore, but Joe dreaded their last Bible study. Now he knew for sure that he wanted to see her even after she was freed.

Karen twirled a lock of hair around her forefinger. "I plan to live with my aunt. She has a spare room. I figure I'll get a job and save up some money."

Joe couldn't contain his curiosity. "Where does she live?"

"The most beautiful place in the world." Karen stared into Joe's eyes, but she clearly didn't see them, just her home. "It has acres of farmland, hills, and pines."

"That sounds kind of like Mercy."

Her eyes widened in surprise. "It *is* Mercy."

"You're from Mercy?" they asked in unison.

They both nodded, grinning at each other.

Joe frowned in bewilderment. "I thought you knew what church we were from."

"Actually," she whispered, "we're not supposed to know for the church's safety. The prison doesn't want to be liable for any angry prisoners getting out and harming anyone from a particular church."

Joe nodded. "Silly liability reasons."

She shook her head in amazement. "I grew up in Mercy."

"Me too. I've lived there all of my life. Well, with the exception of college and vet school."

Karen's interest visibly peaked. "You're a veterinarian?"

He hesitated. The fact wasn't part of his pick-up line. "Yes, I'm a vet."

"That's great, Joe. What made you decide to become a vet?"

Joe wondered how much he could open up to her. The words came naturally, though. "My mom says I have a gift for caring for animals. When I was about eight years old, I was walking home from school. I heard yelping and whining, so I followed the sound. It was a lab puppy stuck in a box. Someone put the box on the train tracks behind Main Street. I couldn't believe it. So I moved the box, and I tried to take her out. She was really scared, though. When I went to pick her up, she bit me."

Karen leaned forward in her seat. "You weren't afraid she was rabid?"

"No, I knew she didn't trust me yet. She was protecting herself. So I tried again, and she let me hold her. After that, I took her home. She had been abused, so I nursed her wounds. She healed up really well, and we still have her today."

Karen smiled, appearing impressed. Then a curious expression came over her face. "Hey, if you grew up in Mercy, you must've gone to the schools. What's your last name?"

"Aldridge. Joe is short for Joseph."

Suddenly, with his words, all of the color drained from Karen's face. Her mouth sat ajar, and she stared at him for a moment. She hopped up from the bench, holding her stomach.

"Guard," she called in a quaking voice.

Joe jumped up. "Karen, what's wrong?"

"I'm not feeling well," she said as the guard came over. "I want to go back to the dorm."

The guard took Karen by the arm gently and led her to the door. She exited the room without looking back at him.

*   *   *

"You look like someone ripped out your heart and dropped an anvil on it," Aunt Val said.

Karen sat at a table across from her in the visiting room. "That's pretty much how it went."

"What happened? Did they say you're not getting out? I've talked to them ten times, and they told me ten times—"

"No, I'm getting out on time."

"Then what is it? Did my fudge make you sick?"

"No."

"Come on. Out with it," she said, watching her niece intensely.

"I've been going to Bible study."

Her aunt's eyes narrowed. "Are they harassing you again? I told you what to tell them."

"No, Aunt Val. I met this guy, and he—"

Aunt Val pointed a slender finger at her. "Don't even finish. He thought he was better than you 'cause you were in jail, and he

57

started harassin' you! That jerk! You give me his name, and I'll be on him like syrup on pancakes!"

Karen sighed heavily. "Joseph Aldridge."

"What?" Aunt Val's jaw looked ready to fall into her lap.

"He didn't harass me, though."

"How in the world do you even know him, let alone, even speak to him without him harassing you?"

She dropped her heavy chin in her palm. "He doesn't know who I am."

Her green eyes flashed confusion. "Whoa, Nelly! Let's back track here. Tell me what happened."

"He was my Bible study partner for one-on-one Bible study through the church," she explained. "He said his name was Joe. I didn't know his last name or that Joe was short for Joseph or that he was even from Mercy. They don't tell us what church the people come from."

"And why not?"

"Silly liability reasons. Anyway, all I knew was that he was the sweetest guy I'd ever met," she said, picturing his soft, brown eyes. "He's been teaching me for the last few studies, but I didn't find out who he was until yesterday."

Aunt Val tapped her ruby red nails on the tabletop. "So you've got a crush on the wrong guy."

Karen could feel her cheeks burning. "It's not a crush. He would have been a great friend, but once he knows who I am, he won't want anything to do with me."

"Hon, first of all, that look means crush, not friend. Second, it's been nine years. Maybe he'll be able to leave the past in the past."

"I'm responsible for his grandfather's death! How can he just forget that?"

Aunt Val shrugged. "Some people are more forgivin' than others."

Karen sighed heavily, her chest aching. "I can't go back to Bible study, and I can't go back to Mercy."

"You are coming back to Mercy. I refuse to let you give up your home because you're afraid of some unforgiving people. Now going back to Bible study is up to you, but I will not let you run away from home again."

"Fine, fine," Karen muttered.

"So whatcha gonna do?"

"I don't know. How long I can hide who I am?"

* * *

"Joe, you look thoughtful. What's on your mind?" his mother asked at Sunday dinner.

"Just the clinic," he lied, poking at his pork chop with his fork. The fried meat smothered in gravy, which he normally devoured like a starving stray, didn't look so appetizing.

Karen, Karen, Karen, he thought. She'd been on his mind non-stop since their last meeting. *Had she really gotten sick? Why did she run off like that? Was it me? Does she hate vets? Why would anyone hate veterinarians?*

"How's that coming along, Joe?" Uncle Robert asked from across the table.

With Karen on the brain, Joe hardly remembered his aunt and uncle seated at the table. It was customary for them to come over for Sunday dinner. After church service, the meal was more like a late lunch or early dinner around three o'clock. Joe guessed the tradition didn't break while he was at college. That was the funny thing about Mercy. Despite who came and left, old traditions died hard.

"What?" Joe's thoughts finally arrived at the table with his body.

Joe's father looked at him from the end of the crowded oak table. "The clinic, son."

"Oh, it's going well. The plans are all set, and the permits will be ready tomorrow. I'm going in on Wednesday with the contractors."

"Mrs. Perdy says she's bringing Choo-choo as soon as you open up," Aunt Connie said.

A look of surprise came over his father's face. "She still has that little, yippy dog?"

Aunt Connie nodded. "Yes, she's had him for some years now." Her blue eyes brightened. "You know it's been nine years since that Denwood girl went to prison, Rich."

Joe's father shrugged. "So?"

"So her sentence will be up soon." She grimaced. "What if she comes back to Mercy?"

Joe's mother shook her head. "I don't think she will. Her father left town and never came back."

"Not Valerie Denwood," Aunt Connie said. "That's her aunt. She still lives here."

"Yes, Valerie Denwood," Uncle Robert said thoughtfully. "She's a good woman. She helps with all of the church picnics."

Aunt Connie cleared her throat. "Well, I wouldn't know. I don't speak to any kin of that *girl.*"

The tone in which she said 'girl' sent chills down Joe's spine. He had pushed the memories of his grandfather's death as far back in his mind as they would go. Even now, he still found it hard to believe that a young girl could have killed his grandpa. *Denwood,* he thought. *Katie Denwood? No. Carrie Denwood? What was that Denwood girl's name?*

"You really shouldn't hold her niece's actions against her," Joe's mother said. "It's not even Christian to hold such a grudge with Karen Denwood."

At the mention of the forgotten first name, Joe's eyes shot up to look at his mother.

Aunt Connie's face grew flush. "Excuse me." She hurried from the dining room, and Uncle Robert rose to follow her.

"Well, I think she needs to find some forgiveness in her heart," Mrs. Aldridge whispered. "We were all hurt. We all miss him, but you shouldn't dig up the past."

"Please, dear," Joe's father whispered back gruffly.

Blue eyes. Blonde hair. Karen, Joseph thought. He suddenly rose from the table.

"You too?" his mother asked.

"I have to make a quick phone call," Joe said, darting from the room and up the stairs.

In his small bedroom, he shuffled through papers, searching desperately for Emily Bailey's telephone number on his old, wooden dresser. To his relief, he found it and dialed.

"Hello?" Emily's eternally cheerful voice answered.

"Emily, it's Joseph."

"Joe? Hi! How are you?"

"Good. Listen, who is that girl you paired me up with at the prison?"

"Karen."

"Her last name."

The name that came over the phone seemed to enter his ear in slow-motion. It was what he feared.

"Denwood," she said, "Karen Denwood."

He sighed heavily. It all made sense now.

"Emily, did you know who she was?"

"What do you mean?"

"Don't you remember the incident with my grandfather?"

There was silence over the phone for a moment.

"Oh, Joe, I had no idea!" she cried, her voice becoming shrill. "I mean, I thought her name sounded familiar when we met, but I didn't realize . . ."

Joe sank down on his bed. "It's okay."

"She looks so different now," Emily said. "If you don't want to go there anymore, we can make other arrangements."

"I need to think it over."

"Joe?"

"Yes?"

"Why don't we talk about it over coffee tomorrow morning?"

"I can't, Emily. I have a lot to do tomorrow. I'm sorry." He dropped the phone on the cradle and fell back on his old boyhood bed. "What am I going to do?"

Joe's eyes searched the room as if he were looking for the answer written on his bedroom walls. His eyes stopped on a dark book on his dresser across the room. He couldn't remember what book it was and curiosity brought him to it. It was his grandpa's old Bible. He returned to his bed, sat down, and flipped through the worn, thin pages. The pages stopped flipping on their own, and his eyes landed on a certain verse from Proverbs 21:21: "He that followeth after righteousness and mercy findeth life, righteousness, and honour."

"Is that your answer, God?" he whispered. "Be merciful? She took away my grandfather. If it hadn't been for her, he might still be here with us now."

Joseph sat hunched over his grandfather's Bible, sighing. He could remember now so clearly the grief in his father's eyes when Sheriff Wilson had arrived with the news. The funeral was like a quiet nightmare. Everyone in town had attended. His grandfather had looked so strange in that coffin. He missed Grandpa Frank. He missed his smile and his wisdom.

"But I'll see him again," Joe told himself. "God promises that."

On Tuesday, Joseph entered the women's prison with hope and forgiveness in his heart for Karen. He only hoped she would be at the Bible study to receive it.

They waited in their usual meeting room for the prisoners. He began to chew his nails, which was not a normal habit for him. He looked at Emily and noticed she was very quiet for the first time that evening. They exchanged glances, and she quickly looked away. *She's mad at me. No, maybe she's disappointed,* he thought. He really couldn't tell and, at that moment, he didn't care. Right then, he just hoped Karen would walk in.

The door opened, and the usual troupe of ladies came in with the exception of one—the one he feared.

Joe turned to the guard. "Where's Karen?"

She shrugged. "She didn't want to come."

"Can I see her?"

"Only if you're registered as one of her visitors, sir."

He groaned in frustration, and he knew their Bible study was over.

* * *

With each stroke of the paint brush, Karen felt as if gentle hands massaged her soul. Each color represented some part of herself she was releasing. With every stroke of blue, she let a little bit of sadness slip away. With each stroke of red, some of her anger emptied out on to the canvas. The colors were a part of her that could form a beautiful picture when worked together with the brush.

Karen was grateful for every moment she could spend on her art. Aunt Val brought her new supplies every week in exchange for what her aunt called another "masterpiece". To Karen, painting was a way to find some relief and peace in a place that was often stressful and chaotic. She was certain any art dealer would find her works worthless.

Typically, nothing short of a tornado could break Karen's concentration when she was painting, but she couldn't focus this time. Her painting was supposed to be of Mercy Church, but she accidentally added too many windows. The cemetery was on the wrong side.

The metal door to the activity room creaked open, and Karen nearly dropped her brush.

She turned to see Maria enter and make her way among the tables where other inmates were reading books, playing cards, or writing letters.

"Well? Was he there?" Karen asked.

A mischievous grin formed on her bunkmate's face, making her dark eyes sparkle. "Sí, Señorita."

"And?"

Maria began to reply in speedy Spanish.

"Maria!" Karen found herself unable to keep from smiling at her teasing friend.

"You need to brush up on your Spanish, Karen."

"Out with it!"

"He was looking for you. He seemed desperate."

"He knows. What happened?"

"We came in," Maria said, "and he asked the guard where you were. Then he wanted to know if he could visit you."

"Did he seem angry?"

"Nope. He looked really disappointed after that. He never looked mad."

Karen bit her lip. "Maybe he doesn't know."

"I don't think he does. He didn't look like a man who was ready to lash out at someone. He just looked really eager to see you."

Karen sighed. This report sounded good. Whether he knew or not, for the moment, Joseph Aldridge wasn't angry. Relief swept over her. They had only met a few times. It seemed strange that he would be so eager to see her. Was it possible Joe had an interest in her? Her heart skipped a beat, but she immediately snapped back to reality. It didn't matter. It would only be a matter of time before he knew who she was. Then she would get what she deserved, nothing less than his complete loathing.

Karen grabbed her large, flat-handled paintbrush dunked it in white and with each blanketing stroke, watched Mercy Church disappear.

Chapter Six

The front entrance to the general store put up quite a fight for Joe on Wednesday morning. This made him all the more anxious to see the interior and begin the old building's transformation.

Tuesday night had felt more like the night before Christmas. He couldn't sleep, thinking about all of the renovations and plans he had for his grandfather's store. This had been Joe's dream since college. Mercy had been home for so long that he couldn't imagine not returning to practice among the people he knew and loved. His college buddies thought he was crazy to return to such a small town. Business was booming in the metropolitan areas when it came to pet care. After all, people were getting pet insurance these days. Big money never appealed to Joe, though. He cared more about being near family and giving back to the community that had given him an almost perfect boyhood.

Joe gave the front door a determined shove with his right shoulder. It finally gave in to the pressure and creaked open. The sound instantly brought him back to those good, old days.

familiar smell lingered in the dusty air, flooding in memories of sweeping the dark, hardwood floors. Rays of morning sunlight managed to sneak in passed the boards over the front window. He would have to rip those rotting boards down to let in more light. For now, he reached for the light switch by the door. With a click, florescent lights flickered on across the length of the little store. Some shelves still remained, hidden under old bed sheets. He remembered stocking those shelves with canned vegetables, bags of potato chips, and boxes of pain reliever.

Despite the warm, late spring air outside, the store was chilly. Joe crossed his arms over his chest as he walked in, examining the room. His imagination ran circles around him as he envisioned where the receptionist would sit. He had to hire one. This one large room would be split into at least three. He would need a waiting area, a reception area, his own office, an examination room, and a small kennel room. Because the main floor had plenty of space for all of this, Joe had decided he would leave the upstairs office and storage space untouched.

Joe walked toward the back of the store, curious to see what was left in his grandfather's office. He came to the infamous staircase and stopped in his tracks. He'd heard his grandfather died on the wooden platform. Imagining such a sight sent chills down Joe's spine. The staircase was once filled with great memories. He used to race his little brother down them. He once tripped and would have tumbled down if it had not been for his grandfather's quick reflexes.

Looking at the dusty, wooden staircase, Joe couldn't bring himself to climb it. A pain returned that he hadn't felt in years. He took a deep, quaking breath and walked to where the front counter still stood, draped with flowery bed sheets. With one swift movement, Joe yanked the sheet down to the floor, revealing the glass case counter and his grandfather's cash register. He remembered the first time his grandpa let him ring up a customer. He was seven years old.

"Now push the red button there, Joe," Grandpa had said in his gentle voice.

Upon pushing the red button, the register's draw popped open with a resounding ding.

"Cool!" Joe had exclaimed.

"Now take her money, son."

A younger Valerie Denwood had smiled at him as he carefully took the bills from her hand. Back then, none of them had any idea Valerie's niece would be responsible for his grandfather's death.

Joe pushed the red button on the register, and the draw popped open with the same enthusiastic ding it had sounded in better days. The sounds, sights, and smells of the general store tugged at his heart, bringing back memories he had thought could never be relived. He had tucked them away, buried them in the deepest recesses of his mind. They were too painful to drudge up, even now. He felt his eyes begin to sting. The sheet had kicked up some dust. It must have landed in his eyes. A lump in his throat told him it wasn't the dust at all.

Wiping his eyes, Joe hurried to the front door, hoping to get out into some fresh air. That would give him a second wind, help him to get some work done. Outside the front door, Joe took in a few deep breaths, pushing back more memories of his grandfather. The memories were slipping away, but other thoughts lingered. He wondered where he would have set up shop if his grandfather were still alive. Would he still be living at home with the family? Would Grandpa still be reading the Bible to the family every Sunday evening?

A longing for what could have been overcame Joe. He was finding it harder and harder not to become emotional. He closed his eyes tightly, feeling a hot breeze dance across him and down Main Street. Why did Karen have to go into his shop? Why did she have to go up the stairs?

To his surprise, another emotion began to rise up inside of Joe. It burned in his belly and tightened his jaw. It forced his tears back and reddened his normally carefree face.

Fists clenched, Joe opened his eyes. He was so sure he had forgiven Karen. Now the pain seemed fresh all over again. His wound was reopened, and it seemed to hurt worse than it did before. Maybe he wasn't ready to forgive her after all.

* * *

From the moment Karen's eyes opened on that Thursday morning, her hands wouldn't stop shaking. The strange combination of nervousness, joy, excitement, and hope could only escape through her sweaty palms, gyrating fingers, and chattering teeth. She clinched her jaw, and her hands shook more violently. As she watched the clock in the dormitory count down to her very last hour, she silently prayed.

Lord, thank You for getting me through my sentence. I think I turned out okay, all things considered. You really have been faithful. I know there was a reason why I had to go to jail. I'll understand that someday. I'm just glad that it's finally over. Please help me adjust to the world outside, so I can do Your will and glorify You with each new day of freedom.

Maria hugged Karen tightly, grinning from ear to ear. "You're free, girl."

Karen swallowed. "I'm scared."

"You've got your auntie who loves you." Maria pulled back and gave her a comforting smile. "And you look so pretty. Orange was never your color."

Karen was wearing a long, baby blue dress decorated with pink roses. Matching pink sandals adorned her feet. Aunt Val gave the dress and shoes to Karen as a gift for her big day.

Tears burned Karen's eyes. "You're the only thing about this place I'm gonna miss."

The two friends had met the day after Karen's eighteenth birthday. Karen had moved from the juvenile detention center to the women's prison as required by state law. Maria was twenty at the time.

"One more year. I'll go to Mercy lookin' for you and turn the place upside down."

They laughed and embraced again.

A light bulb flipped on in Karen's mind. "I can't believe I almost forgot. I have a present for you."

"For me?"

Karen reached under the bottom bunk and pulled out a colorful canvas. "I hope you like it."

Maria took the painting and gasped. "Karen, this is beautiful."

They both gazed at the brightly colored portrait of Maria's grandmother. The old woman smiled in front of a purple backdrop.

"I used the picture of her that you love."

Tears glimmered in Maria's eyes. "She is smiling down on you from Heaven, Karen." She hugged her tightly again. "Thank you."

A guard approached them. "Time to go, Denwood."

Karen turned back to her friend. "I'll come see you next week. I promise."

Maria put a hand on each of Karen's shoulders, a stern look in her eyes. "Karen, get out of here and don't look back. Just write me, and I'll see you in a year."

Maria knew all too well how much Karen didn't want to come back. She nodded at her friend, turned and followed the guard out of the dormitory for the last time.

The guard led Karen through the narrow corridors of white cement block walls to the front lobby.

At the front desk, Officer Bright smiled at Karen. "Congratulations, Denwood." Her smile faded suddenly with the words, "Stay out of trouble."

"Yes, Officer."

The guard led Karen through a metal detector and two metal doors before they finally reached the brilliant May sunlight.

Karen squinted to see a long cement walk ahead. Standing about ten feet away, Aunt Val grinned at her. She wore a bright red dress suit and red pumps. They contrasted a bouquet of white daisies in her hands.

"There's my girl!" she squealed, throwing her arms in the air. "Free at last!"

Aunt Val ran to meet her niece as Karen stepped out into the hot sunlight. The metal door closed heavily behind her. *I'm free*, she thought in disbelief.

Aunt Val threw her arms around Karen in that tight embrace she hadn't felt in nine years. Aunt Val seemed so small and fragile now. Karen had been the small and fragile one the last time they embraced. Hot tears fell down Karen's cheeks as her heart boomed in her ears. She sighed loudly, and a sudden burst of grief and joy made her feel as if she would collapse in her aunt's arms. She began to heave and sob as Aunt Val pulled back to look at her. Her aunt's eyes were wet with tears, and she sobbed right along with Karen.

"Oh, honey," Aunt Val said, wiping Karen's tears. "It's okay now. We're going home. I brought you these."

Karen's hands finally stopped shaking as Aunt Val placed the daisies in them. She smiled at her aunt, speechless. The wait was finally over.

In her aunt's new Pontiac, Karen nestled into the front seat with much excitement, like a child riding in a brand new car. It was actually five years old, but the four-door was new to Karen. She remembered Aunt Val driving a two-door Chevy throughout Karen's childhood. The only trips Karen had ever taken out of the correctional facilities were in dingy, old vans with bars over the windows. Those trips only allowed the slightest glimpses of freedom. Afterward, Karen would return to the prison and paint the images she saw along the roadway, holding on to every shrub and cloud as if she would never see the real thing again.

On the road to Mercy, the path hadn't changed much in the past nine years. Acres of pines still paralleled the highway. Some of the fields had been cleared for farmland in recent years. They passed Wiley's Bar. To Karen's relief, the horrible establishment was weather-beaten and abandoned.

Not long after seeing Wiley's, they entered Mercy. She was thrilled to see that her little hometown looked almost exactly the same as it had ten years before. There was one change. Mr. Aldridge's store was renovated and had a new, freshly painted sign that read "Mercy Veterinary Clinic, Joseph W. Aldridge." A plastic sign hanging below read "Coming Soon."

"Joseph." The name escaped under her breath.

"What?" Aunt Val asked, driving past the clinic.

"Nothing."

"He's opening it in a couple of weeks."

"What? Who?"

Her aunt giggled. "Give me a break. I know you're still pouting over him."

"I am not."

"You better forget about him, kitten. He'll just realize who you are, and the past will come right back up to haunt the both of you."

"I thought you said some people are more forgiving than others," Karen said in jest.

Aunt Val's lips tightened. "I don't want you to get hurt."

Her sudden seriousness startled Karen. "You're being silly. I'm not looking for a relationship or a friendship right now. All I want to do is make some money and go to art school."

Despite her attraction to Joe Aldridge, any type of relationship, even a friendship, was impossible to fathom. There was Ricky, though. The memory of his photo forced its way into Karen's thoughts. He was so handsome. Becoming friends with him and Maria had made her sentence a little easier to endure. The desire to meet him in person was hard for her to ignore. Now that she was free, the possibility of falling in love didn't seem so unrealistic.

As if reading her niece's thoughts, Aunt Val said, "What about that Ricky guy?"

Karen immediately changed the subject. "Do you think I should start looking for a job tomorrow?"

"I think you should lay low and relax a while. Besides, some people might think you're an out-of-towner. You know how bias Mercy locals can be."

"Do they know I'm coming home?"

"No one but me should know unless you told Joe Aldridge."

Karen groaned.

Aunt Val's jaw dropped. "You didn't."

"I didn't know who he was at the time."

"Oh, Karen, now he's going to have his whole family waiting with pitchforks at my house!"

To their relief, no Aldridges waited on Aunt Val's front lawn, only her fluffy gray cat, Muffins.

"There's my Muffins!" Aunt Val squealed, slipping out of the car and running to the lounging cat. "I thought you got away from me!"

Aunt Val scooped Muffins up in her arms and cuddled him as Karen slipped out of the car with her one small duffle bag.

"He was teasing my Choo-choo again," said a cranky, female voice. "Just strolling along my fence while Choo-choo barked."

Aunt Val and Karen found the source of the raspy voice. It was Mrs. Eva Perdy. Karen couldn't believe her eyes. The woman had to be, at least, ninety years old now. When she was thirteen, Karen didn't think the gutsy, elderly woman would live another year. Yet, there she stood in her front yard. She leaned over her wooden cane with a gardening hat on top of her brown, curly wig. Already a small woman hunched over, she was only about four and a half feet tall standing upright. She wore a purple sweatshirt with matching purple sweat pants.

"Sweats in May, Mrs. Perdy?" Aunt Val asked.

"There's a chill in the air," she croaked, pushing her big sunglasses up her nose. "Who's your friend?"

Aunt Val was silent for a moment, and Karen suddenly remembered why. Mrs. Eva Perdy was Mercy's town gossip. If word got to her that Karen Denwood, the "delinquent," was back in town, all of Mercy would know by bedtime.

"This is Kar, uh, Carrie. She's a relative," Aunt Val said. "She's staying with me for a little while."

Mrs. Perdy cocked her head. "Why?"

Aunt Val walked toward her front door with Muffins under one arm. "She needed a place to stay."

"Why?" Mrs. Perdy was as inquisitive as a four-year-old.

"Her house burned down. Come on, Carrie. You need to get in and rest." Aunt Val turned to Mrs. Perdy again. "She's all worked up, lost almost everything in the fire."

The old widow hummed suspiciously.

Karen rushed to the front porch where her aunt opened the front door and dropped Muffins in the front foyer.

Aunt Val waved. "Talk to you later, Mrs. Perdy."

"Nice to meet you, Carrie."

"You too, Mrs. Perdy," Karen said, entering the house behind her aunt.

Karen pushed the door shut behind her. "Aunt Val, you lied!"

"The woman is so nosy! What was I supposed to say? She'll tell everyone you're here."

Karen would have protested longer, but she could hardly believe her eyes. Her aunt's house looked so different. She hardly recognized it. Everything had changed, right down to the carpet under her feet.

"Where am I?"

Her aunt strolled through the front foyer and across the living room toward the kitchen doorway. "I know it's a big difference to you. I changed things so gradually that I'm just used to it all."

The living room walls that were once patterned with flowery wallpaper had been striped and painted a striking shade of lavender. The old, blue carpet was replaced with a light and fluffy beige one. She had a completely new set of living room furniture. Karen took some comfort in the fact that a few wall hangings remained where she had remembered them, including a European-made coo-coo clock.

"Come on and see the attic."

Karen followed her excited aunt through a very familiar kitchen. Only the wallpaper and countertops had changed in this room, much to Karen's relief. After years of being locked up in a place that changes very little, familiarity and consistency had become something of a security blanket to her.

A door stood closed at the top of the attic staircase. At this door, Aunt Val stopped and turned to her niece.

She beamed. "I hope you like what I've done with it. You know you are welcomed to stay as long as you want. No man can put up with my picky nature, but I sure hope you can, sweetie."

"I can, and I will." Anything was better than that cold, sterile prison cell.

Aunt Val pushed the door open. Following her aunt, Karen stepped inside of a huge room painted in a shade of peach. She hardly recognized the once unfinished, cluttered space. A full sized bed covered with a peach and cream quilt sat at one end of the room between a matching white wicker night stand and dresser. At the other end, her eyes fell upon a wooden stool, table with art supplies, and an easel with a blank canvas.

Karen gasped as she recognized the images all around her. On every open space of the walls, her aunt had hung her paintings. Karen nearly buckled over at the sight. There must have been at least three dozen sixteen by twenty paintings decorating the room from floor to ceiling.

"This is your studio."

Karen gasped. "Aunt Val, you saved every one of them."

"What else would I do with them? They're all beautiful."

Tears began to fill her eyes. "Thank you. This is more than I deserve."

"Kitten, don't ever say you deserve anything less." Aunt Val placed her arms around Karen. "Don't punish yourself anymore. That part of your life is over."

Chapter Seven

"Why aren't you at the prison this evening, Joe?" his mother asked, looking up from her full dinner plate.

Once again, Joe's mother went all out, preparing meatloaf and yeast rolls from scratch for a delicious family feast. She arranged bowls of green beans and rice pilaf neatly around the meatloaf in the center of the table. He wondered if she had cooked so thoroughly when he was away at college. Joe wished he could ask her about it right then and avoid her question.

Instead, he shrugged. "I guess I've been doing too much lately. I needed to cut back."

"Oh, Joe, did you hurt Emily's feelings?"

"No," he lied, "she understood."

Whether she had understood or not, he saw the look on Emily's face when he said he couldn't go back. The old guilt that plagued him after dumping her had returned.

"I'm amazed at how quickly the renovations are going," his mother said. "I can't believe the grand opening is in one week."

Joe smirked. "Well, Dad's been a strong influence."

"You've gotta get on the ball and stay busy with it," his father said. "Idle hands, as they say."

She shook her head. "Oh, Joe, you shouldn't mind your father. Starting a business should be a slow process. No wonder you got so stressed." She grimaced at her husband at the other end of the table. "Shame on you, Rich."

His father frowned, chewing on his yeast roll. "The boy needs to get out on his own."

"Amen, Dad," Eric chimed in with a mouth full of meatloaf.

Joe's mother wagged her finger. "You agricultural men have awful table manners."

The telephone rang, and everyone paused to look at Joe's mother. She hated any interruptions during family dinner. She once spent half an hour telling a door-to-door salesman how important the family meal was and how he needed to be at home eating with his family. He never came back.

She rose from her seat, tossing her cloth napkin on the table. "Well, they're going to get an earful for calling at suppertime."

She left the dining room to answer the phone in the kitchen. The Aldridge men sat quietly, anticipating an ugly confrontation between her and the caller.

"I hope it's a telemarketer," Eric whispered gleefully.

Joseph rolled his eyes, still listening.

"Aldridge residence," Helen answered. "What's wrong? . . . Cool down. What's going on? . . . Who? . . . Oh dear . . . Well, who told you that? . . . Then it maybe true . . ."

The conversation remained vague. Joe couldn't tell who was on the other end of the line. Finally, his mother hung up the phone and returned to the dining room. She nonchalantly took her seat as the men watched her with inquisitive glances.

"Who was it?" her husband asked, returning to his food.

She picked up her fork. "Connie. We'll talk about it later."

"She never calls at suppertime. What did she want?"

"We need to talk about it alone, Rich," she said, taking a bite of rice.

"They're men now. They can hear it," he said, setting down his fork.

"Rich, it's not them."

"Tell me."

Joe's mother sighed loudly and looked down at her plate, perching her fork on the edge. "She said Karen Denwood is in town."

Joe's heart nearly stopped. He dropped his rice-covered fork, and it fell with a loud clang on his plate, sending rice in the air like confetti. His mother nearly jumped out of her skin.

"Sorry," he apologized, picking up his fork.

"That girl's got a lot of nerve," his father said, returning to his food. "Who told her this?"

"Mrs. Perdy told Angela Bailey who told Mrs. Satterwhite who told Miss Parson who told her."

Joe couldn't believe his mother could say all of that with a straight face. It was quite a serious matter, though.

"Then it may be true," he said, echoing his wife's words from the phone conversation.

Joe's mother nodded. "She said Mrs. Perdy saw her arrive at Valerie Denwood's house this morning. She's very upset. I'm meeting her for lunch tomorrow."

Joe's father shook his head. "The sheriff will hear about this. She'll be booted out of town in no time."

Joe was suddenly torn. He had struggled with his anger over the past couple of days, reading the Bible to get up the courage to forgive. He still didn't know for sure if he could do it. The more time he spent in the general store, the more memories returned. Yet, as walls were being put up and the floors ripped out, those memories were melting away. It was as if his memories were sheltered in that old building, the old being pulled out to make room for the new.

He thought of those tender blue eyes and Karen's soothing laugh. He wanted to defend her. He wanted to tell his parents how wonderful Karen was. They had to know how smart she was, how she could explain even the most challenging passage of Scripture. She wasn't that thirteen-year-old delinquent anymore. Yet, seeing the anger and pain in his father's eyes made him want to be mad at her too. *Why did she have to break into the store?* he thought angrily. *And why did Grandpa have to die because of it?*

Joe could see sympathy in his mother's eyes. "It was nine years ago, Rich. Don't you think she's gotten what she deserved? She should be able to go on with her life."

Joe sighed under his breath. *Thank God for Mom.*

He saw his father's jaw clench. "My father can't go on with his life!"

He stormed out of the dining room, and they all listened to his loud footsteps as stomped through the kitchen and out the back door.

Joe's mother sighed heavily. "Boys, clean up the table for me, would you?"

She rose slowly from her chair and headed outside.

"Let's go egg Valerie Denwood's house," Eric said with a goofy grin.

Joe groaned. "That's so juvenile, Eric."

"But Dad's really mad. How could she come back here like everything's okay?"

Joe thought for a moment about his brother's question. "Maybe because she hoped everything *was* okay."

* * *

The early Sunday morning air was enough to make Karen want to burst with joy. She finally had the freedom to relax outdoors. Over the past four years, her time outside had been spent on the community work squad, completing various clean-up and landscaping duties from early morning to late afternoon. Out on her aunt's back porch, Karen lay on a folding lawn chair, watching the chickadees dance among the bushes. She was quite sure she looked like some kind of starlet there on the porch, tanning in a bikini and wearing her aunt's rhinestone-studded, black sunglasses. It didn't matter, though. All she could think about was the gorgeous backyard surrounding her.

The hydrangeas and day lilies in Aunt Val's garden were unbelievably beautiful. They reminded Karen of the flowers she'd seen a few weeks earlier. She was collecting trash on an interstate median abounding in red and yellow tulips. It took everything in her not to pick one of them. God's glory seemed to beam from every bright petal. But she didn't want to see it die and wither behind the prison walls like so many prisoners and their hopes.

Her first few days of freedom were more than she could've hoped for. Her only disappointment was her inability to oversleep. In jail, all inmates had to wake up at six o'clock in the morning to start the day. She always promised herself that on her first day of freedom, she would sleep in. Six o'clock came the morning after she was released, and Karen was wide awake. Finally, after two early mornings, she rose at eight o'clock. To her, it was a slice of heaven.

Still, her prison schedule remained with her when it came to eating. She always got hungry for lunch and dinner at the same time the meals were served in the correctional facility. Aunt Val understood and made sure Karen had something to munch on at those times and then some. Karen felt like she had already gained ten pounds. The past few days were spent eating treats she had missed for nine years. She was surprised that between all of the overindulging, she had found time to paint and read.

A rustling noise on the other side of Aunt Val's short, wooden fence caught Karen's attention. She glanced over to see Mrs. Perdy watering her azalea bushes with a plastic, yellow watering can.

Karen offered her a wave and a smile. "Good morning, Mrs. Perdy."

Mrs. Perdy met eyes with her under a large, round gardening hat and scowled. "I know who you really are. You can't fool me, criminal."

Karen lost her breath as she watched the old woman hobble back into her house, slamming the back door behind her.

"Well, Miss Priss," Aunt Val said, stepping out of the sliding glass door and on to the wooden deck in her Sunday best, "I guess you're not going to church this morning?"

Still caught up in the last few seconds, Karen didn't answer.

"What's wrong, kitten?"

Karen shook her head, lowering her sunglasses from her eyes. "Nothing. Uh, maybe next Sunday?"

"You haven't left my property since you got out of jail. There's a big world out there. It's called Earth."

"I know about Earth," she said with a sigh. "I'm exploring one place at a time."

Her aunt swatted a bug from her face. "Well, I'm going with or without you. At least take some time to look at your Bible."

"I will."

Karen had been doing a devotion everyday for about two years. Her newfound freedom only increased her desire to study and pray more. She was grateful for things that most people took for granted. Yet, she couldn't help but feel a little guilty about hanging around Aunt Val's house and neglecting the outside world. It felt so big and unfamiliar. She was out of her element.

Aunt Val picked up a strand of her niece's hair. "Just how much time have you spent outside lately?"

"More than enough. Why?"

"I think your hair is already starting to lighten some. You should grow it out again."

Karen grinned, pushing the sunglasses back up her nose. "Maybe I will."

"Well, I've gotta go. Water my garden, would you, babe?"

"Sure."

The sound of the telephone ringing from inside the house cut through the natural melodies of summer like a knife.

"I'll get it!" Aunt Val rushed back into the house, only to emerge ten seconds later with the telephone. She frowned, offering it to her niece. "It's Ricky."

Karen's relaxed and steady heartbeat suddenly shifted into overdrive as she reached for the phone. Her aunt waited and listened as Karen put the phone to her ear. "A little privacy?"

"You're no fun," her aunt said, sticking out her tongue playfully. "I'll be back after service."

Karen watched Aunt Val wave and disappear back into the house, closing the sliding glass door behind her.

"Hello?" she greeted in a fluttery voice.

"Hey, Karen. How's sweet freedom?" that familiar voice asked over the line.

"It's so great!" she said, not meaning to sound so unreserved. "That was my aunt who answered."

"It's totally cool that she's letting you stay with her." He sounded more like a sixteen-year-old than a twenty-five-year-old sometimes. Karen liked his youthful nature.

"So you'll be released on Thursday, right?"

"No. Actually, the date got moved up," he said, his tone wavering between calm and mischievous.

"When?"

"I'm out now, girl!"

Karen's heart nearly stopped as she sat up in the lawn chair. "What? Really?"

"Yeah. Give me directions, and I'll come over."

She could hear her heartbeat in her ears, drowning out the sound of his voice. "Hang on a sec." Karen scurried to the door and hopped into the cool house air. She fumbled through directions while studying a map she'd rummaged from one of the kitchen drawers. After about five minutes of trying to map out a path to Mercy with Karen's help, Ricky seemed confident he could find the way.

"I should be there in about an hour," he said. "See you soon."

"Okay, Ricky."

Karen set the phone down with a shaky hand. She took a deep breath, trying to calm her nerves. The time had finally come, the moment she had waited so long for. The man who was once just a picture was going to be right in front of her in the flesh. What would she wear? What would he think of her? What would they do when he came over? Her head was spinning. She rushed up to her new bedroom in a panic.

*   *   *

There was no assigned seating in the Mercy Church, but everyone seemed to have their place. The Aldridge family always sat about halfway down the chapel from the altar on the right side. Joe felt comfortable seated between his mother and brother as in old times. After several weeks at home, he felt like he hadn't missed a single day in Mercy. Sundays were the same as they had always been. His uncle's sermons were no different than they had been when he was growing up. Some Sundays he preached in an uplifting tone. On other Sundays, he was more convicting. In the end, he managed to get some of the congregation to the altar to renew or begin their relationship with Christ.

As Joe waited for the service to begin, he turned in his seat to watch the church members file in. His eyes fell on one face in particular. Valerie Denwood slipped in, wearing a bright blue dress suit. Her red hair was up in a conservative bun. For a second, their eyes met. She forced a small smile, and then turned to squeeze down an aisle to her usual seat. Joe sighed, watching the door hopefully. Karen was no where in sight, though. He had done a lot of praying after the news of her arrival in town. It sounded like the only person who had caught sight of her was Eva Perdy. Joe hoped to see her out of the orange inmate uniform and in some attire that suited her personality better.

Maybe I should talk to her aunt after the service, he thought.

The past few days had been full of emotional rollercoasters and more recollections of good times with his grandfather, but Joe felt ready to put the past behind him. He knew it was time to let go of the anger and extend the same forgiveness God had extended to him when he accepted Jesus at age eight.

Eric turned to Joe, smirking. "That Denwood girl still hasn't shown up. I guess she knows better."

"Eric, let it go. She did her time," Joseph whispered, not hiding the irritation in his voice.

Eric's brow dropped. "Why are you sticking up for her?"

As Joe was about to respond, he saw Eric's eyes shift upward and his angry expression melt away into one of a deer caught in headlights. Joe turned to follow his brother's glance.

"Hey, Joe," Emily said with a little, Miss America wave. "How are you?"

Emily stood in the aisle in front of Joe wearing a yellow sun dress.

"Oh, hi, Emily. I'm good. How—"

"Hi, Emily," Eric said in a strange tone that Joe hardly recognized.

"Hey, Eric." Emily smiled at him but immediately returned her attention to Joe. "I'm having a dinner party in a few weeks.

It's for my birthday, a little get-together with old friends. Would you like to come?"

Joe shrugged. "Sure, that sounds good." He silently gathered this would be a nice way to make up for dropping out of her Bible study group.

"Great! I'll put you down on my list."

The piano at the front of the church began to echo melodies across the chapel. The congregation settled into their seats on cue. Emily gave Joe one last giddy smile and turned to take her seat. He sighed with relief. Every time they spoke, he couldn't wait for the conversation to end. A pang of guilt hit him hard. He couldn't understand why he found Emily so unappealing. After all, Eric seemed enamored with her. Joe stole a glance at his little brother. Eric was staring at the back of Emily's head with a look that reminded Joe of Eric's expression when his favorite team loses.

"Hey, why don't you go to that dinner party with me?" Joe said. "I bet she wouldn't mind."

Eric's expression quickly changed, and he shifted in his seat. "What? I don't go to dinner parties! Who do I look like—*you*?"

Joe shook his head at Eric's pitiful save. As long as he was too proud to admit his feelings, Emily would never give him a second glance.

* * *

The doorbell sent a loud ding-dong all through Aunt Val's house. Karen nearly tripped and tumbled down the attic stairs when the sound hit her ears. She caught herself on the wooden railing along the wall and straightened up. It was her aunt's heels. The two women wore the same size, but Karen wasn't used to anything but standard-issue prison sneakers. She tugged at her aunt's long pansy-covered, white skirt. She thought the purple blouse fit her well. Her only hope was that Ricky thought so too.

In the living room, Karen combed her blonde hair with her fingers and took one last look at herself in the foyer mirror. She smiled to check her teeth for any lingering food particles. Satisified, she took a deep breath and pulled the front door open.

Karen's eyes met a tall man with dark, spiky hair. He wore a small, silver hoop ring in the center of his lower lip. A black t-shirt with cut-off sleeves and black jeans covered his slender figure. A large tattoo of a tiger climbed up his exposed left arm.

"Hey, Karen!" the man greeted with a grin, opening his arms.

"Ricky?" Karen didn't know whether to embrace this Gothic-styled stranger or slam the door and lock the deadbolt.

He seemed to sense her unease and dropped his arms. "Yeah, I know I look pretty different from that old prom picture."

Karen pulled back slowly, feeling forced to let this odd-looking version of Ricky in. He made his way through the door past her. "Come on in."

He turned back to her as she closed the front door. "You look just like that drawing."

"Thanks," Karen said, leading him into the living room.

"Wow, this is nice." Ricky scanned the surroundings as they both sat on the couch.

Karen was still in shock at the Ricky that sat before her. She only recognized his eyes and voice. Little else seemed to match the image she had gotten used to over the years.

"Can I get you a drink?" she said after a moment of awkward silence.

Ricky shrugged. "How about some orange juice or something?"

"Okay." Karen was relieved to have an excuse to leave the room.

As she approached the doorway to reenter the living room with the drinks, Karen thought she heard rustling. When she entered, Ricky sat on the couch, stretching his arms.

She handed him a small glass. "Orange juice all around."

"Thanks." Ricky gulped his down.

Karen took a seat on the loveseat adjacent from him.

"So what did you think of Mercy when you drove in?" Karen asked with genuine curiosity.

"Well, I'm city folk, Ms. Denwood," Ricky said, mocking a thick, Southern accent. "I'm used to somethin' with a little more entertainment."

Karen nodded, releasing an uneasy chuckle. "I guess if you're used to a bigger place, it can be pretty boring here."

Ricky nodded.

"So what are you doing after this?"

Ricky set his glass on the coffee table. "I'm going around visiting some old friends."

The sound of the front door opening interrupted their dull conversation much to Karen's relief. Aunt Val entered the living room, obviously startled by the presence of this less conservative-looking guest.

Karen practically jumped from her seat. "Hey, Aunt Val. This is my pen pal friend, Ricky."

Ricky gave her a wave.

"Hello," Aunt Val greeted, forcing a friendly smile. "Karen, can I speak to you in the kitchen for two seconds?"

Karen nodded and followed her aunt into the kitchen.

"What is Dracula doing in my living room?" she whispered in a frazzled tone.

"He got out early. We're just chatting."

"I really would have preferred that you two met somewhere in public. You don't really know him," Aunt Val said.

Karen rolled her eyes. "We're adults having a conversation."

Her aunt sighed in defeat, shaking her head. "I'm going to fix some sandwiches, so ask him to stay for lunch."

When Karen returned to the living room, her guest was standing.

"I'd better hit the road, Karen," Ricky said.

Genuine disappointment hit her. "But we're fixing lunch. Wouldn't you like to stay?"

"Like I said, I'm visiting people, so I've got other places to be."

That's it? she thought, a hole forming in her gut. It wasn't necessarily the fact that he was leaving. It was the whole visit. She sensed their relationship wasn't going anywhere.

Ricky opened his arms to her. "I'm so glad we finally met in person."

Karen forced a smile and embraced her friend. "Me too."

He pulled away from her. "We should get together and do something when I've got more time. Let me give you my cell number."

Hopeful, Karen grabbed a pen and an old, used envelope from the coffee table. She jotted down the number as he recited it to her.

Karen opened the front door. "Drive safely."

"Bye, Karen," Ricky said, his blue eyes sparkling. Despite the Gothic look, she could still feel herself melting from his warm glance.

She waved and closed the door behind them.

Karen found her aunt in the living room waiting for her. "Is he gone?"

Her niece frowned. "Yeah. Thanks to you."

"I didn't do anything!" she said with her hands on her hips.

Karen huffed, watching her aunt's eyes move from her to the end table past her.

"There's my pocket book!" she said with relief. "I was lookin' all through my purse for this."

Aunt Val picked up the little black combination check book and wallet from the table and unzipped it. "I couldn't tithe because I couldn't find the thing. I'd been holdin' thirty dollars in here all week to put in the basket."

Upon pulling the wallet open, Aunt Val's jaw dropped. She gasped.

"What's wrong?" Karen asked, approaching her.

"My thirty dollars is gone!"

Her aunt flipped through the pocket book again. There was no sign of the cash.

An uneasy feeling rose in Karen's gut. "Are you sure you had it there?"

"Of course, hon." Aunt Val's eyes grew wide in realization. "Ricky!"

Karen shook her head frantically. "No, he wouldn't have done that."

"He's a criminal! Of course, he would have and he did!"

"You're jumping to conclusions, Aunt Val," Karen said, but the feeling in her gut told her that her aunt was right once again.

She surrendered with a heavy sigh. "It was my fault. I let him come over. I'll pay the money back to you."

Aunt Val put a hand on her hip and cocked her head. "It wasn't your fault. You're too trusting."

Karen collapsed on the sofa, dropping her face in her hands. "I was really hoping . . ."

"What? That he would be your Prince Charming, Cinderella?"

Her niece looked up at her and nodded solemnly.

Aunt Val smiled. "There's hope yet, kitten. You haven't even been to the ball."

Chapter Eight

As Karen walked toward Main Street, she took in deep breaths of the fresh air. Leaving her aunt's property was easier to do than she thought. Perhaps the mishap with Ricky on Sunday had given her incentive to get out into the world and meet people she could feel more comfortable around. Either way, she awoke on Wednesday morning finally motivated to start her new life in Mercy by getting a part-time job. With the money she would earn, perhaps she could afford to take one art course at the community college in the fall.

At the intersection of Main and Blooming, she paused to look at the street ahead. The main road of Mercy was home to a variety of businesses. Karen hoped that at least one needed some help. With no work experience, she felt Bailey's Coffee Shop, Aunt Maggie's Books, Mercy Variety Store or Mercy Town Deli & Bakery could offer some hope.

There is hope, she reminded herself, starting to walk down Main Street.

Her first stop was Mercy Variety Store. To her relief, a "Help Wanted" sign graced the window. She slipped into the small thrift shop, a rusty bell on the door jingling as she entered.

The store, filled wall to wall with used clothing and miscellaneous items, smelled of dust. All of the sights dazzled Karen. Shelves of old books, antique wedding gowns, racks of pants and shirts, and boxes full of old toys marked "50% OFF" filled every open space. She made her way to the checkout counter at the back of the store where an old woman sat behind a glass case of old jewelry.

She looked up from some notebooks before her and squinted at Karen.

She pushed her thick glasses up her small, wrinkled nose. "Hello, young lady. How are you?"

"Great," Karen replied, curiously eyeing the jewelry in the case.

"You're not from around here," the woman said.

"I came to town a few days ago. I saw your help wanted sign."

The woman squinted at her again. "So you're that Denwood girl. I filled that position yesterday."

Karen felt as if she'd been bulldozed. She took in a deep breath.

Karen turned toward the door. "Thank you anyway, mam."

"It's *Ms. Parson* to you," the old woman snapped.

Karen sighed and hurried out of the store without a word.

That Denwood girl? How did she know who I was? Karen wondered, heading to the next shop. How many more people knew about her? *This was a bad idea,* she thought, feeling a tug-o-war start in her brain. *No, I can't give up. I can't let her get to me.*

In the next window, Karen could see a "Cashier Needed Fridays and Saturdays" sign for Bailey's Coffee Shop. She smiled hopefully until she saw a woman in the window. She was about fifty, talking on a cordless telephone and watching Karen's every move. As Karen stepped closer to the door, the woman snatched the sign from the window, frowned at Karen, and turned away.

Karen stopped in her tracks. *No. That was just a coincidence.*

Deep down, she knew that it wasn't. The old lady from the variety store must have called the coffee shop to tell them to look out for "that Denwood girl."

Hurt and frustrated, Karen started toward the next store, Aunt Maggie's Books. She hoped that maybe the variety store or coffee shop hadn't warned Maggie. She jogged to the entrance. No sign sat in the window, but she would ask anyway.

Inside the newly renovated bookshop, Karen made her way to the cashier's counter. A gentleman in his mid-forties sat behind it, reading a book. He looked up at the sound of her approaching footsteps.

"Are you hiring?"

"Yes," he said, reaching under the counter, "we need some help."

Karen smiled with relief. She watched him dig under the counter, and a sudden fear swept over her. *I hope he's not looking for a gun,* she thought. She sighed as the man placed a job application on the counter.

She reached in her pocket for a pen. "Can I fill it out here?"

"Sure."

She took her time filling out the application, careful to make it look as professional as possible. When she finished it, she couldn't help but frown at all of the blank spaces.

With a flicker of hope, she handed the form back to the cashier. "All done."

The man took it and glanced over it. His eyes paused on one section.

"Nine years in prison?"

Karen was silent. She nodded.

His eyes went back up to the top of the application.

"I forgot," he said, handing it back to her. "We've been having to cut back. No new hires for at least a month."

All of the color drained from Karen's face as she looked at him in disbelief.

"It was an accident. I didn't mean for him to get shot."

The man looked startled and rose from his chair. He lifted his hands in front of him in surrender. "I'm gonna have to ask you to leave, Ms. Denwood."

Karen's sudden feelings of weakness and desperation boiled into anger. Her face began to burn. She stormed out of the store, accidentally bumping into a greeting cards rack. A few cards scattered to the floor. She didn't pick them up or apologize. She wanted to escape the rejection and lies.

Outside on the sidewalk, she sat down and wanted to cry. Instead, she took in several shaky, deep breaths. Three more businesses sat uncharted. She had to keep trying.

A noise across the street made her look up from her miserable state. Joseph's clinic was right across the two-lane road from her. In front of the two-story brick building, she saw a familiar face. Joseph Aldridge was setting up a ladder with two other men, one about his age and one much older. With panic, she realized that the other two men had to be his brother and father.

I've got to hide, she thought, rising up from the curb.

As she searched for something to duck behind, she imagined the horrible things they would do to her. She pictured raw eggs, pitchforks, angry shouts and rotting vegetables. She finally found a dead payphone booth and jumped in. Through the filthy glass, she watched him hold the ladder as his brother climbed up. She froze when his head turned in her direction.

After a brief glance toward the phone booth, Joe returned his attention to his work. Karen sprang from the booth as soon as all three men had their backs to her. She couldn't remember the last time she'd ran so fast. She took a glance back. The men were still distracted as the Main Street strip disappeared behind her.

Karen arrived in front of Mercy Pond breathless, her sides fiercely aching. She dropped her head between her knees and sucked in the air hard and fast. A trickle of sweat ran down the side of her face. She wiped it away with the back of her hand as she rose up to look at the pond of her childhood.

With each step across the small, dirt parking lot, Karen stepped back in time. She remembered the old wooden playground. The warped, metal slide would get so hot in the summer that Karen and her friends would have ice cube races on it. The kid with the ice that lasted the longest runs on the scolding slide would win. At some point in the last nine years, the town had installed a new playground set. This one was a metal and plastic combination shaped like a castle. Two girls chased each other up and around every crevasse of the structure, giggling musically.

The pond itself looked exactly as Karen remembered it. She could feel the slimy bottom under her toes again. The summers had been magical at Mercy Pond, filled with splash wars and chasing ducks along the shore. She would give anything to have those moments back, to be a carefree child again.

"Hey, lady!" The voice was raspy and youthful.

Karen turned to meet eyes with a freckle-faced boy of about thirteen. His braces glimmered in the sun, covering an oversized grin. A group of preteens, probably his buddies, stood about ten feet behind him. They snickered in a huddle, watching him.

"Are you that chick who stabbed Old Man Aldridge?"

Karen blinked, the question replaying in her mind. "What?"

The curious kid let out a nervous laugh and glanced back at his friends with a grin. The other kids burst into uncontrollable laughter.

Karen could feel her fists balling. "No!"

The boy's grin fell away, and alarm covered his expression.

"Where did you hear such a thing?" Karen demanded, taking a step toward him.

The boy raised his hands defensively. "Chill out, lady."

His friends became silent, curiosity freezing them in place.

"I want to know who told you that." She spoke slowly and purposely, trying to keep her anger at bay.

Without a word, the boy darted toward his friends. Like frightened gazelle, the whole group of kids scurried into the woods and disappeared.

* * *

"I've been getting rude hang-up calls," Aunt Val told Karen the next Sunday morning.

"What?"

She braided her niece's hair in front of the long mirror in the attic. "I didn't want to tell you, but it's really getting on my nerves. I think it's Mrs. Perdy, maybe Eric Aldridge too. I don't know. I'm not good with voices."

"I shouldn't be going to church then."

"It will show the town that you are a good, Christian woman who has turned her life around."

Karen released a groan of aggravation. "There wasn't anything to turn around. You know I've never been a terrible person. I was just a stupid kid."

She watched herself in the mirror with curiosity. Even after almost a week and a half of freedom, she hardly recognized herself in anything but a prison uniform. She wore mostly her aunt's clothing since they were relatively the same shape and size. Some of the clothing didn't match her tastes at all, but a few pieces here and there looked nice. Karen preferred to wear muted shades. Most of her aunt's wardrobe consisted of bright, screaming colors. She was relieved to find a nice pastel pink dress to wear to worship service.

Aunt Val finished the French braid and wrapped a hair band around the end. "I know, kitten. These people don't understand that, though. They just need a little more convincing."

These people, Karen thought bitterly. *These people used to be my life, all that I had.*

She had spent the rest of the week fruitlessly trying to get a job in Mercy. No one in town would hire her. She even tried to volunteer at the local public schools as a tutor, but she was turned away because of her criminal record. Her situation seemed hopeless.

What's the use? I have no one in this town but Aunt Val, she thought, her mind drifting to the one other person she had longed so much to have in her life again.

She turned to her aunt. "Where's Dad?"

Aunt Val sighed as if she expected this question. "What was the date on his last letter?"

"The fifth of May."

"Last time I talked to him was just before you got out. He was in New Hampshire, and he didn't know when he'd be through the Carolinas again. He really wants to hear from you, though, as usual."

Karen wasn't sure what to say. They had discussed her forgiveness issues many times before. Aunt Val knew where Karen stood.

She tugged Karen's arm. "Come on. It's almost time for church."

Mercy Church seemed smaller now to the grown Karen. A new, freshly-painted steeple adorned the church's roof. Karen hoped that this place of God's grace and mercy would offer her shelter from the town's rejection.

"Be very quiet," Aunt Val warned as they headed up the church steps. "They've already started."

Her aunt slowly pulled the bulky wooden door open, and they slipped into the empty main lobby. From a table beside the door, they each grabbed service programs and headed to the open doors of the chapel.

Pastor Bell had already begun the service, asking the congregation to stand with their songbooks. The pianist started playing "I'll Fly Away" as the congregation joined in with the verses. Karen was relieved to see that the left side of the last row was empty. The two women almost slipped in unnoticed to join the chorus.

Unfortunately, a familiar face noticed Karen in the opposite last row. It was the woman from Bailey's Coffee Shop. She looked at Karen, frowned and tapped the man in front of her on the shoulder. She whispered something to him. Then he looked at Karen, frowned, and whispered to the woman next to him.

Oh, no, she thought in horror.

Like a snake slithering through the congregation, this pattern of listen, look, frown and whisper made its way to the front of the right side. Karen watched, wide-eyed, as the man sitting beside the aisle in the right front row, leaned to the woman beside the aisle in the front left row. By that time, the song was over, and Pastor Bell asked everyone to be seated.

As Karen started to take her seat, she saw a more pleasant familiar face. Joseph Aldridge, standing in the middle of the right side, looked back at her with surprise on his face. Karen cringed when she noticed Joseph's brother and father each giving her a look that could stop a train.

After everyone was seated, a deafening silence in the room gripped Karen by the throat. She looked up at Pastor Bell. He was leaning over the stage down to the woman who had been sitting beside the aisle on the left front row. Pastor Bell had a look of helplessness on his face as the woman rose and walked briskly down the aisle. As she passed Karen, she gave her the worst evil eye Karen had ever received.

Then Karen remembered her. She was Frank Aldridge's daughter, Constance Aldridge Bell. She had her father's eyes. Karen's stomach twisted into a thousand knots. She searched the crowded pews for the other Aldridge family members and didn't have to look for long. The two men who Karen had suspected were Joe's brother and father rose from their seats. Her eyes met Joe's face. He threw her an expression of concern which took her by surprise.

As they marched bitterly past Karen, Frank Aldridge's son and grandson gave her just as hateful looks as his daughter had. Karen's head dropped. She stared down at her hands in her lap, feeling as if every eye in the church were on her. Aunt Val put a comforting arm around her. Without a word, Richard and his son left the chapel.

Pastor Bell continued his announcements, desperately trying to ignore the distractions.

Joe had turned back to the front. Karen couldn't believe that he and Mrs. Aldridge were still seated. *He doesn't hate me?* she wondered with hope.

When she returned her attention to Pastor Bell, two other people on the right side rose from their seats and exited the chapel, glaring at Karen the whole time. She didn't even recognize them. A moment later, two more, then a third, then a fourth rose from different sections of the chapel and did the same. Pastor Bell noticed these people leaving and started to stutter but continued reading. A family of six rose and left the chapel without even looking at Karen. Then, almost all at once, three rows exited, some people glaring, others ignoring her. She recognized all of the shopkeepers who had turned her away. She even recognized volunteers from the prison Bible study.

Pastor Bell paused and sighed into the microphone. "If there's anyone else who plans to leave, do so now so I can continue the service uninterrupted."

In a large wave, congregation members rose and moved to the center aisle. After one minute of dirty looks from the quiet, exiting crowd, the sound of footsteps and rustling fell silent with the closing of the doors. Only six people remained in the chapel, including Pastor Bell and the puzzled pianist. Besides Karen and her aunt, Helen and Joseph Aldridge were seated in the pews.

Pastor Bell appeared uneasy. Suddenly, the door came open, and Constance Bell reentered the chapel.

She looked at her husband but pointed at Karen. "Robert, it's her or us!"

Aunt Val rose to defend her niece, but Connie marched back outside.

"She can't do this!" Aunt Val shouted to Pastor Bell.

The pastor sighed. "She's my wife. She can do whatever she wants. Karen, I'm going to have to ask you—"

"Rob!" Mrs. Aldridge protested, rising from her seat. "All are welcome in God's house. Your flock should know this."

"I realize that, Helen, but I can't lose my whole congregation for one woman."

Her face became flush. "Does not the Word say—"

"I know what the Word says," Pastor Bell said, "but I can't. Connie would be very upset with me."

"She should be more forgiving," Joe chimed in.

He's not mad at me, Karen realized.

Ignoring his nephew, Pastor Bell returned his attention to Karen.

"I'm sorry, Karen, but you'll have to leave."

As Aunt Val was about to give him a piece of her mind, Karen rose. "Thank you, Joe and Mrs. Aldridge, for staying in here and defending me."

At a pallbearer's pace, Karen exited the chapel with her aunt following behind.

Outside the church doors, the congregation had gathered around the church steps, talking amongst each other heatedly. Upon the sight of Karen and her aunt, they all fell silent. A path through the crowd opened up for the two women who headed in the direction of the parking lot.

"Murderer," an almost inhuman voice hissed.

Karen couldn't tell whose voice it was or where the word came from. She only hoped she had imagined it.

Chapter Nine

Joe's father gave him and his mother the cold shoulder for the rest of the day. Thinking of Karen, Joe found little reason to care. Sitting at the kitchen bar that evening, he appeared to be reading one of his animal anatomy books, but he was really deep in thought about Karen. This day had been no different from the past week. In the midst of his busy renovation schedule, he couldn't focus on the tasks at hand. He was sure he was going crazy since he had imagined seeing her across Main Street on Wednesday. From then on, he seemed to see her face everywhere.

His mother was busy at the sink, working on the Sunday dinner dishes. She turned off the water and came to the bar, wiping her hands with a dishtowel.

"How did she recognize you after nine years?" his mother asked suspiciously.

Joe tried to appear calm, but the question obviously caught him off guard. "Who?"

She raised an eyebrow at him. "You know who. Karen Denwood."

"I don't know. Good memory, I guess."

She leaned over the counter. "I saw the way you were looking at her, Joe. A mother knows."

He shrugged. "Knows what?"

"That was the first time you didn't side with your father, and I know you didn't do it for me."

"Mom!"

She smirked. "I know puppy love when I see it, Joseph William."

"It's not like that," he said, setting his book on the counter. "We met at the Bible study at the prison."

"I should've known! That was her prison?"

"Shhh," Joe hissed. "Dad can't know. He's already too mad at me."

"I knew something was odd about you," she said thoughtfully. "You seemed so distracted all the time, and I knew it wasn't the clinic. For a minute, I thought it was Emily."

"Emily?" Joe scoffed.

"Only for a minute. You definitely didn't have that look in your eyes when you talked about her."

"Mom, I've never met anyone like Karen," he said, feeling silly but eager to share his feelings. "For a while, I was mad at her, but it was all a terrible accident. She couldn't be a murderer."

"Awww."

"Mom! This is serious."

She looked deeply into his eyes for a moment and smiled. "A mother knows, Joe."

* * *

"Ice cream heals all wounds," Aunt Val said, eating a spoonful of Rocky Road.

The aunt and niece duo were watching sitcom reruns and pigging out on ice cream and popcorn. Even hours after the church incident, the whole ordeal left Karen wallowing in self-pity, trying to treat her burdened heart with chocolate chip mint ice cream. It wasn't working. She remained quiet, appearing to be watching TV, but really lost in thoughts of Joe.

"I'm not all that wounded," she told her aunt, surrendering to her full stomach and placing her ice cream bowl on the coffee table.

"Really?"

She smiled. "He stuck up for me."

For Karen, all of the snubbing and dirty looks were worth it, knowing that Joe knew who she was and still didn't hate her.

"I was amazed at that. I really thought we would be the only two left in the chapel. So are you going next Sunday?"

Karen rolled her eyes dramatically. Aunt Val looked back at her with a big grin. "Just kidding."

After another hour of TV, Karen was ready for some light reading and a long night of sleep. She rose from the couch and stretched, eager to face another day, only because of Joe.

The chime of the doorbell suddenly jerked them from their routine.

"Mrs. Perdy?" Karen said.

"No," Aunt Val replied, rising from the sofa. "She would call. Let's hope I don't find a burning paper sack on my porch."

Aunt Val walked into the foyer as Karen waited out of sight on the sofa and listened from the living room.

"Well, hey there," she heard her aunt say.

"Hi, Ms. Denwood," a familiar male voice said. "Can I speak to Karen?"

Karen nearly tripped over the coffee table as she rose in a flurry. It was Joseph Aldridge, and she looked a mess in Aunt Val's gray, cotton shorts and oversized, paint-stained t-shirt. *I'm not here!* her conscience cried.

"I don't know." Aunt Val wavered at the door as if hearing her niece's thoughts. "You have good business with her, right? No eggs will be thrown at her when she comes to the door?"

"No eggs. Has that happened?"

"I found them on my porch yesterday morning. Fortunately, that was as close as they could get to her."

"It's awful that they're doing that to her, Ms. Denwood."

"It makes me ill as a rattlesnake. They don't have to take it out on my porch! I'll get her. Hang on."

Aunt Val walked through the foyer and met Karen inside the living room.

"Guess who's here."

Karen grimaced.

"Go talk to him. He won't bite." This was probably true, although Aldridges were capable of some very nasty glances.

Karen took her aunt's advice and headed to the front door, messy hair and all.

"Hey, Joe." She stepped on to the front porch, closing the door behind her. The wood was warm on her bare feet. The sun was setting behind the pines. In the remaining glow over a pink horizon, Joe smacked at his bare calves.

He cracked a smile. "Hi. I guess I should've sprayed on some repellent."

She let out a nervous chuckle. "Looks like they're having a buffet on your legs."

He chuckled back.

Karen bit her lip. "You didn't change your mind and decide to come chew me out, did you?"

"No, of course not." He rubbed the back of his neck with one hand. "Look, I'm so sorry about everything."

Karen frowned. "You're sorry? I ran out on our Bible study. I was afraid that if you knew who I was, you would hate me, and your family would come after me with pitchforks and—"

"Pitchforks?" He laughed. "Are we *that* country?"

Karen smiled and took a seat on the front step. "I mean, why are *you* sorry?"

He sat beside her. "Because I should've told you this sooner." He looked deeply into her eyes. "I forgive you."

Her heart nearly stopped pumping. She caught her breath in a sigh. "Why?"

"Well, for a lot of reasons, but mostly because I don't see a murderer in you."

"That's because I'm not. Joe, don't you remember the trial? You were there. It was an accident."

"But the gun expert—"

"He was an old friend of your grandpa's."

"What?" Joe's expression instantly changed, filling with confusion and anger.

"After the trial, my attorney found out a lot of things. The supposed gun expert was your grandpa's old war buddy."

"Why didn't anyone know?"

"The judge knew, but he sided with Mercy and your grandfather. They refused to believe the truth because they were out for revenge."

"Did my parents know this?" Joe asked.

Karen's eyes lowered. "I think they did."

His expression melted into one of pain.

Karen began to explain in detail the night of his grandfather's death. By the end, her face was drawn and pale as though she were reliving the incident. "I'll never forget the look on your grandpa's face, Joe. That whole night was the biggest mistake of my life."

Joe was silent. She feared how he might respond to her sudden outpouring of emotion.

He shook his head. "I can't imagine how tough it must've been for you. And yet, you kept your faith in Christ."

Karen sighed. "I can't take credit for that. I pretty much rejected God the whole time that I was in juvenile detention. I was angry at Him, my dad, everyone. You can ask my aunt. She saw me at my worst."

Joe looked shocked but sympathetic. "How did you come back around?"

"Well, when I turned eighteen and went to the women's prison, my cellmate, Maria, was saved. She was the force behind my complete recommitment to Christ." Memories of their friendship made Karen miss Maria right then. "My whole sentence was pretty lonely, though. Aunt Val was the only person in the outside world who stuck with me. She visited me at least twice a week. She brought me books, mostly goofy romance novels. You know, a princess gets saved by a knight after he kills a fire-breathing dragon. She brought me canvas and paint all the time too."

She could've smacked herself on the forehead right then. Her love of art was so personal. She never meant to let that detail slip.

"You paint?" A shimmer of interest lit up his face, surprising her.

Karen shrugged. "It's only a hobby of mine."

"That's great, Karen. I'd love to see your work."

"It's nothing, amateur art. It's a good thing I have my reading and my hobbies. I guess I didn't have much else to come home to."

Joe frowned, staring at the darkening horizon. "Did you expect it to be this bad?"

She shook her head. "I thought everyone would have forgotten me. I was sure I could start over. I missed Mercy so much in jail. I guess this little town likes to keep old grudges."

They both listened to the still evening quiet. Stars glittered over the horizon. The wind blew gently. Crickets chirped, and birds fluttered to their nests.

Joe turned to her with a hopeful expression. "To really prove to you that I forgive you, I want to offer you a job at my vet clinic."

She felt a surge zip through her.

"It would mean a lot to me if you would be my receptionist."

"Joe, I don't have any job experience. I don't know the first thing. I'd make a mess of your clinic."

"It's easy. You answer the phone, order supplies and make my appointments."

Karen thought for a moment, hesitating only because she feared she would embarrass herself and make Joe regret his decision. Then another thought came to mind.

"What would your father say?"

He shook his head. "It doesn't matter. It's my clinic."

She sighed in resignation. "Okay, but please forgive me if I'm terrible at every task you give me."

"That's easy to forgive."

"When do I start?"

"Tomorrow, " he said. "It's the grand opening. The whole day is booked, so it might be a little hectic."

Karen felt her jaw drop. "Booked? Joe, people aren't going to like me working there." She imagined an angry mob gathering outside his little clinic.

"Then I don't want their business."

"You never cease to amaze me," she said, falling into his brown eyes.

They smiled at each other for a few seconds. It was a few seconds too long. They both looked away awkwardly. Karen could feel her cheeks growing warm. She felt funny around Joe. It had been years since she'd felt butterflies dance in her stomach like this.

She finally broke the silence. "I'd better get to bed then. We'll have a long day."

Joe rose from the steps. "Be there at 8:45. The clinic opens at nine."

Karen stood and inched toward the front door. "Good night, Joe."

"Good night."

As Karen started to open the door, she realized she'd forgotten one thing.

"Joe?"

He turned to her.

"Thank you."

He smiled and that smile overwhelmed her thoughts until she fell asleep.

Chapter Ten

"This can't be right," Karen said, looking miserably at herself in her aunt's long mirror.

She wore a purple dress suit with matching pumps. Her shoulders looked about as wide and padded as a linebacker's.

Aunt Val yanked at her suit coat and grinned. "You look great."

Karen unbuttoned the coat. "This is too much. I need something more casual."

Aunt Val collapsed on her bed with a deep sigh.

"I don't want to look like a goof, okay?" Karen said, removing the coat and kicking off the purple pumps.

"You wanna look good for him, don't you?"

Karen glared at her aunt. "It's not like that. He's my friend, my only friend in this town."

Aunt Val jumped up from the bed. "I've got it!"

She went into her walk-in closet and returned to Karen with a long, black skirt, black flat sandals and a violet, short-sleeved blouse. She put the skirt and blouse up to her niece's figure. "How's this combo?"

Karen gladly took the outfit from her. "Now that's what I'm talking about."

"You sure are nervous about dressing for a friend."

"It's my first job."

Aunt Val raised an eyebrow at her. "Well, your *friend* is the most eligible bachelor in Mercy. Ever since he came back into town, the girls have been talking."

A knot formed in Karen's stomach. "What girls?"

"Well, some of the ladies he went to high school with have come back from college. I heard Emily Bailey has a crush on him again."

"Again?"

"They were high school sweethearts."

"That's the woman who ran the Bible study at the prison," Karen realized aloud.

"She was really disappointed when he stopped going," Aunt Val said.

Karen smirked and pointed an accusing finger at her aunt. "You're just trying to shake me up!"

Aunt Val shrugged. "Maybe, but it's the truth."

Karen sighed, jealousy aching within her. "Does he like her?"

"I really don't know. Girls talk about their feelings more than guys do. That's how word gets around."

Karen finished dressing, lost in thoughts of Joe. Maybe she *was* dressing for him. *No. I'm dressing for me,* she thought defiantly.

She returned to the mirror for a final look. "This is much better. Perfect."

Aunt Val came up and stood beside her in front of the mirror. Her eyes shimmered in the morning light piercing through the window beside them. "I think he likes you."

"What makes you think that?"

"He was a bundle of nerves last night. People aren't nervous about seeing friends unless they have something to hide."

"What if he's hiding something else?" Karen turned to her aunt. "What if he's playing nice to win me over so he can eventually get revenge?"

This possibility hadn't struck Karen until now. She suddenly imagined Joe with that angry expression on his face like his brother and father had at church. It sent a shiver down her spine.

Aunt Val put a comforting arm around Karen's shoulder. "You have to trust him."

Ten minutes later, in front of Joe's vet clinic, Aunt Val gave Karen one last encouraging wave through the car windshield as she pulled out of her parking spot. Karen waved back halfheartedly. Butterflies spun about in her stomach. She looked at the beautifully restored building before her. The new front door had the words "Mercy Veterinary Clinic, Joseph W. Aldridge" delicately painted in white on the glass. She took in a deep breath and pushed the door open.

Inside, a gold bell jingled on the door, announcing her arrival to anyone within earshot. The cool, office air was marked with the smell of fresh paint and new carpet. Karen walked slowly through a large, pale blue waiting area complete with an elegant living room suite and a magazine rack. Beyond the waiting area, Karen stopped at a blue and black marble top counter. Leaning over it, she could see a telephone, a slim, black computer monitor and a few forms on the desk below. Behind the desk, there was a chair, a few feet of space and a hallway with several doors on each side. One was open, and the room was lit.

"Karen?" a familiar voice called from the room.

"Joe?"

Joe popped his head into the hallway and grinned at her. She felt goose bumps all over as she watched him approach the desk. The handsome, young bachelor was wearing khaki pants and a solid, green dress shirt with a white lab coat over it.

He smiled at her. "You're right on time. Come around. I'll show you the phone."

She slipped through the swinging half-door to the right of the front counter. "It looks great in here. I don't even recognize it. It looks so different."

"Everyone did a great job on it." He gestured for her to sit at the chair behind the desk. "It's a four-lined telephone."

He began to explain the phone system to her. "Oh, and have each pet owner fill out this form before the pet comes back."

Relief swept over Karen. "Okay, this sounds easy. What about the computer?"

"I bought some basic accounting software. We can learn that together when there's a little free time. Can you use a computer?"

"Of course," she said. "I haven't been dead, just in jail."

"Right. Sorry."

She smiled and shrugged. "That's okay."

They were both quiet for a moment. Karen noticed that Joe looked oddly pale. He was sweating bullets.

"Joe, are you okay?"

He wiped his brow with the back of his hand. "Is it hot in here?"

"No, not to me."

He frowned. "Geez, I'm a mess."

"What's wrong?"

"I've been thinking about this day for years. Now here I am, and I've never been so scared in my life."

She smiled, suddenly relieved. "You had *me* scared. I thought you were sick. Everything's gonna be fine."

"What if I misdiagnose or give out the wrong prescription?"

"You can't dwell on those possibilities. You just have to do your best," she said, rising from the chair. "Here, sit down and take some deep breaths."

He took her advice. Karen gently placed a hand on each of his shoulders and began to firmly push and pull like a baker loosening dough.

"This should ease the tension. Relax your muscles."

She felt Joe relax as her hands more easily navigated his neck and shoulders.

"I didn't know you were a masseuse," Joe said.

"My friend, Maria, showed me how. Her mother is a masseuse."

Karen pulled away, seeing that the wall clock read 8:59. "When's the first appointment?"

"Nine o'clock." Joe rolled his shoulders back. "Thanks. That really helped."

"Good." She gave him a reassuring smile. "Don't worry about anything. You went to school. You know what you're doing."

"Oh, I almost forgot." He reached into his pocket and pulled out a small, plastic nametag and handed it to Karen. She read it and smiled. It read "Karen, Receptionist."

She pinned it to her blouse. "Thanks, Joe."

"It looks great on you." He blushed, apparently not meaning to compliment her on a nametag. She couldn't help but let a giggle escape.

As soon as the clock struck nine, the front door opened. Joe and Karen turned to see an elderly white-haired woman enter, holding a Yorkshire terrier. She walked slowly, neck craned, to the front. She set the small dog on the counter top. It looked around the room with wide eyes, hair dancing on its shaking legs.

"Good morning," Karen said with a smile, grabbing a clipboard, pen and the form Joe talked about.

The old woman looked at Karen curiously through thick glasses.

Joe smiled at her. "Good morning, Mrs. Bailey. How's Mickey today?"

"Mickey needs a check-up," she said, staring at Karen's name tag.

Karen offered the old woman a pen. "We need you to fill out this form first, Mrs. Bailey."

"I can go ahead and weigh Mickey and check his heart while you do that," Joe said.

She frowned at Karen. "Does your Aunt Connie know about this, Joseph?"

Karen's heart nearly stopped as she looked at Joe. He appeared just as shocked. Then his expression turned angry.

"It's none of her business who I employ in my clinic. Karen is a good person."

Mrs. Bailey scooped Mickey up in her arms.

"Shameful," she muttered, turning and walking slowly back to the door.

"Mrs. Bailey," Joe said. "She's a good person. Have forgiveness in your heart."

Mrs. Bailey turned, scowled, and shook her head, "Your granddaddy was such a good man. You should have more respect."

Joe appeared speechless as Mrs. Bailey and Mickey exited the clinic.

Karen's stomach turned. "Joe, I'm so sorry."

"I don't want her business."

Karen could see how hurt and frustrated he was. *This is my fault,* she thought.

Karen rose from the desk chair. "This was a bad idea. I'm going home."

"No, Karen. You deserve to live your life. These people need to get over it."

"Does anyone in your family know that I'm working here?"

Joe's eyes dropped to the floor. "My mom actually suggested that I hire you. She thinks it's the right thing to do, but she also said it wouldn't be easy."

"Have you and your dad been fighting about me?"

"No, he just ignores me. Eric tries to ignore me, but he's not good at it. He keeps asking me why I stuck up for you. I don't know what to say to make him understand."

Suddenly, the front door burst open, and Emily Bailey entered at a swift pace. Karen swallowed hard.

Emily walked briskly to the front counter. "Joe, what happened? Grandma won't say a word to me. Did something happen with Mickey?"

Karen rose from her seat and met eyes with Emily.

"Oh. Hi, Karen," Emily said awkwardly.

"Hi, Emily."

Emily returned her gaze to Joe. "She works here?"

"Yes, she does. Is there a problem with that?"

Karen cracked a smile. Her stomach started to untie itself.

Emily's mouth dropped open. "You two are friends?"

"Of course," Joe said. "Why do you think I stayed in the church yesterday?"

Emily shrugged. "Because your mother stayed?"

Joe rolled his eyes as he let out a sigh of frustration.

"This was probably not a good idea, Joe. Grandma is very upset. I was at the coffee shop waiting for her and Mickey when she came in."

"Karen doesn't deserve to be treated this way."

Emily shook her head in disapproval. "You know our grandparents were very close friends. They grew up together. It's no wonder she's so angry."

"Well, Karen's staying, and there's nothing you can do about it."

Emily lifted her hands in surrender. "I came to see what was going on. Do as you please."

She turned and started to walk out of the clinic but stopped and turned back to them with an unexpected smile. "Joe, my birthday is coming up. Don't forget about my dinner party."

"I know," he said, looking disinterested.

Karen could see the hurt on Emily's face. *She does have a crush on him.*

Emily exited the clinic without another word.

A loud, unfamiliar ring startled both of them from their thoughts. It was the telephone. Karen dropped back into the desk chair and picked up the receiver.

"Mercy Veterinary Clinic. This is Karen," she answered in a professional tone.

"Karen who?" the female caller asked suspiciously.

Karen paused. "How can I help you?"

"Are you Karen Denwood?"

Karen sighed. "Yes."

"This is Joanna Cartwright," the woman said, anger piercing her tone, "and I want to cancel my appointment for Harper at two o'clock."

Karen heard a loud click. Joanna had hung up on her.

"Who was that?" Joe asked as she set down the receiver.

"Joanna Cartwright. She canceled her appointment because of me."

"Mrs. Bailey! She told Mrs. Cartwright you were over here."

"How do you know?"

"She runs the coffee shop for the Bailey family."

Karen put her face in her hands and released a loud sigh. Joe put a comforting hand on her shoulder.

"Don't worry. I'm booked up today. Not everyone's going to cancel their appointment."

* * *

113

At 10:25, the front door opened again. Mrs. Thorpe entered, pushing a walker. Joe was surprise to see her looking so well. She had to be in her seventies by now. He remembered his mother saying that Mrs. Thorpe would change his diapers in the church nursery. Then he remembered how her hearing started to go out before he left for college.

"Good," Joe whispered to Karen. "It's Mrs. Thorpe. She's so old, she never remembers anyone."

Karen sighed. He was glad to see some inkling of relief in her face. She'd spent the last hour and a half looking rather depressed and concerned. He felt guilty for putting her in such a position.

Joe watched the door and recognized Mrs. Thorpe's daughter coming in behind her with a calico cat in her arms. "Oh, no."

"What?" Karen whispered, paranoia flooding her expression.

"Her daughter, Jane Ramsey, reminds her of everything."

"Well, hello, Dr. Joe," Mrs. Ramsey greeted, following her mother's slow pace to the front.

"Good morning, Mrs. Ramsey."

"I told Mother I would bring Trixie in for her check-up, but she insisted on coming," Jane Ramsey said. Her voice grew louder as she turned to her mother and said, "Isn't that right, Mother?"

"What?" the old woman croaked.

"I said you were too stubborn to stay home."

Mrs. Thorpe finally arrived at the front counter. "I want to be with Trixie."

Mrs. Ramsey set the cat on the floor. It remained still, looking around curiously. Mrs. Ramsey followed suit. "Your clinic looks wonderful, Joe. Doesn't it look lovely, Mother?"

"What?"

"I said doesn't Joe's clinic look lovely?"

"It's very clean," she remarked, watching her cat.

"Well, I should call you Dr. Aldridge now, shouldn't I?" She giggled, returning her attention to Joe.

"Whatever you prefer."

Karen handed Mrs. Ramsey a clipboard, form and pen. "We need you to fill out this form before Trixie gets her examination."

Mrs. Ramsey finally noticed Karen, smiled and took the items from her.

"Mother, let's go sit down while I fill this out," Mrs. Ramsey told the aging woman, helping her to the armchair closest to the desk.

As they settled in, Joe became hopeful. They didn't seem to notice Karen at all, and she looked relieved. She and Joe exchanged smiles.

"I think you're in the clear," he whispered to her.

Karen nodded.

Joe looked back at the pair of ladies in his new waiting area. Mrs. Ramsey looked up at Karen inquisitively. Joe's jaw tightened. He cringed as Mrs. Ramsey turned to her mother. She attempted to whisper, but Joe could clearly hear every word.

Jane Ramsey drew close to her mother's ear. "Mother, it's that Denwood girl."

"Who?" the old woman said loudly.

"Karen Denwood, the delinquent girl who killed Frank Aldridge. Do you remember yesterday when we walked out of church because of her?"

"Yes, I remember. Let's go."

Karen and Joe watched as the two women rose. Mrs. Ramsey picked up Trixie who had been rubbing affectionately against her leg. She left the clipboard on one of the side tables.

"Where are you going?" Karen asked.

"Mother isn't feeling well," Mrs. Ramsey lied in a curt tone, following her mother to the door.

Joe and Karen looked at each other with a mixture of disappointment and frustration.

Joe returned his glance to the two women. "I hope she'll get to feeling better."

"She will," Mrs. Ramsey said, helping her mother out the door.

The women disappeared into the bright daylight outside.

Chapter Eleven

Around eleven o'clock, the clinic front door opened again. Karen and Joe looked up expectantly from their seats behind the front desk. Karen saw Joe shrink back when a man not much older than them stuck his head into the clinic door. He wore dusty work pants and a faded baseball cap, looking like he'd been working outdoors for a several hours.

Joe forced a smile. "Hey, Tim."

"Don't you 'hey, Tim' me, *Doctor*." He said the word "doctor" in a mocking tone.

Joe's jaw dropped.

Tim poked his head out of the door without a word and disappeared.

Karen frowned. "Who was that?"

"Timothy Gardner. He's a part-time farmhand for my dad."

"Oh, no. Will he tell him?"

Joe sighed. "Most definitely. Dad probably sent him over to confirm the rumor that you're here."

"What will your dad do?"

He shrugged. "Disown me, I guess."

"Joe, I have to leave," she said, rising from the desk. "I can't keep tearing your family apart."

He gently took her arm. "No. Please stay, Karen."

His physical contact startled her. Joe must have noticed because he immediately released her arm from his grasp.

She crossed her arms. "Honor your mother and your father, Joe. You're breaking a commandment here."

"Do unto others," he reminded her. Then a look of remembrance came across his face. "I brought something for you."

"For me?"

Joe hurried to one of the back rooms. "Hang on."

The phone rang once again and a sense of dread came over Karen. If only she could let it go to voice mail.

She settled back into the chair and picked up the receiver. "Mercy Veterinary Clinic."

"This is Mr. Keller. My dog has an appointment at 1:30," a deep male voice said. "I want to cancel that appointment."

"For what reason?" Karen asked, not withholding the suspicion in her voice.

There was a pause.

"You know why, Denwood."

Mr. Keller hung up loudly, and anger rose up in Karen's chest, closing her throat. She slammed the receiver in its cradle.

"Hey! I just bought that."

Joe stood behind her with what looked like a picture in one hand.

"I'm sorry," she said, struggling to keep the fire in her belly from raging.

He dropped down in the chair beside her. "I'm only kidding. Who was it this time?"

"Mr. Keller."

"Word is getting around."

Karen looked at the photo in his hands. "What's that?"

He handed it to her, and Karen felt herself taken back to a time she had nearly forgotten.

She looked at the picture of grinning school children. "My fourth grade class."

Joe pointed to a little blonde wearing a pink dress. "There you are."

Karen laughed. "I looked so silly."

"You looked cute. Can you find my brother?"

As Karen's eyes swam through the small faces, they stopped on a more familiar one.

Karen's smile faded as she stared at a beautiful blonde-haired woman in a yellow dress.

"I know you lost most of your things after you went to jail," he said. "I didn't know if you still had any pictures of your mother so I wanted to give you this one."

Karen stared at her mother's face, remembering and longing for her touch, her voice, just her presence. After years without her, the memories had faded away. The pain of remembering was often too much for her to handle. Her eyes began to burn like hot coals.

"Karen, you okay?"

She could see the deep concern in his eyes. It had been so long since she'd seen such an expression for her on a man's face.

Karen wiped her eyes with her free hand. "I'm fine."

"I shouldn't have brought it."

"No, I haven't seen her picture in almost four years."

She sat the picture on the desk. "Someone stole the last one I had and ripped it up."

Joe grimaced. "How could they do such a thing?"

"I got picked on a lot when I was moved to the women's prison."

"Why didn't you get another picture of her from your aunt?"

His question stirred up a flurry of emotions. "I had my reasons."

Her reasons were too delicate to tell him. After all, they really hadn't known each other long. She couldn't tell him that she didn't get another picture because sometimes she would stare at the old one and cry during the darkest hours of the night. She couldn't tell him that she was angry at herself for not protecting the picture and allowing it to slip into the hands of a bully. She couldn't tell him that she didn't feel worthy to possess another photo of her mother within the prison walls. She couldn't tell him because it would only lead to tears.

Joe returned his eyes to the picture. "Your mom was my favorite teacher out of every teacher I ever had. She was the best."

Karen jogged her memory back to that time and place. She remembered the days under her mother's instruction. She remembered wanting to be just like her. She wanted to be smart, kind and pretty like her. She was the best elementary teacher in the entire county. She was the best mother in the county—at least in Karen's eyes, she was. But that terrible evening came like a thief and stole her life away.

Dad, she thought, her heart aching, *why did you have to do it?*

No one outside of Mercy knew the truth of that night. In the papers, people read about a terrible car accident. People read that Lillian Hart Denwood was killed when she swerved off the road and hit a tree, but few people knew that she wasn't even the driver. A drunk driver killing the county's finest school teacher was one thing, but her drunk-driving husband killing her was completely different. Sheriff Wilson didn't want the bad press for Mercy, though. He reported that Karen's mother was driving and lost control of the car on the slick road in the pouring rain. Mercy locals knew the shameful truth, though.

"I haven't stopped at her grave yet," Karen said.

"I haven't been to Grandpa's since before college," Joe admitted. "Your mother's has the angel statue, right?"

Karen cracked a smile. "Yeah. The whole town donated money for that angel."

"This town has a good side and a bad one."

"I'm sorry that I had to learn that the hard way." Her eyes returned to the picture. "Thank you for the photo."

"It's yours. Literally."

"What do you mean?"

"My mom bought it when they auctioned off your dad's house."

After the trial, Karen's father never came back to Mercy. After a month, the house was foreclosed on, and all of its contents were declared abandoned and sold off at auction. Aunt Val attended the auction and fought tooth and nail for any family heirlooms and pictures. Mercy residents, still bitter about the death of Frank Aldridge, bought the items to spite Aunt Val and drive her out of town. She had told Karen that she spent nearly a thousand dollars at the auction and never once thought about leaving her hometown.

"My mom was a little angry back then," Joe said, shame covering his expression. "She put everything she bought at the auction in a box. I remember she told me she was packing up her anger with it, and she wasn't going to ever open it again. Then last night, she remembered it and decided I should give it back to you."

"What else does she have?"

Joe rose from his chair. "I brought all of it. Come on."

Karen followed him into a messy office. A large, old wooden desk sat in the center of the room. Boxes were scattered here and there. Joe walked to the cluttered desk and opened an old shoe box. Karen hurried over and peered in.

Memories poured back into her mind with the sight of a girls' pink hair brush, multi-colored bows, a small plastic doll in a blue dress, and a little girl's diary.

Karen's eyes grew wide. "It's my stuff. I hid all of these things when I turned twelve. I decided I was getting too old for them."

She picked up the small baby blue diary and flipped through it. It contained only fragments of sentences, misspelled words and scribbled drawings. She smiled down at the little box of treasures.

"This is my diary from when I was little. Mom made me save it. She said someday it would mean a lot to me."

"She was right, huh?" Joe asked.

"Mothers are always right."

Joe chuckled. "My mom is always saying that."

Karen closed the shoebox as the telephone's high-pitched ring once again startled them both. They hurried out of the office and back to the front desk.

Joe reached for the phone. "Let me answer this time."

Rather than picking up the receiver, Joe hit the speaker button. "Dr. Aldridge speaking."

"Joe?" a female voice asked.

"Mom?"

"Dear, your aunt knows. She just called me," Mrs. Aldridge said, sounding alarmed. "She's really angry with you."

"I didn't see that coming," Joe quipped.

"I think she's on her way over there."

Karen's heart nearly stopped.

"I can handle her," he said, looking at Karen. "Does Dad know?"

"I'm not sure, but I didn't tell him."

"Is Tim over there?"

"I don't know. I haven't been out to the barn. Why?"

"He knows."

"Oh, Joseph," she murmured, worry saturating her tone. "Let's hope he's not got to your father. Have things been bad up there?"

"Vacant. Canceled appointments left and right. People have walked out."

"Hang in there. If your aunt comes over there, you mind your words and send Karen into another room if you have to."

"I will, Mom."

"Love you."

Joe glanced over at Karen who was watching intently.

He hesitated then mumbled, "I love you too."

Karen smiled to herself at his embarrassment. *He still says it. How sweet.*

Joe hung up the phone and sat down in his desk chair.

Karen sighed. "She'll be here any minute now, won't she?"

"You don't have to worry, Karen."

"Are you kidding? She hates me. She might call the sheriff on me and make up a story," she sputtered, horrible fears crowding her mind.

"She's after me, not you. I'm an Aldridge. To her, I shouldn't have anything to do with you. She thinks I'm practically spitting on my grandpa's grave by befriending you."

Karen frowned, guilt overwhelming her. She was causing a family feud. Then she realized that Joe really was choosing to be her friend. He was also choosing to suffer the consequences. He didn't have to have anything to do with her. "What does befriending me mean to *you*?"

Joe was silent for a moment, looking thoughtful. "I'm honoring my grandpa's memory by befriending you. What I remember the most about him was how forgiving he was toward people."

A memory flashed in his eyes. "Tim Gardner used to be a big troublemaker when we were about thirteen. One time, he stole some candy from Grandpa's store. Grandpa knew, and he confronted him. Tim denied it. A few months later, Tim tried to drive his dad's car and ran it into a mailbox. He needed money to pay for the damages, so he came to Grandpa for a job. Well, my grandpa made him admit that he stole the candy. Then he hired him like nothing ever happened."

"That's pretty forgiving."

"I could name a dozen other times Grandpa forgave someone for doing him wrong. As much as this town loved him, they didn't always treat him like it. He felt their bad side too."

Karen frowned, thinking of her father.

"Kind of ironic how the good ones always suffer," Joe said with a shrug.

Remorse covered her face.

"I'm sorry, Karen. I didn't mean anything by it. Hey, you're one of them. You didn't deserve all of that time in prison."

"The world is an ironic place," she said, her eyes glancing at the wall clock.

Joe followed her gaze. "I guess my next appointment isn't coming either. They didn't even bother to cancel."

"Wanna play tic-tac-toe?"

They ended up playing the game for an hour without interruption. Karen won sixteen out of nineteen games.

"Maria and I used to have tournaments," Karen said. "When we got really competitive, we'd draw a bigger grid."

"Well, I'm done. You're officially the tic-tac-toe champion in my book."

Karen laughed. "That's probably the best title I'll ever receive."

He frowned. "I doubt that."

"Joe, I've spent the last nine years of my life in prison. I only got my GED last year. I have no work experience, and I don't even know how to drive."

"You have work experience now, and I can teach you how to drive."

"You want to teach me how to drive?" It was hard to believe that he would want to spend any more time with her, considering the mess she had made of his first morning as a veterinarian.

He grinned. "Sure."

"When?"

"Whenever you want."

Karen thought for a moment. Then a mischievous grin formed on her face.

"In about three weeks," she said. "It'll be your birthday present to me."

"Your birthday's coming up?"

"Yep. Two weeks from Friday."

"Okay, you've got it, one driving lesson."

They were both quiet for a moment, listening to the wall clock tick away the seconds.

"Do you think you're going to see anyone's pet today?" Karen asked.

Joe twirled a pen between his fingers. "Probably not. We'll have to give them time. Eventually, they'll come around."

"Before or after you have to declare bankruptcy?"

He looked deeply into her eyes. "We can't give into them."

Karen found herself suddenly in awe of Joe. It wasn't just his kind, brown eyes, his adorable smile, and the fact that he *was* Mercy's most eligible bachelor. His confidence and faith in her were more than she could've ever dreamed. He wasn't merely befriending her. He was boldly protecting her.

The sound of the front door opening broke into Karen's thoughts, and they both turned uneasily to see who was entering.

"You are so dead, Joe!" Eric Aldridge said, rushing to the front desk.

He was dressed in overalls, a sweaty t-shirt and dirty work boots.

Joe jumped from his chair. "What do you want?"

"Dad's outside, and he said if you don't send that Denwood girl out of here in the next two minutes, he's coming in here himself."

"Her name is Karen, not 'that Denwood girl', and she's not going anywhere! Why don't you sit down and make yourself comfortable for two minutes."

Eric's jaw dropped. "Joe, why are you doing this? She killed Grandpa!"

Joe walked around the desk to meet his brother face to face. "It was an accident. I've already told you that."

"You've got a lot of nerve," Eric said, daring to get into Joe's face. "This is Grandpa's store, and you think you can just bring her in here like everything's okay?"

"Please listen to me, Eric," Joe said, trying to back away from Eric's threatening advances.

"No, she's got you brainwashed! She's a liar and a murderer!"

"No, she isn't!"

Eric stared into Joe's eyes intensely. "Yes, she is, Joe."

Joe finally stood his ground. "You don't scare me, Eric."

His brother's face began to turn red. This statement had angered him even more. He pushed Joe back. Karen watched in silence, debating between staying in the middle of the Aldridge feud or retreating to her aunt's house.

"What's wrong with you? You were always the smart one!" Eric shouted as his brother stumbled back at the force of his shove.

Joe managed to keep his footing as Karen rose from her desk chair.

"You wanna fight me?" Joe asked like a bold teenager.

Eric started toward Joe with a menacing look in his eyes. "Yeah, I'd like to knock some sense into you!"

"Stop!" Karen cried.

Both men turned their attention to her. She leaned over the desk, gripping the counter so tight that her fingers were white.

"Stop it," she ordered firmly. "I'm leaving."

Karen snatched the shoebox of her childhood treasures and headed around the desk.

"No, Karen," Joe called after her. "You have to stand up for yourself."

"What's to stand up for?" Eric said. "She knows she killed him."

"Shut your mouth!" Joe yelled. He turned back to Karen. "Karen, don't listen to him. He doesn't understand. This is your home. You belong here."

Karen kept walking toward the door, trying to ignore Joe's pleas.

"From the moment I first saw you," Joe said desperately, "I knew you didn't belong in that prison. I knew you belonged here in Mercy."

Karen stopped in her tracks, puzzled and touched by his words all at once. She turned and remembered that first moment that their eyes met, how rude she was and how he only responded with patience and kindness. Ever since they first met, he had showed her nothing but both. He believed in her. She couldn't turn her back on him now.

Her eyes met Joe's. "Then I'll stay here."

Eric scowled at her.

Just then, the door opened again. The jingling of that little bell had never before sounded so ominous to Karen. They all looked over in unison to see Richard Aldridge standing in the doorway. He wore blue jeans, grimy work boots and a dirty t-shirt that matched Eric's.

"Son, you wanna tell me what's going on here?" Mr. Aldridge asked Joe calmly.

Karen couldn't help but notice that Joe's whole demeanor changed with his father's presence in the room. He shrunk back a little, lowering his head and shoulders. At the same time, he appeared defensive like a pug before a Great Dane. She thought that perhaps she even saw some sweat on his brow.

"I hired Karen as my receptionist," he said meekly as his father slowly walked toward Karen.

Karen's heart began to pound in her ears. *You've taken on bigger women than him,* she told herself. *Yeah, but Maria was with me.*

He looked at the box in Karen's hands. "What's that?"

"My things," she said as meekly as Joe. "Joe gave them back to me."

Mr. Aldridge frowned and ripped the box from her hands. Karen nearly jumped out of her skin. He opened the box and frowned at its contents. With an angry grunt, he threw the

126

shoebox and its lid on the floor. The girlhood items scattered around Karen's feet.

"Dad!" Joe cried, shock and anger heightening his pitch.

Mr. Aldridge looked at Joe. "I want you out of my house or her out of my town. And if you don't make the decision quick, I'll make it for you."

He stormed out of the clinic without another word.

Eric headed for the door. "Don't be stupid, Joe." Eric narrowed his eyes at Karen as he passed her. "Get out of our town, *murderer*."

Karen could feel tears burning her eyes. She put her hand to her chest as if it might help her pulse to slow. It didn't.

"Get out, Eric!" Joe yelled.

Eric hurried out, and Karen stood there in shock, looking down at her childhood. Her entire world seemed to be spinning in the wrong direction once again. She only wanted to come home and start over. Now everything was scattered, out of place, just like her little treasures on the floor.

Joe hurried to her side. "Karen?"

Karen looked at him, anger burning her chest. "I want to go home."

Chapter Twelve

Karen's eyes opened. The morning light poured into her studio bedroom, draping across her paintings like a bright, yellow sheet. She blinked a few times, realizing with regret that she had slept for over twelve hours. A knock at her door made her also realize that it was probably not the morning light that had stirred her from her deep, forgetful sleep. Her door creaked open, and Aunt Val peaked in from the other side.

She entered the room in her pansy-spotted bath robe. "Hey, kitten."

"Good morning," Karen greeted unenthusiastically.

Aunt Val plopped down on the bed beside her, jarring Karen into an even more wakeful state. "How are you?"

Memories of yesterday's horrifying encounter with Richard and Eric Aldridge unfolded in her mind. She couldn't shake their angry expressions and harsh tones.

"I wish I were dead," she finally said, covering her head with her pillow.

Her aunt yanked the pillow away and tossed it on the floor. "I don't. Funerals are expensive these days."

Karen sighed, remembering the better part of yesterday: the long conversations with Joe, tic-tac-toe, and his adorable smile. After the day went south, Joe closed up the shop early and walked her home. The walk was awkward between them. She could only recall Joe assuring her that things would get better. When she reached home, she collapsed in bed and tried to bury her emotions with sleep. The incident with Mr. Aldridge had stirred up shock and anger. On top of that, the tiny remnants of her girlhood made old memories fresh. A deep sadness had washed over her. This mixture of sour emotions left her weary with self-pity. She wasn't sure how she would be able to press on in Mercy. After such an outburst from his father, Joe couldn't possibly have her back at the clinic again.

"Get dressed and come down for breakfast. I have a surprise for you," Aunt Val said, planting a big kiss on Karen's forehead.

Karen heard the sound of the pipes creaking downstairs, a sign that someone was using one of the bathroom sinks.

She sat up. "Who's here?"

Aunt Val giggled. "Get dressed, and you'll see."

Karen watched her aunt skip out of the room, still grinning mischievously. She frowned and listened, hoping to hear some familiar voices. She heard nothing but water running through the pipes, and Aunt Val traipsing down the attic staircase.

Who is it? she wondered, climbing out of bed. *Is it even anyone I know? What if it's Dad?*

Her heart began to race as she flipped through clothes in her closet. To her relief, she found the new blue jeans and orange, v-neck top that Aunt Val bought her over the weekend. She threw on her clothes, her mind buzzing with a million questions. What if it was her father? What would she say? Would she be angry with him? What did he look like now?

After throwing her blonde hair up in a pony tail, Karen raced down the attic staircase, landing in the kitchen. She froze when her eyes met the man at her aunt's kitchen table.

"Joe?"

"Good morning," he said with his usual adorable smile.

He was dressed for work and reading the morning paper with a cup of coffee.

"What are you doing here?"

Aunt Val brandished a cheesy grin. "Didn't ya hear? Joe is my new tenant."

"What?" Karen sputtered, wondering if perhaps her aunt was speaking in some Chinese dialect.

He smirked at her. "Well, my dad said I had to choose."

"Joe! They kicked you out?"

"I left." His expression grew serious. "I want you to be my receptionist, Karen."

"Joe, scrambled eggs okay?" Aunt Val asked, greasing an iron skillet.

Joe nodded.

Karen put her hands on her hips. "But you're not getting any patients."

Joe sipped his coffee. "I told you, Karen. If they don't forgive you, I don't want their business."

"No, Joe! This is crazy. You can't just leave home and risk your clinic for me."

"Don't flatter yourself, honey. It's the principle of the matter," Aunt Val said, cracking eggs into a blue, ceramic bowl. "Joe is setting an example of forgiveness. They need to follow it."

Joe nodded. "Yes. Thank you, Ms. Denwood."

"Oh, call me Val, darlin'."

"Miss Val."

She blushed. "That'll do."

Karen was flabbergasted. "So you're gonna live here?"

"Why not?" Aunt Val shot back. "I have a spare room and bathroom for him. The rent is cheap, and I can definitely use a handyman around my house."

Karen finally dropped down into a chair at the table. She wasn't sure why she was fighting the whole idea of having Joe around the house. He was her friend after all. The idea actually sat very well with her. Then she realized that it always had. Her outburst had actually been a means of disguising her excitement.

"So we'll need to be heading to the clinic in about half an hour," Joe said, looking up at the rooster clock on the kitchen wall.

Karen bit her lip. "Are you sure about this?"

"I've never been so sure of anything in my whole life."

* * *

Joe felt guilt sweep over him as he recalled lying to Karen at breakfast. He wasn't sure about bringing her back to the clinic. He actually feared he was going to start some Mercy town civil war with his antics. Yet, seeing the look of peace and relief on her face made him want to continue to stand by her. He wanted to do everything in his power to make the town accept Karen and forgive her. It was his new crusade.

The first few hours of this crusade, however, were unsuccessful. Two canceled appointments and two walk-outs left Joe and Karen feeling discouraged. He decided to show her some of the games on the desk computer to pass the time. Leaning over her shoulder to peer at the monitor, he could smell her vanilla-scented perfume. As he leaned in to explain his best gaming strategies, he felt her loose, blonde hair tickle his cheek.

The sound of the clinic door opening startled Joe as if he were caught in a floodlight trying to escape up a prison wall. They both turned to see Joe's uncle enter with Paul under his arm. Paul, named after the apostle, was Uncle Rob's treasured golden cocker spaniel. The dog's long, heavy tongue hung from his mouth, legs kicking in every direction.

"Good morning, Joe!" his uncle said with a grin.

Joe released a sigh of relief. "Hey, Uncle Rob."

Uncle Rob set Paul on the floor. "I heard you were accepting walk-ins."

"As long as I'm here," Karen quipped with a smirk.

"Karen, please forgive me," his uncle said, regret weighing on his face, "I wanted to be on your side when you came to church. My wife has had a terrible time with all of this. She was very close to her father."

"Have you tried talking to her?" Joe asked, hoping for some good news.

"I try everyday. I think she's coming around. I always have to remind her how forgiving her father was." He laughed a little, his eyes glazed over by a memory. "I remember the day I met him when we were dating. I was a bumbling fool! I mean, I did *everything* wrong. I knew I would never be able to marry Constance."

"What happened?" Karen asked, leaning forward.

"Well, I went to him and told him my intentions. I told him that I loved the Lord, but I loved his daughter too. I asked him to forgive me if I didn't meet his standards, but, I said, I think love is all she needs. He said he would be honored to have me as his son-in-law."

Karen smiled, and the look in her eyes reminded Joe that she was a sucker for tales of romance.

Joe offered his uncle a clipboard to sign-in. "What can I do for Paul today?"

"He's got a limp. I thought it was a burr in his paw, but I couldn't find one. I hope it isn't serious."

"We'll check it out," Karen reassured him, peeking over the counter to look at Paul. "What a handsome fella. I always wanted a dog."

"In this job, you'll meet enough to get tired of them," Joe promised her, opening the waist-high door to lead his uncle and the limping pup to the exam room. "Come on and give me a hand with him, Karen."

Karen rose uneasily from her chair. "Are you sure?"

"You can keep him calm for me," Joe said. "Haven't you ever heard of the soothing effects of beauty on the beast?"

He winked at her. She smiled and blushed just as he had hoped she would.

* * *

At dinner that night, Karen couldn't believe how well the day at the clinic had gone. After Robert Bell and Paul showed up, they had five more pet owners stop in. They were even present for the birth of six kittens. She felt overjoyed to be by Joe's side all day, helping him like a professional assistant. Despite her lack of experience or education, Joe insisted that she help. He made her feel capable and even worthy of every task, even the ones she didn't think she could do. Warming newborn kittens and calming a frantic bird were a far cry from painting quietly in a studio, but she couldn't wait to get back to the clinic.

Aunt Val passed her famous glazed yams across the table to Joe. "I am so glad today went better. I knew people would start to come around. God is good. He answers our prayers."

"How was work for you, Miss Val?"

She sighed dramatically. "Well, those preteens were monsters as usual, but I set them straight. It's always tougher teaching summer school. All they want to do is go outside." She shook her head and turned to Karen beside her. "Your mother had more patience with kids than I could ever dream of having."

Karen only nodded, munching on her country fried steak. After many tears the day before, she wasn't ready to touch on the subject of her mother again.

"Oh, Karen!" her aunt cried. "You have to show Joe your studio bedroom. I am so proud."

Karen nearly dropped her fork.

"Studio?" Joe gave them a puzzled look.

"Karen is a painter. She didn't tell you?" Aunt Val gave her niece a look like she had committed another crime.

"She said it was a little hobby of hers."

Karen shrugged at her aunt's accusing glance. She could feel her cheeks burning. Her paintings were so personal, her heart and soul on canvas. If only Aunt Val could read her thoughts.

"You're an artist, Karen?" Joe asked.

Karen poked at her yams with the fork. "Hardly."

Aunt Val nearly choked. "Hardly! This little lady has over fifty paintings to her name. Most of them are on the walls in the attic. They are stunning!"

"Aunt Val, please," Karen murmured, staring down at her half-empty plate.

"She is too shy about her talent," her aunt said. "She could be famous."

Karen raised her eyes to meet Joe's. He smiled. "I'd love to see them."

She could feel her heart racing in her chest.

"Why don't *you* take him up to see them, Aunt Val?" she suggested, trying to tone down the urgency in her voice.

"I have a church meeting tonight," her aunt said with a wink.

Karen watched her rise from her chair at the table, gather her dish, and head for the kitchen sink.

134

Karen's heart sank. What if he didn't like what he saw? What if he thought her paintings were ugly? Worse yet, what if they offended him? Karen swallowed hard and prayed a short prayer.

* * *

Joe followed Karen up the narrow attic staircase. He felt as though he were part of a funeral procession. Karen didn't seem at all eager to show off her talent. If anything, she seemed embarrassed and even a little nervous. Despite her hesitation, he was on her heels all the way up the stairs, eager to see this new side of her.

"I never took any art classes outside of grade school," Karen said, pausing at the door and turning to look down at him. "It's something that I do for fun."

"Fifty paintings for fun?" he said with a disbelieving smirk.

She shrugged. "Well, it helped me pass the time in jail."

Karen returned her attention to the attic door and slowly pushed it open. She flipped on the ceiling light as she entered the room. He followed behind, stepping into the attic with child-like curiosity.

The long room was typical of a country girl, adorning shades of cream and peach, quilt patterns, and white wicker furniture. The only difference was the walls. They were covered with beautiful paintings unlike any Joe had ever seen before. Some were images of landscapes and natural settings. Others were buildings, ones he even recognized like her aunt's house and Mercy Church.

"Wow," he whispered, walking up to them. "Like Thomas Kinkade meets van Gogh . . . with a dash of Monet."

Karen laughed. "You know more about art than I thought."

"I may be a math and science kind of guy, but I like a pretty picture." He turned to her and saw that her once fearful expression was now softening. "Karen, this is unbelievable."

"Really?"

He returned his gaze to her work. "Yeah, you *are* talented."

He began to walk along the length of the room, pausing to look at each piece like an art critic in a gallery.

He pointed to the one nearest to her bed. "A self portrait?"

"My mother."

"Of course. You look just like her now," he said, walking around the bed to get a better look at her painting of children playing on a playground.

Joe followed the rest of the paintings around the room until his eyes fell upon a familiar face. He could feel his jaw drop slightly at the sight.

"I'm sorry." Her voice cracked. "I needed to paint him."

Joe stared into the painted eyes of his grandfather almost forgetting to breathe. It was a perfect portrait of him. His eyes were bright and warm. The smile on his face was tender and sincere. This was exactly how Joe remembered his Grandpa Frank. It was as though his grandfather were standing in the room with them.

Joe's emotions turned raw within him. "No, don't apologize. It's the best picture of him I've ever seen. You did this from memory?"

She nodded, looking uneasy.

"Karen, it's beautiful," Joe said, mustering up the courage to ask her for a huge favor. "Could I—"

She stepped closer to him, nodding her head. "I want you to have it, Joe."

It took every ounce of his strength not to break down in front of Karen. Fearing she might notice his struggle, he kept his eyes on the painting. "Thank you."

"I had to paint him," she said. "All I could ever remember was how he smiled when he . . ." Her voice trailed off, and Joe could hear her breaths becoming uneven. He turned to see her drop on the bed with one tight fist over her mouth. She avoided his eyes, but he could see that hers were forcing back tears. Joe walked over and sat beside her.

"Did it help to paint him?" he asked, fighting the urge to put a consoling arm around her shoulder.

She swallowed. "It helped a lot."

"I think my family will love that painting of him." His eyes avoided the portrait. It stirred up too many wild emotions, too much pain. Karen didn't need to see him that way. "I'll have it framed and hang it in the clinic."

"I'm so glad you like it. I was afraid you would be offended."

He shook his head, gesturing to the works of art. "Is this what you want to do? Do you want to be an artist?"

Karen scoffed. "I'm not talented enough to make a living from my work."

"Are you crazy?" Joe said, funneling his pain into disbelief. "These are amazing!"

"Joe, I would love to have my own studio and gallery. I would love to teach art to kids," she said in a tone of surrender. "But no one is going to buy my art, especially not in this town."

There was a deep-seeded sadness in her eyes that Joe could see she was trying to hide. This was her dream. He could feel it. He wanted nothing more than to build her the biggest and best art gallery in the whole state of North Carolina right then. He could renovate the clinic into a gallery for her. These thoughts were not ordinary and hardly rational for Joe. The realization hit him like a freight train. He cared deeply for Karen, enough to care about her dreams. He even cared enough to make sacrifices for this once troubled, young girl from his past.

Karen hopped up from the bed and lifted the portrait of Joe's grandfather from the wall. She offered it to him, and he gently took it from her as if handling a newborn child.

She smiled. "I guess this is our official peace offering."

He returned the smile and then met eyes with his grandfather again. The emotion was hardly more than he could handle. Joe unintentionally let out a small breath that seemed to start a domino effect through him. His eyes burned. He closed them as tightly as he could.

Karen lifted the painting from his hands and propped it against the end of the bed. "Joe?"

Joe opened his eyes. Memories of his grandfather washed over him yet again. He missed him more than he could ever tell her. Karen placed a comforting hand on his shoulder. It was more than enough to keep his emotions at bay.

Chapter Thirteen

"Pet insurance?" Karen huffed, flipping through the stack of papers on her desk.

After three days at the clinic, another new day as Joe's receptionist had filled her with excitement and anticipation until the first pet owner left her with a mountain of paperwork.

Joe shrugged. "Yeah, it's a new fad. I know there are a lot of documents to fill out, but it's actually the same information on different forms."

"I'm not complaining." The last thing she wanted was for Joe to think that she was ungrateful for her job.

He laughed. "Of course, you are! I don't expect you to love everything about this job, Karen. Be glad that only a few people in Mercy even know what pet insurance is."

Karen returned her attention to the papers and began to sift through them with a heavy sense of dread. She had hoped for another thrilling day of births and rescues, not insurance claim forms and filing. She knew she had to buckle down, though, and get the job done. She couldn't let Joe down.

Karen heard the veterinarian drift back into his office. They were both waiting and wondering if the next appointment would show up. A part of her almost wished that they wouldn't. Karen couldn't help but enjoy the alone time they had to talk. *Who am I kidding? Talk? You mean flirt,* she reminded herself, smirking. Her thoughts meandered and so did her eyes. They met the painted eyes of Frank Aldridge. Joe had her work framed the day before and found a spot for it on the waiting area wall. On the bottom of the frame, on a small gold plate, were the etched words "In memory of Frank Aldridge."

Karen couldn't have been more relieved at Joe's reaction to the painting. She had feared the worst when she brought him up to the attic room. When he nearly broke down in tears, she felt sick. It was her fault that Joe and his family had suffered so much pain. She wished that she could turn back the clock and change everything. All she could do now, though, was be grateful that God had placed forgiveness in Joe's heart. That painting, which was once a symbol of pain, was now one of forgiveness and mercy.

Feeling encouraged once again, she returned her attention to the task at hand. After about twenty minutes of filling out forms, her fingers felt cramped. She dropped the pen on the desk and cracked her weary knuckles. At the same time, the clinic door came open, the bell on the handle jingling. She expected to look up and see Mrs. Leitha Yarborough. Instead, she saw a familiar face that sent a shock wave through her.

"Hey, girl!"

"Ricky!" Karen exclaimed, the confusion and disbelief practically dripping from his name.

Ricky approached her desk, a silver chain dangling from his waist down the side of his black jeans. He looked exactly as he had when they first met, spiky hair and that awful black getup.

"What are you doing here?" She tried desperately to make the question sound like one of curiosity, but it came out in a more unpleasant tone.

He winced. "Sorry, I barged in on you at work."

She rose from her chair. "No. Uh, that's fine."

"No hug?" he asked, opening his arms.

She forced a smile. "Of course." Karen met him with a weak hug on the other side of the desk.

"I went by your place and your aunt didn't want to tell me where you worked," Ricky said, perplexed. "What's up with her?"

"Uh, she's feeling a little under the weather, I guess. Listen, why don't we go talk outside?"

If Joe saw Ricky, what would he think? She couldn't let that happen.

"It's raining like crazy out there. Why don't you let me take you out to lunch?"

"Uh." She couldn't think of what to say as she heard Joe's approaching footsteps.

"Hi," Joe said from behind the desk.

Ricky offered him a goofy grin. "What's up, Doc?" He laughed at his own joke, and Karen felt her stomach turn.

Joe extended his hand. "How are you? I'm Joseph Aldridge."

"I'm Ricky, Karen's boyfriend," Ricky said, shaking his hand.

Karen could feel her face turning white. *Boyfriend?*

She let out a nervous laugh. "He's such a joker. We were just pen pals in jail."

"You're too shy, Karen." Ricky put his arm around her waist and pulled her close. She tried to pull away, but he was stronger than she had anticipated. "She used to draw pictures for me and call me all the time."

"Really?" Joe said in a rather robotic tone.

"So you wanna get some lunch, girl?" Ricky asked, finally releasing her waist.

She met eyes with Joe. "You know, I really can't. I have a lot of paperwork today."

Ricky took her hand. "Oh, come on. Only a bite. We have a lot to catch up on." He turned to Joe. "What do you say, boss man? Can she come out and play?"

She could die right then. She could just crawl into a hole and die.

Karen tried to protest, yanking her hand from his grasp. "Really, Ricky, I—"

"Sure, she can take a break. Have a nice lunch," Joe said, bitterness covering his tone.

Ricky grinned. "Cool! Let's go."

Melissa McGovern Taylor

"Wait, but, Joe," Karen sputtered, watching Joe head back into his office and close the door.

Ricky tugged at her arm. "Come on, Karen. Lighten up. You've got all afternoon to work."

She could've tumbled off of Mount Everest and not felt worse than she did right then. It could've been the pained look in Joe's eyes or her own severe humiliation, but it was probably both that sucked the energy out of her. She didn't have the fight in her right then to resist Ricky any longer. With a weight on her shoulders, she grabbed her purse and followed him out of the clinic.

The first car that Karen saw on the street was the one she'd guessed correctly to be Ricky's. It was a tiny black hatchback. As she hurried through the rain to the passenger side, she saw a skull with vampire teeth painted on the door.

Ricky noticed her puzzled expression. "It's my brother's car. Oh, and he smokes, so it kind of stinks."

God, please get me out of this! Somehow Karen knew God wasn't going to bail her out.

By the time the two arrived back, Karen was out of patience with her former pen pal. Ricky's idea of taking her out to lunch was a greasy taco joint outside of Mercy. To make matters worse, he conveniently forgot his wallet, and Karen had to pay for both of their meals. Their conversation during lunch consisted mainly of his interest in gory movies. It didn't matter to her. She couldn't focus on a conversation with him anyway. All she could think about was Joe alone at the clinic fuming over how flirty Karen Denwood neglected to tell him she had a boyfriend. When they reached the clinic, she planned to politely break off all ties with Ricky.

"So lunch was nice," Ricky said, walking her to the clinic door. "I hope we can do that again."

"I'm not sure we should, Ricky," Karen said gently.

"What do you mean?"

She bit her lip. "I know we bonded while we were in jail, but we're very different people with very different interests."

He gave her a cheesy grin. "Opposites attract, remember?"

She shook her head. "Not these opposites."

142

He looked thoughtful. "Well, uh, can I borrow like twenty bucks? I'm almost out of gas."

"Anything for my fellow Christian *friend*," she said, overemphasizing the word 'friend'. She seemed to be talking to herself, though, feeling the need to remind herself that despite their differences, he was still a person.

"Christian?" He laughed. "Right."

Karen froze. "What do you mean, 'right'?"

"I'm not a Christian."

Her heart nearly stopped. "What are you talking about? That day on the phone, you accepted Christ, remember?"

"Give me a break, girl!"

"You lied to me?" She could feel a knife twisting in her gut.

"You wanted me to be saved. I was just going along with your little Jesus thing to make you happy."

Karen could feel her hurt and disappointment boil into anger. She pulled a twenty-dollar bill from her purse and shoved it in his direction.

"Just leave," she ordered through gritted teeth.

His brow dropped. "Oh, so now you don't want to be friends because I'm not a Christian?"

Karen shook her head. "It's not that at all. You betrayed my trust."

He shrugged and snatched the bill from her grasp. "Adios."

She watched him climb into his hatchback and rev up the tiny engine.

"And I know you stole my aunt's money!" she screamed as he pulled away.

His car disappeared down the road. Karen could only hope she would never see it again.

* * *

Joe stared down at his desk, listlessly sifting through papers. His thoughts were a million miles away from work. His lunch, a peanut butter and grape jelly sandwich, sat half eaten on a napkin. He had lost his appetite about an hour earlier.

He heard the clinic door open.

"I'm back," Karen's familiar voice echoed from the front.

He said nothing. He didn't want to even look at her. Too many mixed emotions were brewing inside of him. *Ricky? A boyfriend? Nice of her to mention it.* He'd thought this to himself ever since her Goth lover boy came waltzing into the clinic.

Why was he so bitter and angry? Karen wasn't his girlfriend. He knew why, though. It was all jealousy. He was too proud to admit it to himself. When he saw that clown putting his hands on Karen, he felt like his heart was being ripped out. *How could she not mention Ricky?*

He heard the clinic door open once again.

"Hi, I'm Annie Starling," a familiar voice greeted. "My cat has a neutering today."

Joe hopped up from his desk and made his way to the front. Karen turned to him, but he intentionally ignored her.

"Hey, Mrs. Starling," he said, meeting eyes with his old high school math teacher.

She gasped. "Joseph Aldridge. You've grown up!"

Joe walked around the desk and embraced the fifty-something woman.

She released him from her arms. "I am so proud of you!"

He shrugged. "It's all thanks to my teachers."

She turned to Karen. "Still a teacher's pet, and he's not even in school anymore!"

Karen smiled as she and Joe met eyes for a split second. Joe dodged her glance like a stray bullet.

He turned his attention to the kennel on the floor beside Mrs. Starling. "So is Harry ready for his neutering?"

His owner laughed. "Is any cat ready?"

Joe spied a small, black cat with piercing green eyes through the metal bars of the door. It hissed at him, showing its threatening fangs.

"This should be fun," he noted with sarcasm.

Karen giggled. As much as he wanted to see that giggle, Joe couldn't set aside his bitterness for the sight.

Mrs. Starling smiled at Joe. "Harry was a stray. He's still getting accustomed to being a pet."

He lifted the kennel and headed back around the desk. "Karen, I'll need you to scrub down and assist me with this one."

He heard her rise from her chair. "Okay."

Her voice sounded uneasy. Nonetheless, he remained monotonous and instructive. "Get the anesthesia from the locked cabinet in my office and bring it into the exam room."

Even twenty minutes later, when Joe and Karen stood over a very unconscious Harry the cat, he still couldn't make eye contact with her. Thoughts of Ricky and Karen overwhelmed him.

Joe looked over the cat's shaved skin. "Okay, he's prepped. Scalpel, please."

Karen placed the scalpel in his gloved hand.

He began to make the first incision, trying hard not to think about Karen's eyes penetrating him from across the table. To make matters worse, this was his first neutering since college. Sweat began to form on his brow. His breath was hot around his cheeks and chin under the surgical mask. Joe decided to sneak a glance at Karen, only one. Maybe then he could clear his thoughts.

To his surprise, Karen was not staring him down. She was wide-eyed, staring down at the cat. Her face looked unusually pale. He wondered if it was simply the light they were under. He followed her gaze back down to Harry. All seemed normal. Why did she look like a deer in headlights?

"Karen, what's—"

Before he could finish his question, he saw Karen's eyes roll up to the back of her head. She fell limp and hit the exam room floor.

* * *

"Karen?"

She opened her eyes, letting in the florescent light above her.

An old, familiar face smiled down at her. "Welcome back."

The green-eyed man was stout and chubby with salt and pepper hair. He wore a white coat and a stethoscope around his neck like a doctor straight out of a Norman Rockwell painting.

"Doctor Whitfield?" she whispered, trying to sit up.

The doctor took her by the shoulders and gently pushed her back down. "Woh, little lady, it's not time for you to get up yet."

Karen looked around and found herself in the waiting area of the clinic, stretched out on one of the sofas. She still wore her medical gloves and a surgical shirt over her own. She and the doctor were not alone. Mrs. Starling was still there. Her face reminded Karen of what had happened.

"I passed out," she remembered aloud.

Dr. Whitfield nodded at her. "Yes, you did. Joe called me over."

Karen searched the room. "Where is he?"

"He's finishing up with Harry," Mrs. Starling said.

Regret and embarrassment engulfed Karen like a fog. She should've admitted to Joe that she was squeamish, but her pride had gotten the best of her. Even when he was delivering kittens, she had to avoid the sight. Ever since the incident with Frank Aldridge, Karen couldn't stand the sight of blood or gore. She would simply lose consciousness when faced with it head on.

"You had quite a fall when you knocked out," Dr. Whitfield said, taking her pulse with his stethoscope. "Does anything hurt?"

"No."

The sight of old Dr. Whitfield brought back so many memories for Karen, her days with the flu and chicken pox. She could remember when Dr. Whitfield treated her broken arm from a fall on the playground.

He smiled. "Good."

Karen pulled off her gloves. "Do you remember me?"

He nodded with a wise expression on his face. "Little Karen Denwood."

There was silence between them as Karen tried to sit up again. She felt stiff and wondered how long she had been lying on the coach.

"You've been unconscious for ten minutes or so," the doctor said as if reading her thoughts.

He allowed her to take a seated position.

"Now, if nothing's wrong, I'll be heading back to my office."

Suddenly, Karen remembered seeing Dr. Whitfield. He was in church that Sunday when she attended. He had walked out with the rest of the crowd. Now here he was, not denying her aid when she needed it.

The doctor approached the door. "Give me a call if you need me."

"Wait."

The doctor stopped in his tracks, looking slightly alarmed. "Something hurting?"

"Why did you walk out of church that Sunday?" She couldn't believe how bold she was being, but she had to understand why she was facing so much rejection.

He gave her an expression of resignation. "Frank was my best friend growing up."

Karen felt a lump climb up her throat. "I'm sorry."

He nodded, expressionless, and disappeared through the clinic door.

Fighting back tears, Karen pulled off her surgical shirt and folded it.

"I left too, Karen," Mrs. Starling admitted, sitting on the sofa across from her.

Here we go, Karen thought, wanting to go home and try to sleep away the rest of her terrible day.

Mrs. Starling fiddled with the hem of her brown purse. "My mother was best friends with Mrs. Aldridge. Of course, his wife passed away before he did, but nonetheless, my mother insisted on leaving the church with everyone else."

Karen nodded, rising from her seat. "I understand."

Mrs. Starling rose with her. "Don't give up hope, Karen. In time, everyone will be able to forgive you."

The reassuring words of this stranger surprised Karen. Yet, she was warmed by Mrs. Starling's attempt to encourage her.

"It could be a very long time," Karen muttered, frowning.

"Well, in the mean time, I'll try to talk some sense into my mother."

They exchanged smiles.

"Thank you." Karen headed back around the desk. "I'll go check on Harry and Joe."

Down the hall, Karen remembered Joe's tone with her before she had fainted. He had sounded so unemotional and cold. She could only assume that he was angry about Ricky's visit. But why would he be angry? Was he jealous? She shook her head as if to rid her mind of such ridiculous ideas. She couldn't shake the hurt that she felt, though. He almost treated her as badly as his brother and father had.

Karen slipped into the examination room where Joe was completing the procedure.

He looked up from the table and met eyes with her again after what had felt like an eternity of scorn. "Are you okay?" Before she could answer, he turned back to Harry.

"I think so," she said, feeling her cheeks warm. "I'm a little squeamish."

"You should have said something." Again, he gave her that cold tone.

She stepped toward him. "Is something wrong, Joe?"

"No."

"Talk to me. I can't—"

"I think you need to take the rest of the day off," he interrupted.

Karen felt as if someone punched her in the gut.

He set some of his instruments on the rolling cart beside him. "You fell pretty hard on the floor. You need to go home and lie down."

She could've buckled over right then. Instead, she held herself together. Without a word, she stormed out of the exam room and down the hall.

"Something wrong?" Mrs. Starling asked as Karen flew through the waiting area.

Karen pushed back tears. "Have a nice day, Mrs. Starling."

She hurried out into the hot June air and as far away from Joe Aldridge as possible.

* * *

"You two are unusually quiet," Karen's aunt said, buttering her corn muffin. "How were things at the clinic today besides Little Miss Woozy taking a spill?"

"Fine," Joe and Karen replied in unison.

They shared a glance for a split second, but quickly looked away. Joe couldn't believe she wasn't telling her aunt about Ricky. Was Karen lying to her too?

Miss Valerie set her butter knife on the edge of her plate. "Well, I don't believe that for one second. What happened?"

Karen stared down at her plate, pushing her corn around with her fork. "Nothing happened."

Her aunt sighed. "Well, that Ricky boy came over looking for you. Did he come by the clinic?"

From the corner of his eye, Joe could see Karen nodding.

A light bulb seemed to beam over Miss Valerie's head. "Oh, I see."

Great, Joe thought. *Now her aunt is going to think that I'm jealous and that's why I'm not talking to Karen.*

"I was just surprised that Karen never mentioned that she had a boyfriend," Joe said.

Karen's eye widened. "He's not my boyfriend."

Joe turned to her. "I don't understand why you're not opening up to me. I thought we were friends. What else are you hiding?"

"Nothing, Joe! I'm not hiding anything!"

Aunt Val raised her hands. "Okay, kids. Not at the dinner table. We'll eat in peace. Then you two can go outside and talk about it, okay?"

"There's nothing to talk about." Joe rose from his chair, plate in hand. "Thank you for dinner. I'll be in my room."

He set his plate in the sink, left the kitchen, and headed for his bedroom. He had to get away from Karen, from the thoughts and feelings that swallowed him whole in her presence. They were so new to him. Growing up he'd had crushes and girlfriends from time to time, but this time was so different. His feelings for Karen were unusually strong. He wanted to run and hide from them, deny them. That was easier than embracing them and facing the possibility of hurt or rejection. What would she want with a goody-two-shoe veterinarian compared to a bad boy rocker like Ricky? He had thought that maybe Karen's feelings for him were mutual, but now he couldn't be sure of anything.

In his cozy furnished bedroom, Joe watched TV from a comfortable spot on his bed. The room was comparable to his own at home with deep blue walls and solid, oak furniture. After only a week, he felt right at home in Valerie Denwood's house. He had already helped her fix her dishwasher and replace a broken window. It was nice to find a home away from home.

After two hours of sitcom reruns and game shows, Joe still couldn't shake thoughts of Karen. TV was a decent distraction. He often hated and loved it for that very reason, but it wasn't enough right then. Turning off the TV, he decided to crack open his Bible and do a devotion.

About five minutes into his reading, Joe thought he heard a thump over his head. Then another thump resounded. He paused from the devotion and listened. There it was again. Something was on the roof.

Joe rose from the bed and approached his bedroom window. It was dusk and a torch of orange sunlight remained on Mercy's horizon, glimmering through the trees. He pushed his rather stubborn window open and felt the warm, summer air creep into his cool bedroom. He poked his head out of the window to take a look around.

There was a small overhang under his window and the roof of the house sat above him. He pulled himself up to sit on the window sill and get a better look above. In the dim sunlight, surrounded by pink sky, Joe's eyes fell on Karen. She lounged on an old quilt on the rooftop beside the attic window, staring up at the sky above her. Stars were beginning to sparkle as the night sky approached.

"What are you doing?" Joe called to her.

Karen seemed startled. She sat up. "Star gazing."

"Are you out of your mind? You could fall off the roof."

She returned her attention to the sky. "For the stars, it's worth it."

A sudden thought came over Joe that he knew came straight from God. *Maybe you should get up there and talk with her.*

Taking in a breath, Joe stepped out onto the overhang below his window.

Karen must have heard him because she looked at him again. "You really should come up through my window. It's a little safer."

Joe shrugged, his pride taking over. "It's a short climb."

Karen shook her head, smirking. "Boys will be boys."

Joe clumsily managed to pull himself from the overhang on to the roof. Carefully, he crawled across the shingles toward her. Karen laughed.

"Laugh all you want," he said. "This is the safe way."

She pointed at the attic window. "I told you the safe way."

"Well, I made it," he countered, sitting down on the quilt beside her.

She was quiet, watching the sky above them again. It was growing darker, and the stars were becoming brighter and more numerous. In the remaining sunlight, Karen looked forlorn but beautiful nonetheless. He knew her gloomy mood was his fault.

"I was out of line, Karen."

She stretched back down across the quilt. "I guess I should've said something about Ricky, but I thought I would never see him again."

"So he's not your boyfriend?"

"At one time, I would have been happy to say 'yes,' but now I'm glad to tell you 'no.'"

Relief washed over Joe, surprising him. He still wanted to deny his feelings.

"Was he ever your boyfriend?" He surprised himself with the question.

"The only boyfriend I've ever had was Teddy Garmon in the seventh grade," she said, the unhappy memory showing on her face. "He dumped me after a week."

Joe shook his head in disapproval. "Ted never knew how to treat a lady."

Karen shrugged. "I've never had much luck with love."

"There's no luck involved."

Karen seemed to shift uncomfortably. "Ricky and I have nothing to do with each other anymore. We're not even friends."

"That's not my fault, is it?" Joe asked, wondering exactly how much he had revealed his jealousy that afternoon.

"No. He stole some money from my aunt. He even pretended to become a Christian just to impress me. Aunt Val was right about him from the beginning."

"What is it? A woman's intuition? My mom pulls it on me all the time."

Karen cracked a smile. "Whatever it is, it must have skipped me." She looked up at the sky, narrowing her eyes. "Do you ever watch the stars?"

Joe reclined back on the warm quilt beside her and met eyes with a countless number of twinkling, little lights. "It's been a long time."

"I missed this so much while I was in prison. In all those years, I probably felt the night air and saw the stars about three times."

Joe felt guilty for not taking advantage of his freedom to star gaze. "I guess you do this every night now, huh?"

"Just about. Don't tell Aunt Val. She hates it when I'm on the roof."

"I think you gave yourself up with the loud stomping."

"Was I really that loud?"

"I thought Santa was early."

Karen cracked up. It was a sound he had missed almost all day.

She gave him puppy-dog eyes. "So I guess you're not mad at me anymore?"

"As long as you don't have anymore skeletons in your closet."

"Well, I do have a friend from jail, Maria. When she gets out, she plans on coming into town. She's a welcomed visitor, though."

"Maria was in the Bible study group, right?"

"Yeah." Karen's expression grew somber again. "I miss her."

"I could take you to see her."

Karen looked away from the stars to meet eyes with Joe. Her eyes seemed to sparkle even more than those shimmering, celestial bodies. They were more brilliant, more colorful. They drew him in.

"She made me promise not to come back, but thanks."

The two were silent for a moment, gazing into each other's eyes as if there weren't any stars to look at. Every part of Joe wanted to lean over and kiss her. What would she do? Would she pull away?

The next thing Joe knew, he wasn't bringing his face to hers, but Karen was bringing her lips to his. His heart began to pound loudly in his ears, blocking out the sound of crickets. He closed his eyes and felt her warm lips meet his own. Her fingertips gently touched his cheek. Joe wanted to pull her in closer and make the moment last well into the morning hours, but a familiar voice cut through the romance like a hot knife through butter.

"Joe! You out there? Your mother is on the phone for you!" Miss Valerie called from inside Karen's room.

Karen pulled away like a turtle retreating into its shell. She looked stunned, perhaps by her aunt's interruption, perhaps by her own forwardness. Joe couldn't tell which. He gave her an awkward smile and hopped up from his spot on the roof. He nearly lost his balance, forgetting half way up that he was well above ground level.

"Joe!" Karen cried in fright as he fluttered about, trying to regain his balance.

He steadied himself. "I'm okay. I'll be right back."

With his heart still pounding a mile a minute, Joe shimmied to Karen's window and climbed into her room, longing to go back out.

* * *

Karen watched Joe disappear into her bedroom to answer the phone call from his mother. She took in a deep breath for the first time in what felt like forever. *What have I done?* Her cheeks grew hot. *I kissed him.*

Her heart raced like she had just finished a marathon. She could hardly believe her behavior. What was she thinking? What was *he* thinking? It all happened so fast. She wasn't sure if Joe's response was positive. He didn't pull away, but he didn't fall into the kiss like she had hoped he would. She had longed for him to put his arms around her, but he stayed in place like a mannequin. Maybe she had been too impulsive. This was so unlike her. Karen always thought things through first. Yet, right then, her emotions took over. She couldn't look away from his eyes.

Joe's behavior all afternoon seemed to scream jealousy. Had she read him completely wrong? What if he was telling his mother right now? She could imagine his horrifying tale.

"Mom, Karen Denwood is seducing me! She's got this rocker guy on the side too!"

Karen shook her head. That was ridiculous, but she still wondered if she had been too impulsive. He did say he would be back. Maybe he would be back to tell her, "Sorry, I think we should just be friends."

A feeling of heavy regret consumed her. Karen sat up and climbed back up into her bedroom, dragging the old quilt behind her. She shut the window and got changed to go to bed.

Chapter Fourteen

Most of the morning at the clinic consisted of awkward exchanges about the slow computer, the next appointment, and the weather. Joe couldn't understand it. After the quick "just checking up on you" phone call from his mother, he returned to Karen's room only to find the door shut and the lights out. Did he do something wrong? The complexity of women reached a new height for him. He wanted desperately to know what Karen was feeling all morning, but she seemed distant. This woman seemed so unlike the warm, loving one he'd shared the rooftop with the night before.

Joe had spent much of the morning trying to come up with an icebreaker. It finally hit him when he went outside to help Mr. Faircloth get his horse of a dog, Brute, into his Cadillac. On the way back to the clinic door, Joe glanced at the clinic's street sign.

He slipped back into the clinic. "Karen."

She looked up at him expectantly.

"My sign out there for passing cars is pretty drab. Does the artist have any advice?"

She shrugged nonchalantly. "Not really. It does the job, doesn't it?"

"Well, yeah," he said, leaning over the front counter, "but it needs a special touch."

He offered her a hint-hint smile with raised eyebrows.

She blushed a little and lowered her eyes. "I guess it could use some colorful pets."

"So you'll make me a new sign?"

A mischievous grin formed on her face. "Is that an order from my boss?"

"A polite request."

Her expression became forlorn as she twisted a lock of hair around her fingers. "I don't know, Joe."

"What are you afraid of?"

The question visibly startled her. She remained silent and thoughtful for a moment. "Okay, but I get to paint on the clock, and supply costs come out of the office budget."

Joe grinned. "You play hard ball, don't you?"

"I learned a thing or two in jail."

Karen returned her attention to the computer monitor on her desk. Joe returned to his office, relieved that the air between them was clear once again. Still, many questions about the night before floated through his mind. More than that, the memory wouldn't stop repeating. He wondered if, in her mind, Karen, too, was still kissing him on that warm rooftop.

* * *

Saturdays outside the prison walls were becoming more numerous for Karen. In prison, she used to imagine all of the fun things she would do on her weekends. She pictured herself visiting other towns in North Carolina, shopping and going to the beach. Now that she was free, Saturdays consisted of television and reading. She felt like an ungrateful hypocrite as she lay on her bed reading a fantasy romance.

The scene of a princess dashing across a field to her prince played out in Karen's mind. She could see the prince embracing his princess until her stomach growled, interrupting the typically romantic moment. She glanced at the digital alarm clock on her wicker nightstand. It was quarter after nine o'clock. With a sigh, she sat up in bed, still clothed in her pajamas. The smell of bacon and biscuits hit her nostrils.

Humming to herself, Karen gathered up her robe and slipped it on. As she approached the door, a thought stopped her in her tracks. *Should I look like this in front of my boss?* It was a valid question. She certainly didn't want to scare him with her bed head. She grabbed her hair brush and attempted to make her rat's nest a little tamer.

Why should I care what Joe thinks? He can't fire me for wearing a bath robe in my own home, she told herself.

Other thoughts began to creep up. Was she really concerned about what her boss thought? Or was she worried about looking good for an attractive, single guy?

Karen frowned at herself in the mirror. "I look fine."

In the kitchen, she found her aunt and the attractive, single Joe sitting at the kitchen table. Three plates of biscuits, bacon, eggs and grits graced the spots in front of each chair. Embarrassment hit Karen when she realized that she was the only person in the kitchen still in pajamas.

Aunt Val smirked at her with raised eyebrows. "I figured the enticing aroma of my oh-so-good cookin' would bring you down in time for the blessing."

"It looks delicious," Karen said, taking her seat.

Aunt Val lowered her head. "Let us pray."

Joe and Karen followed suit.

"Lord, we thank you for this meal that you have blessed us with. We pray that we can accomplish many good things on this beautiful day. Please bless this food to our bodies. In Jesus' name, we pray. Amen."

"Amen," Joe and Karen said in unison.

The trio dug in. The first bite of Aunt Val's scrambled eggs melted in Karen's mouth. She tried to show lady-like restraint as she scooped up another forkful.

"What are you two doing today?" Joe asked.

Aunt Val layered butter and grape jelly on one half of her biscuit. "I'm shopping for a new swim suit. I was a little too optimistic about my diet when I bought the first one in March. Did you want to come along, Karen?"

The thought of shopping didn't sound so appealing, especially when Karen was trying to save every penny she had. "No, thanks. I think I'll hang around the house."

Aunt Val cocked her head. "Again?"

"Sure, why not?"

"You should come with me, Karen," Joe said, eating a forkful of grits and eggs.

Aunt Val turned to him. "Where are you goin'?"

"Not shopping."

Curiosity overwhelmed Karen. "Then where?"

He shot her a mischievous grin. "Why don't you come along?" The sparkle in his eyes seemed to add, "I dare you."

She smirked. "So it's a surprise?"

He nodded.

"Okay. I'll go."

Aunt Val looked perplexed. "Go where?"

Joe grinned. "We'll tell you when we get back."

About forty-five minutes later, Joe and Karen rode in his mother's Mustang along the highway outside of Mercy. With the top down, the air whipped in around them, flipping Karen's hair to and fro. She imagined it would be a tangled mess by the time they arrived at their destination.

"So you don't have your own car?" Karen asked him, fighting the wind for his attention.

"Nope. I took the bus in college," he said. "I'm thinking of getting a Beetle when I have the money, though."

He offered Karen a goofy grin, and she chuckled in response. "Neon green or pink?"

"Oh, definitely pink. I might even have my name painted on the side."

The pair laughed.

"Whenever I learn to drive, I think I'll get one of these," Karen said.

"Good choice."

Karen settled back into her leather seat. She could hardly wait to find out their destination. Maybe they were going to an art gallery or a museum. Maybe he wanted to take her to the movies. The suspense was killing her.

"So seriously, Joe, where are we going?"

The Road to Mercy

He grinned. "Don't you have any patience?"

His question called for a rather snippy answer, but she held her tongue. He meant it in a teasing way, probably not realizing how much patience a person has to learn during a prison sentence.

"I'm not a big fan of surprises," she finally said.

"Well, it's nothing exciting, but I always have a nice time when I go there."

Joe pulled the car down a long, winding road until they came to a single-story, brick building nestled among azalea bushes and pine trees. A sign in front of the building caught Karen's eye.

"Whispering Winds Nursing Home," she read aloud.

Joe pulled the Mustang into a parking space near the front entrance. "I haven't been here in a few months."

"Do you have a relative here?"

"My great grandmother."

Karen pulled off her seatbelt. "She must be pretty old."

"She'll be one hundred in December."

Karen gasped, wondering what it must have been like to live for a century and see so much change.

"Is she . . . ?" She wasn't sure how to phrase the question.

Joe cut off the engine and pushed his door open. "She loses track of time, but she's in her right mind."

Karen frowned. "I mean, is she your Grandpa Frank's mother?"

Joe smiled and nodded.

Karen froze. "Joe . . ."

"It's okay. Come on."

Joe slipped out of the car, leaving Karen alone with her worries and her now racing heart. *Why would he drag me out here to the see the mother of the man I killed?* She pushed her thoughts away and hopped out of the car.

Joe already held the door to the nursing home open for her.

"I don't think this is good idea," she protested, stopping at the entrance.

"She can't remember what happened, Karen."

Her curiosity peaked. "Really?"

"She thinks it's a different time."

"What time?"

He gestured for Karen to enter. "You'll see."

Karen stepped into the small lobby of the nursing home with some apprehension. Joe's behavior was unusually mysterious, and she didn't like it. As he paused at the receptionist's desk to sign them in, she kept her eyes locked on his body language. He seemed completely at ease, so why was she worried?

He set the pen down and turned to her. "This way."

She followed him down a carpeted, blue hallway. The walls were decorated with paintings of European landscapes and eighteenth century children cradling flowers. The air smelled musty with a tinge of some unrecognizable but unpleasant odor. They turned the corner to a hallway with daisy yellow walls and more of the same style of paintings. A nurse stood at a cart, pouring medicine into a cup. An elderly man in a grey sweatshirt watched her from his wheelchair nearby. Karen smiled at him as they walked by. He stared at her blankly, his mouth ajar. An uneasy feeling came over her. She could still turn around and leave. What was stopping her?

Joe finally paused in front of a door labeled with the name Betty Aldridge. "Here it is."

He disappeared into the dimly lit room. Karen peered in, looking for his great grandmother. The scent of cinnamon hit her nostrils as her eyes met a hunched-over woman in a wheelchair. Betty Aldridge watched her television through a pair of thick glasses. Karen slowly slipped into the undersized room, approaching Joe.

"Hi, Oma," Joe greeted, placing his hand on hers.

The white-haired woman slowly looked up from the television. As she recognized Joe, a toothy grin stretched across her wrinkled face. "Frank, where have you been?"

Frank? Karen was dumbfounded.

"I've been at school. I just finished," he said, sitting down on the single bed beside her.

She nodded. "Are your grades still up?"

"Yes, ma'am."

She squeezed his hand. "You make me so proud, Frankie. Look how handsome you are."

Karen could see tears forming in her light brown eyes.

Joe leaned down and put a gentle arm around her shoulder. "Don't cry, Oma."

"You're such a good boy."

She pulled a handkerchief from the breast pocket of her flowery blouse. As she dabbed her eyes, she saw Karen for the first time.

"Oh, my. Who is this lovely lady? Did you find another girlfriend, Frank?"

Joe smiled at Karen. She returned the smile, blushing.

"This is Karen Denwood."

Karen expected his great grandmother's eyes to grow wide in realization. Then her expression would turn angry, and she would yell at Karen to get out of her room. Instead, the elderly woman smiled and nodded.

"From school?"

"I met her in Mercy around town," Joe said.

She reached her hand out to Karen. "Don't be shy, darling."

Karen smiled at her, relieved to be offered a simple handshake. She stepped up and took Betty Aldridge's hand. It was lighter than she expected and soft like the bristles of a new paint brush.

Karen gently shook her hand and let it slip from her own. "Nice to meet you."

Betty looked up at her great grandson again. "Oh, she's beautiful, Frank. You should marry this one."

Joe grinned at her. "I don't know if she'll have me."

His eyes locked on Karen's. Her stomach did a full summersault. She released a nervous laugh, feeling her cheeks burn.

Betty let out a giggle. "You two have some time yet."

Karen nodded. "That's right. We're still young."

By now, Karen felt fully relaxed. All of her anxiety had dissipated into curiosity at the sight of this remarkable side of Joe. He was a nice guy, but the way that he treated his great grandmother gave Karen the warm-and-fuzzies. This was the first time she'd seen such a personal side of him. He obviously cared very much for his Oma.

Joe reached into his back pocket. "Are you ready for a game of Uno?"

He offered Oma a pack of Uno cards.

She took the deck from him. "That sounds fun."

"Can Karen join in?"

She smiled up at Karen. "Of course. I bet she's a pro."

* * *

Joe couldn't help but wonder why Karen was so quiet on the way back from the nursing home. If he'd offended her by taking her out there, he wanted to know. She didn't seem at all upset, though. Who would be after winning three Uno games in a row?

"So I guess you figured out that she thinks I'm my grandpa," Joe said, breaking the silence between them.

Karen turned away from the window to look at him. "She did call you Frankie the whole time."

"She thinks that my dad is him too. Like I said, she gets confused about the time."

"Did she ever know about . . . ?"

Joe nodded. "She went to his funeral, but she thought she was reliving her husband's."

Karen hummed in understanding.

"I'm sorry I dragged you out here. It was wrong of me not to tell you."

"Don't apologize. I really enjoyed meeting her." Her tone was firm yet honest.

"Good. I know it wasn't as interesting as shopping, though."

Karen shook her head. "I hate shopping."

"You do? I thought all women loved shopping."

Karen huffed. "So we're all alike?"

Joe froze, regretting his words. "No, I mean . . ."

"I know what you mean, Joe," she said with a grin.

"Sorry. You're not all alike. Neither are men. Actually, my brother really likes shopping, oddly enough."

Karen burst into laughter. "Your brother the farmhand?"

"Yeah, he goes with my mom all the time." The thought made Joe crack up as well. "Don't tell him I told you that."

Karen nodded. "I promise."

Just then, Joe realized how much he'd enjoyed his day with Karen. He loved talking to her and sharing a few laughs. He hadn't laughed so hard in a long time. He could be himself around her. In college, he often pretended to be smarter than he was around classmates and professors. Around his father and brother, he pretended to be tougher and stronger than he was. Even with this great grandmother, he had to pretend to be his grandpa. Only a handful of people saw the real Joseph Aldridge. After knowing Karen for only a month now, he was surprised she was part of that handful.

Karen's laughter tapered off. "How often do you visit with your great grandmother?"

"I like to go once a month, but I missed a lot of visits while I was in college."

"I'd like to go with you next time."

Joe smiled. "That would be nice."

"Then it's a date."

*   *   *

Karen's second week at the clinic went by without another hitch, much to her relief. Only a few appointments were canceled, and even fewer did so because of her presence. Every pet owner who met Karen was polite and respectful toward her. A few could recall her mother and mentioned how Lillian Denwood was still deeply missed. Their comments were bittersweet for Karen and drudged up thoughts of her father. She missed his letters desperately. There had been no word from the road in weeks, but Aunt Val assured her that this was the norm.

"He loves his job," she had said to Karen. "It makes him feel important. He doesn't get a lot of time off these days, but I know he'll be in town to see you as soon as he gets a chance."

In the mean time, Karen was elated to have Joe's sign project as a healthy distraction from concerns about her father and her and Joe's unpredictable friendship. The kiss had been on her mind constantly, and although they had become more comfortable around each other again, she couldn't shake the embarrassment for her rash behavior that starry evening. Painting the sign had helped her forget her attraction to Joe, at least temporarily. She hated to see that distraction completed, but by Friday morning, she was prepared for the unveiling.

"Should I do a drum roll?" Joe asked, standing outside the clinic before a sheet-covered sign.

Aunt Val fanned herself with her outgoing mail in the early morning heat. "Of course!" She already looked cool in her giant gardening hat, fuchsia tank top and khaki shorts, but her aunt was a fireball in every sense.

Karen stood before them beside her hidden masterpiece as Joe imitated a drum roll with his tongue.

She yanked the sheet from the sign. "Ta-da!"

The new sign was oak with red lettering and cartoonish pets on it. Above the words "Mercy Veterinary Clinic" and Joe's name sat an orange calico cat and a German shepherd dog. A blue parakeet perched on the dog's head between his ears and a black horse stood behind the trio.

"It's adorable!" Aunt Val gushed.

Joe applauded. "Exactly what I had in mind."

"Really?" Karen said.

Joe nodded. "It's great, Karen."

"Thanks."

Aunt Val dropped a scrawny arm around her shoulders. "You are so talented."

Joe squatted in front of the sign, examining the painted animals. "I can't wait for my mom to see it. She's stopping in today."

This news made Karen's gut tighten. She wasn't sure if she could handle any negative criticism about her work. All week she was relieved to earn nothing but rave reviews for her painting of Joe's grandfather. Nearly every pet owner commented on how well it favored him and how professional the piece was. When Joe had pointed to Karen as the artist, she wanted to shrink beneath her desk. She wondered if she would ever get used to her work being in the public eye.

Aunt Val started toward her parked car. "Well, time for work."

"But you took today off," Karen said.

She opened her car door. "I know. I have a ton of gardening to do. See you later, kids."

As Karen waved, she felt her eyes magnetically drawn to the sign. It did look striking in the midst of the ordinary signs on the block. Her hard work had really paid off.

Joe held the clinic door open. "Coming in?"

A feeling of confidence swept over her as she hurried to the door. Then something caught her eye across the street. Was that man watching her? In front of Dr. Whitfield's office, a man sat on a bench now reading the local newspaper. His face was hidden behind it. When she noticed him, he seemed to duck behind the open paper.

"What is it?" Joe asked.

Karen shook her head, wondering if she was being paranoid. "Nothing."

About an hour later, the memory of Karen's suspicions became fresh again.

"Joe!" a pale Mrs. Aldridge cried, bursting into the clinic.

Karen nearly jumped out of her chair. "What's wrong?"

Joe rushed out of his office. "Mom?"

She shook her head frantically. "The sign! Someone ruined it!"

Karen hopped up from her seat, nearly stumbling over her own feet. Her heart raced as she hurried past Joe's mother to the door.

Joe called after her, only a few steps behind her.

The three of them sprang from the door like flood water gushing through a dam.

A crowd of locals had gathered around the front of the clinic, blocking Karen's view of the sign. She gently pushed her way through, fearing what she would see, imagining her sign broken to pieces or burned into an unrecognizable piece of charred wood. What she found, though, was far worse.

The sign was still intact with a cruel addition made to the front. On top of her painted animals, in black spray paint was the word *murderer*.

Karen couldn't believe her eyes. She stood frozen, staring wide-eyed at the horrific graffiti. She could hear the curious whispers of the locals around her.

"What happened?"

"Who did such a thing?"

"Did anyone see who did this?"

"When did it happen?"

Soon the voices turned into a muffle of words and phrases that she no longer tried to decipher. She felt sick, nauseous. A strong arm wrapped around her shoulders, holding her steady. His cologne filled Karen's nostrils as tears burned her eyes.

Joe pulled her close. "Karen, let's go back inside. I'll call the sheriff."

Karen shook her head, the tears blurring her vision.

Mrs. Aldridge took her hand. "It's going to be okay, Karen. We'll find out who did this."

"I want to go home," she said, pulling away from them.

"We're going to find out who did this, Karen," Joe assured her, but he looked completely helpless. "We can fix it."

She pulled out of his grasp. "No!"

Karen pushed through the crowd and hurried down the street.

She could hear Joe walking after her. "Karen, where are you going?"

"I can't do this anymore," she said, the tears falling down her cheeks.

"I'll move out. I can find somewhere else to stay."

She turned back to him, anger filling her chest. "Stop it, Joe! It's never going to work so let it go!"

Karen broke out into a full sprint down Main Street, sobbing and heaving. Running blindly toward Blooming Avenue, she could hear Joe calling desperately after her, but his voice soon fell silent.

The houses at her sides were a fog of colors. She couldn't focus on anything in her sight. She could only keep running. If she ran hard enough and far enough away, maybe the pain would disappear. Maybe she could return to her normal life before prison before that horrible night in the general store, before her mother's death. Her life had never been perfect, but she was happy once.

Karen rushed through her aunt's front door, still crying heavily. Panting, she collapsed on the hard wooden floor inside the foyer. Her heart pounded. Her body ached all over.

"Oh, Karen!" Aunt Val cried, entering the foyer. "What happened?"

Karen was breathing too hard. She couldn't get the words out, and she didn't want to. She wanted to cry and cry. Maybe she could cry it all away. Then she would wake up and realize it was only a nightmare.

Aunt Val helped Karen up to her feet and into the living room on the cool, leather sofa. Her aunt then scurried away for a moment and returned with a cold, damp washcloth for Karen's face.

She wiped her niece's hot cheeks. "Who did this to you? What happened?"

"My sign," she said between gasping breaths. "Someone ruined it."

"Relax. Breathe deep."

Karen obeyed and closed her burning eyes. She didn't want to tell Aunt Val. She didn't want to see that image in her mind any longer, but she had to make her aunt understand why she had to leave Mercy.

"Oh, kitten," Aunt Val said after Karen described the ugly message on her painting.

"I can't do this anymore. I'm ruining Joe's clinic."

Aunt Val shook her head. "This is some man you've got yourself tangled up with."

She sighed. "I'm untangled now. I'm leaving."

"Leaving?"

"This is becoming worse than prison. I can't stay in Mercy anymore. Almost everyone in town hates me, and they always will."

"I was so afraid this would happen." Her aunt appeared ready to debate the issue, but surrender overtook her. "I've seen you blossom into a beautiful, confident woman over the past few weeks, but now . . . I see that broken, little girl again."

Karen said nothing, but she felt exactly how Aunt Val said, wounded and helpless.

Aunt Val broke her solemn silence. "Tell me what you need."

An hour later, Karen hugged her aunt between the front yard and a blue taxi cab. Two suitcases and a purse held all of her possessions, a few borrowed items from Aunt Val, and several hundred dollars of her earnings from the clinic.

Aunt Val gestured to the large, baby blue suitcase that Karen held. "That there is Old Blue. She went with me across four states when I was younger. I was trying to find myself back then."

Karen looked down at the worn suitcase. "Did you find yourself?"

"Not out there," her aunt said, looking nostalgic. "I found myself right back in Mercy."

Karen shook her head, looking down at her feet. Aunt Val sometimes used subtle forms of persuasion, but it wasn't enough right then. Nothing could convince Karen to stay. Nothing could convince her to endure anymore of the pain and rejection.

Aunt Val swallowed, visibly forcing back tears. "Call me when you find a hotel."

"I'll look for a job first thing tomorrow."

An expression of hope filled Aunt Val's face. "Maybe it'll all blow over in a few months. You could come back to my place."

Karen shifted her glance away. She knew that if it hadn't blown over in nine years, a few months wouldn't matter.

"Be very careful."

Karen handed her bags to the taxi driver who dropped them into the trunk. "I'll be fine. I'll call you."

They embraced, and Karen suddenly didn't want to release herself from her aunt's arms. *This is home,* she realized silently. *Why can't I have my home back?* She forced the thoughts away as she slipped into the backseat of the cab.

Forcing a smile, Aunt Val waved as the car pulled away. Karen waved back, wondering how long it would be before she saw her again. *Will I ever see Joe again?* Her heart ached at the thought. All that had happened that day flashed through her mind again. She couldn't forget the image of the black letters marring her work of art. The feelings returned all over again. She felt as if Frank Aldridge's death had only happened yesterday. She could still hear the gunshot and see the look in the dying man's eyes.

I don't want to feel this way ever again. This thought was Karen's driving force for leaving Mercy.

Chapter Fifteen

Joe wasn't sure if he should try to see Karen. After the way she had ran off, she had to be angry with him for placing her in such a situation. Maybe she even blamed him for all of Mercy's rejection. He had been too pushy with her and with the town. It seemed that no one was ready for Karen to be back in Mercy, not even her.

He had decided to return home to the Aldridge farm. Renting the room at Miss Valerie's house only made him miss Karen and long for her return. He doubted that such a return would be possible. It was probably best that he take steps to move on.

Things at home made him feel empty inside, though. Rather than continue to ignore him, his father acted as if nothing ever happened, angering Joe more than anything his father had said or done before.

His mother played receptionist at the clinic for the time being. He was glad to have her there. She was a great source of encouragement, and she helped him keep his head clear. By Tuesday morning, word had spread that Karen left the clinic, and Joe's canceled appointments came back, unashamed and

171

unapologetic. If his mother hadn't been there, Joe would've gladly sent them packing like they had Karen.

"Joe, be forgiving," his mother had said. "Don't be like them. You can't fight fire with fire."

By Thursday afternoon, he felt numb. Each day had been booked since Karen walked out. The clinic was a huge success. Joe even made trips out of the clinic to visit sick livestock. On Wednesday, he was present for the birth of a beautiful Tennessee walker. He was finally doing what he had dreamt of for years, but now it meant nothing.

Joe sighed, filling out another monotonous form for one of his feline patients as he led Mrs. Bailey back to the waiting room.

"Okay, Mrs. Bailey. Astro is completely normal as far as vitals," Joe told Emily's mother who looked more like an older sister. "Get him started on the new food and make sure he exercises more regularly. Sleeping is not exercise."

"My chunky kitty is gonna lose some weight, isn't he?" Theresa Bailey cooed at her fat, orange cat. "Thank you, Joe. You're such a dear. Bye-bye."

Mrs. Bailey took Astro's paw in her hand and made it wave at Joe. It took all of his energy to keep from rolling his eyes at her. She strolled out with Astro under one arm and a bag of cat food under the other.

Joe picked up his clipboard to read off the next appointment.

"Muffins," he read aloud. "Valerie Denwood."

He immediately looked up to see Karen's aunt rising from her chair, holding a small pet carrier.

She approached the desk. "That's me."

As Miss Valerie made her way around the desk to follow him, Joe's eyes met his mother's. She gave him the look.

Don't push it with her, the look warned.

He nodded. *A mother does know*, he thought in amazement.

He looked at Miss Valerie again. "Follow me."

She grinned. "That's what Jesus said to Matthew. Are you going to make me into a disciple?"

Joe genuinely smiled for the first time in days. "Maybe just your cat."

"Sounds like fun."

Despite the distracting banter between them, Joe had a million questions to ask. *How is Karen? Did she say anything about me? Is she mad? Will she ever come back to visit?*

Joe led her and Muffins to the examination room. He took a deep breath and decided to save his questions for last. He would be strictly professional in the exam room.

He closed the door behind him. "How is Muffins doing today?"

She pulled the unhappy cat from her kennel. "I think she ate something she wasn't supposed to. She won't eat anything now."

He jotted down her comments. "When was the last time she ate?"

Joe then realized that he was sweating for the first time that day. He was also frantically tapping his pen on the clipboard when he wasn't writing.

Miss Valerie placed the cat on the exam table. "Karen is fine, Joe."

He sighed with relief. "Where is she?"

"I can't say. I promised her not to tell you or anyone where she was. She doesn't want you tryin' to convince her to come back."

"She's mad at me, isn't she?"

"No, of course not. She felt guilty for leaving you behind."

Joe released another sigh of relief.

"She says she's happier now, though. She got a job waiting tables. She's staying in a motel, but she says she should be able to get an apartment in a few weeks."

Miss Valerie's words echoed in Joe's mind for the rest of the afternoon. As he closed up his clinic for the day, he wondered if he might be able to get Karen's telephone number out of her aunt in a few days. *Probably not,* he thought. Even after he promised her he wouldn't beg Karen to come back, Miss Valerie still wouldn't reveal where she was.

"So did you two talk about Karen?" Joe's mother asked as she shook paper into piles on the front desk.

"Of course."

"And?"

"She won't tell me where Karen is."

His mother rose from her chair and dropped her hands on her hips. "I'm so ashamed to be a local of this town right now. These are people I've known my whole life, and I hardly recognized them when she was here. They remember your grandfather, but how could they forget her mother? People are so quick to remember the bad and so forgetful when it comes to the good."

"I know, Mom."

"Lillian Denwood changed the lives of our children," she said fervently. "She was the best teacher to ever work in North Carolina. I would bet you my life on that."

Joe would never forget Mrs. Denwood. That gentle smile and caring heart would forever be embedded in his memory. He wondered if Lillian Denwood and his grandfather were praising God together in Heaven that very moment. That thought made his troubles seem so insignificant. He started wishing those troubles away the second he realized who Karen really was. Whether he wished them away or dreamed of Heaven, the problem of a merciless Mercy wasn't going away. He needed a solution.

* * *

Recalling the last conversation with her aunt, Karen regretted not being completely honest. It was true that she found a cheap motel room in Raleigh and got a job at a pancake house across the street, but she had lied about being happier. She was just as miserable as she was in Mercy, except now she was alone in her misery.

At first, she was excited about the job. She didn't expect the owner of the restaurant, Mal, to shrug about her jail time, but he did. She started that very day with bussing tables. On Wednesday, she waited on tables. So far, she had broken six glasses and two plates and taken four orders wrong.

"Now, Karen, I can understand a first-timer making mistakes," Mal told her, "but this many broken dishes and angry customers is a little much for your first week on the job."

Karen wiped up the contents of another broken plate. "I'm sorry, sir."

"Don't be so uptight. Just be more careful and don't make me have to tell you again," he warned.

Karen sighed as the chubby, greasy man waddled back to the kitchen. She bent down, collecting French fries and pieces of a plate into a grimy dust pan. *Why does he give me so many chances?* she wondered, frustrated.

Then she realized something awful: she wanted him to fire her. She hated this job. She hated how the other waitresses frowned at her. She hated how the customers frowned at her. It was like being in Mercy all over again, except she had no Joseph Aldridge to run to.

She couldn't get her mind off of him. She partly blamed her broken messes on daydreaming about him. She couldn't wait to call Aunt Val and find out how Muffins' visit went with him. She wondered if he had asked about her or wanted to see her as much as she wanted to see him.

"Karen!" a familiar voice broke into her thoughts.

She looked up at one of the other waitresses, Lois, scowling down at her. "Your orders are up! Get on the ball!"

* * *

The early morning sun peeked through Joe's window. The warm light woke him slowly. He opened his eyes. He couldn't decide what to do with his Saturdays since college. Last Saturday had been spent in Karen's company.

He sat up in bed and glanced at the dusty, digital clock on his nightstand. He had slept in. This didn't surprise him. He'd spent much of the night trying to come up with a way to get the town to forgive Karen. He had been praying hard to God for an answer to the problem of his unforgiving hometown.

Thinking of Karen again got the wheels turning in Joe's brain. Then it hit him: *The Mercy Gazette.* An instant idea popped into his head like some holy revelation. He was sure it was a miracle, although his plan did have a few minor setbacks.

At his congratulatory cookout, Joe got to see his old high school friend, Tommy Parrish. Tommy's father was editor of the Mercy Gazette, and Joe was excited to remember that Tommy had told him he was a new staff writer on the newspaper. If he could convince Tommy to write an article about Karen's innocence, maybe the locals would read it and be willing to forgive and forget.

Joe got the idea on the perfect day. He closed the clinic on the weekend, and he knew that Tommy would probably be at the newspaper office on Main Street.

Joe showered and dressed in a hurry. On his way down the stairs, his mother called him.

"Breakfast, Joe!"

He opened the front door. "No time for breakfast!"

The telephone rang. Curiosity stopped Joe in his tracks. He could barely hear his mother speak into the phone.

"Joe? Telephone!"

Joe headed into the kitchen. "Who is it?"

She offered him the phone. "Tommy Parrish."

"Tommy?"

Weird. Is this confirmation, God? he wondered, putting the phone to his ear.

"Hey, Tommy."

"Hey, Joe!"

"This is so weird. I was just on my way over to see you. I need a favor."

"I need a favor too," Tommy said. "My dad wants me to write an article about your clinic."

"My clinic?" *What could be less interesting?*

"Yeah, my mom brought Elmo in on Wednesday. She couldn't stop talking about how great it was."

"I'm glad she liked it." Among the blur of animals, it took Joe a moment to remember Tommy's shaggy, old sheep dog that his friend had treasured since childhood.

"So can I interview you today?" Tommy asked.

"Sure."

"Come on over."

Joe hung up the phone and hurried for the door.

"Joe," his mother said, "don't forget Emily's dinner party is at three!"

Joe froze in his steps. "Emily's party?"

The memory of her verbal invitation suddenly bounced back into his mind.

Joe poked his head in the kitchen doorway. "I can't!"

His mother frowned, crossing her arms. "Joseph, you know how Theresa is about her parties. Don't you remember what happened when we missed her Christmas party? She wouldn't speak to me for weeks!"

Emily's mother was the most formal hostess in town. She planned every one of her family's parties down to the tiniest detail. When invited guests didn't arrive, their excuses had to be a grave illness or death in order to avoid Theresa's cold shoulder.

"Fine, but I might be late," Joe said. "I have things to take care of."

"I've already wrapped up a gift you can take to her."

After five minutes of biking and sulking over Emily's inevitable dinner party, Joe arrived at the Mercy Printing Press office on Main Street. He parked his old bicycle in a nearby bike rack and made his way into the stuffy, old building.

Inside, Joe immediately entered the reception area, which was humble compared to his clinic reception area. A large, wooden desk with metal legs stood in the middle of the small room. A few photo frames and many papers covered the desktop. An old, stained glass lamp sat on the corner of the desk, illuminating the cup of pencils and pens under it.

Tommy emerged from the door beside the desk with an outstretched hand. "Hey, man!"

Tommy was his usual smiling self that morning, and Joe was glad. A good mood meant smoother convincing.

Joe shook his hand firmly. "How's it going?"

"Same old, same old," Tommy said. "Pull up a chair."

Joe grabbed a wooden chair near the entrance and scooted it to the desk. "What's it like working on the smallest paper in the state?"

Tommy picked up a pad and pen from the desk as he sat down. "This town is hard to write about, Joe. It's Snoozeville. Your clinic opening up is the biggest news since the last tax break."

Joe snickered. "Well, I'm happy to give you something to do."

"Before we start on the interview, what favor did you need?"

Joe hesitated. "Well, you know about Karen Denwood, right?"

"Denwood, Denwood," Tommy repeated, narrowing his eyes. "The lady everyone left church over?"

"Yes."

"So what's the deal with her? I walked out because my parents did," he said. "They wouldn't tell me why they were upset."

"Remember the girl who broke into my grandpa's store when we were kids?"

Tommy thought for a moment. "No kidding."

"She's innocent. My grandfather's death was an accident, and I need you to write about it."

Tommy shook his head. "That's career suicide, man! Besides, our dads are friends. My dad wouldn't print it."

"Tommy, they ran her out of town." Joe leaned forward in his chair. "It's wrong how they've treated her. This is her home too. We have to tell them the truth about what happened that night, the trial—everything."

"I can't. Even if my dad would print it, people could start pulling their ads and stop buying the paper. I can't risk that."

Joe rose from his chair. "Then you can forget my clinic story."

"Come on, Joe. I need this story. Please, man."

He dropped back into his chair. "She's innocent, Tommy. Don't you remember her mother? Mrs. Denwood? Fourth grade?"

Tommy smiled. "Yeah, how could I forget? She was my first crush."

"A teacher?"

"Yeah, man. Girls had cooties back then, remember?"

He shook his head and cracked a smile. It was hard to smile, though. He was trapped by this problem. He thought about Heaven again, and an amazing idea struck him like a lightning bolt.

"That's it! Lillian Denwood!"

Tommy's brow dropped. "What?"

"You can write a story about remembering Lillian Denwood. That won't anger anyone. You can talk about how she changed Mercy and how good of a teacher she was. A tribute."

"A tribute," Tommy repeated with a grin.

"Locals will read it and remember her. Then they'll think of Karen and remember that the apple never falls far from the tree."

Tommy frowned. "But wasn't her father a drunk?"

"Forget her father, just focus on Lillian Denwood," Joe said. "Don't write anything about her death."

Tommy nodded. "Got it. So do I have my clinic story?"

Joe sat back in his chair, a smile still on his face. "Let the interview begin."

* * *

The Bailey House was the second most impressive home in Mercy. It sat across the street and four houses down from Valerie Denwood's much humbler home. The towering fuchsia, Victorian looked like an elephant among elk. Joe stood on its immaculately clean, wrap-around porch and rang the gold-rimmed doorbell.

He adjusted his necktie, nearly dropping the carefully wrapped gift that his mother gave him. In his haste to get dressed, he had tightened the tie in a death grip. He was still trying to work the knot loose when Mrs. Bailey opened the front door.

"Welcome, Dr. Aldridge."

Joe offered her Emily's gift. "I'm still Joe, Mrs. Bailey."

"Of course, you'll always be Little Joe Aldridge to me," she said, accepting the small package. "Come in."

Joe entered the main foyer of the house and looked up to see a chandelier hanging from a twelve-foot ceiling above him. A large staircase before him shined with purple and gold ribbons and bows on the railing. Obviously, Mrs. Bailey had spared no expense on the occasion. To her, all of Emily's birthdays were momentous occasions.

"The ladies are in the parlor," Mrs. Bailey said as he followed her past the staircase.

179

They stepped down into a lavishly furnished parlor with flowery loveseats and cherry, handcrafted tables. Matching pink shames decorated the windows. Five ladies around Joe's age looked up at him from their tea and smiled. He awkwardly returned the expression.

"Joseph is here," Mrs. Bailey announced.

Emily rose from her seat beside an open window. "Joe, I'm so glad you made it."

She wore a pale blue blouse and a multi-colored skirt. He had to admit to himself that she did look pretty. This thought reminded him of their high school days. They had shared many awkward dates and a few kisses. He immediately forced himself to ignore those memories.

"Hi," Joe said.

The ladies stared at him like ravenous dogs at a roasted turkey. He even thought he saw one woman lick her lips.

Emily grinned at her friends. "Joe, you probably remember most of my friends from school. This is Heather Yarborough and Lucy Cochran. You remember my best friend, Naomi Parrish."

Naomi, Tommy's twin sister, nodded at him, feigning interest. Heather and Lucy, dressed in their daintiest attire, nodded politely with blushing cheeks. Joe remembered Heather Yarborough from the seventh grade, a bookworm who bloomed in high school and became a popular cheerleader like Emily. Lucy Cochran looked familiar, but Joe couldn't place her in any exact memories that he had.

Emily pointed to one more attractive woman. "Over here is my former college roommate, Jessica Skylar."

Jessica smiled warmly at Joe and waved. She reminded him of Karen in her shy yet strong demeanor. His heart suddenly ached. Among the beaming, female faces in the room, he was convinced that he might see Karen. This silly and irrational thought completely escaped him when his eyes only met complexions that were incomparable to hers.

"Ladies, this is Dr. Joseph Aldridge, the one I told you about." Emily turned to Joe as she sat back down. "Have a seat, Joe."

Joe followed suit, taking a spot beside Lucy Cochran on one of the loveseats. He couldn't help but wonder exactly what Emily had told them about him.

Mrs. Bailey offered Joe some tea which he gladly accepted, hoping that perhaps this would somehow prevent him from having to speak. Of course, that was a silly notion in a room full of gabbing, inquisitive young women.

Jessica Skylar set her tea cup on a ceramic coaster on the coffee table. "So you're the town vet, Joe?"

"Yes," he said, hoping not to be forced to elaborate.

Lucy Cochran leaned forward in her seat. "That's really fascinating. I bet you had to study very hard."

Joe fingered the teacup handle. "Anyone can do it."

"I love animals," Heather Yarborough said, grinning at him like the Cheshire cat. He got the strong impression that she meant say, "I love *you*."

Joe cleared his throat uncomfortably, feeling five pairs of eyes on him. His mother's comment from his first day back in Mercy replayed in his mind. *"You're the most eligible bachelor in Mercy."*

This memory and the overwhelming female attention would give any man a big ego, but for Joe, the whole situation felt alien and uncomfortable. He longed to be somewhere else in the company of one particular woman, not these five.

Jessica folded her hands in her lap. "Joe, when did you first become interested in veterinary medicine?"

"Back when I was a kid," Joe said, eager to change the subject. "What do you do for a living, Jessica?"

"I'm a child psychiatrist," she said, seeming pleased by his interest.

"I'm a nurse," Heather Yarborough piped in.

"I'm a high school teacher," Lucy Cochran announced.

The women sounded more like young girls competitively comparing shoes or dresses in the schoolyard.

"I work at the newspaper for my dad," Naomi Parrish said. "But you knew that, right, Joe?"

Joe nodded. "I had an interview with your brother today."

Her interest peaked. "Really?"

"He's going to write an article about my clinic and one about Lillian Denwood," Joe said, excitement lifting his discomfort away.

"Lillian Denwood?" Emily echoed.

"Yes. He's writing a tribute for me. I'm hoping that this will help some of the locals forgive Karen."

Emily frowned. "I thought she left town."

"She did. I'm hoping this will allow her to come back."

Emily said nothing. The other women sat in silence. Joe could tell that they all knew the story. It must have been part of what Emily had told them about him.

They steered away from the topic of Karen Denwood during the next couple of hours. Mrs. Bailey served the group her homemade lasagna in the formal dining room. After the delicious meal, they congregated on the back porch. All of Emily's female guests strolled down the porch steps and into the Baileys' elaborate garden. Emily remained with Joe on the porch. The sun still lit up the warm, summer sky. Sunset wouldn't arrive for a couple more hours. Still, the air reminded Joe of that unforgettable kiss he'd shared with Karen.

Emily walked up to the porch rail where Joe stood. "I'm sorry about them."

"What are you talking about?" Joe asked, snapping back into the present.

She giggled. "As soon as I told them that a single guy was coming to the dinner party, they turned into a swarm of bees, and you were the honey."

Joe rolled his eyes. "I hardly noticed."

Emily became serious. "Joe, I want a second chance."

Joe froze, stunned. Did he actually hear those words? He swallowed. It was Emily's birthday, and here he stood about to reject her again.

She fiddled with the collar of her blouse. "I know things didn't work out in high school, but wouldn't you agree that we were different people back then?"

"Well, yes, people change, but now isn't the right time for me, Emily."

This was definitely true. He had a lot on his plate, on his mind, and one particular person on his heart.

Emily's hopeful expression slowly turned grim with each word that he spoke.

"I just opened the clinic, and it's a very stressful time," he explained. "Plus, there are family issues I'm dealing with right now and—"

"It's her, isn't it?" Emily said, tears shining in her eyes.

"No." Joe shook his head desperately. "I can't—"

Just then, the other women marched back up the porch steps.

"Leave!" Emily ordered through gritted teeth.

"Emily," Joe pleaded. Guilt, old and new, burdened his tone. Why did she have to push something that wasn't meant to be?

Naomi hurried to Emily's side. "What's going on, Emily?"

Emily's eyes pierced Joe like daggers. "I want you to leave now, Joe."

Joe nodded in surrender and hurried back into the house, avoiding five accusing glances. As he slid the glass door shut behind him, he could hear Emily sobbing. Guilt tugged at him. If only he did have feelings for her, if only he even feigned an interest in Emily Bailey. The heart, however, complicated things. Right then, he wasn't sure what his heart was telling him. All he knew was that Emily Bailey wasn't Karen Denwood.

Chapter Sixteen

The old, beige telephone on the wooden nightstand rang insistently. Karen hurried from her tiny, motel bathroom, wrapped in a towel and dripping on the carpet.

She picked up the receiver. "Aunt Val?"

"Hey, kitten! Where have you been?"

"Mal has been working me to death!" she said, flopping down on the bed.

"Did he make you work today?"

"No. He's been true to his promise of giving me Sundays off, but I've been working dawn 'til midnight since my first day. He says practice makes perfect."

"You poor thing. Did you make it to a church service?"

"No, I overslept. What happened at Muffins' appointment?"

"He misses you like crazy!" her aunt squealed.

"What? How do you know that?"

"Joe couldn't stop asking about you. He begged me to tell him where you were, but I didn't tell him anything."

Karen felt equal relief and joy. "Thanks. I thought he might be mad about me running off."

"No. He thought you were mad at him. I told him 'of course not.' Oh! They had an article in the Sunday paper on the front page about his clinic. Just this past week, he saw forty-one patients. Pretty good, huh?"

"That's because I'm not there anymore," Karen said.

"I don't think he cares about his success, kitten."

Karen sighed into the phone, not really meaning to.

"You miss him like crazy too, huh?"

"Maybe," Karen admitted, feeling her cheeks grow warm.

"Why don't you try callin' him?"

"No, it's better this way. Why try what can never be?"

"All things are possible through Christ who strengthens me," Aunt Val reminded her. She could almost see her aunt's wagging finger.

Karen was quiet but hopeful, remembering all that faith had seen her through before. "Can you mail me a copy of the paper?"

"Sure. First thing tomorrow."

"Thanks. I'd better get to bed. I have another double shift tomorrow."

"Hey, what're we doing for your birthday?"

"I'll probably be working."

"You tell that boss of yours you need your birthday off."

"Good night, Aunt Val."

"Buh-bye."

Karen hung up the phone and lay back on the hard, motel bed. She stared up at the yellow, smoke-stained ceiling. *Is this really better than Mercy? Maybe I should go back and hide in Aunt Val's house. Maybe I'd be happier as a hermit.*

She decided to get up and start preparing for bed.

No, she thought, digging through her aunt's suitcase, *I'd be a prisoner all over again, trapped in Aunt Val's house instead of a jail. I'd rather work in a pancake house and live in a motel for the rest of my life than be a prisoner again.*

* * *

On Tuesday, Joe sat in his quiet office, tapping his pen on the desk. His hand grew tired from the weight of the heavy ballpoint, so he began to tap his foot. He watched the clock. One-thirty was fast approaching.

C'mon, Tommy, he begged silently. *I have a one-thirty appointment.*

Tommy had a very important one o'clock delivery to make, which he was now sixteen minutes late for. To Joe's relief and joy, Tommy was able to focus solely on Lillian Denwood's tribute article. He promised Joe it would be ready in time for the mid-week edition of *The Mercy Gazette.*

The door to Joe's office flew open, startling him out of his nervous tapping.

"Hey!" Tommy greeted with his trademark grin.

Joe rose from his chair. "Is it ready?"

"Is it *ready*?" Tommy repeated. "It's never been more ready in its whole life!"

Joe smiled. College hadn't changed his friend one bit.

Tommy handed him a folder as he took the seat in front of Joe's desk.

Joe sat down and opened it. His eyes scanned the black type at the top of the page. It read, "Lillian Denwood: Remembering Mercy's Angel."

"Great title!" Joe said, eager to read on.

"It was my dad's idea."

Joe continued to read, grinning all the way through. When he finally finished, he knew his plan would work.

He handed the copy back. "Tommy, this is perfect. I didn't know you were such a great writer."

"I learned a thing or two at State. I'd better get back and get this ready for print."

"Thanks, man. I really don't know what I would've done without your help."

"Hey, I'm just being a friend," Tommy said with a shrug, opening the office door. "Later, Joe."

Joe relaxed in his leather desk chair as Tommy closed the door behind him. He tilted his head back and closed his eyes for the five minutes he had before the next appointment. He had been tense for the past few days, wondering if they would be able to pull it off. Tomorrow was the big day. It would be in print, and he hoped the Mercy locals would read it and have a change of heart.

Please, God, let this work, he prayed.

* * *

Karen rose on Wednesday morning with her usual backache and crick in her neck. The motel bed was hardly more suitable for sleeping on than the floor, but financial restraints left her little choice of where to stay. She constantly reminded herself that, in one more week, she would have enough money to put a deposit down on a furnished studio apartment. She could finally stop eating carryout and leftovers from work and cook in her own kitchen. She could rest in a more comfortable bed. She could finally stop paying the motel owner for her room every week.

Today was another of those days. She needed to make a quick stop at the motel office to pay her bill.

After she long, soothing shower, Karen slipped into her blue waitress uniform. A sudden flash of memory came to her as she looked in the mirror. It wasn't a real memory. It was the memory of a dream from the night before. Her uniform had reminded her of a dream in which she was working and irritating everyone as usual. Then a familiar young boy entered the restaurant. She knew that this boy was a much younger Joe. He took Karen by the hand and without a word, led her outside. The parking lot and busy street that she expected to see outside were gone. Her motel was no where in sight. She and Joe stood on the elementary school playground from her childhood.

The young Joe sprinted off toward the swing set. "C'mon, Karen! I'll push you! You won't fall, I promise!"

"I'm too big," Karen said.

Still dressed in her work uniform, she was a young girl again. There was no questioning this strange situation. All Karen knew was that she wanted to get on a swing. She hurried after Joe.

"Karen!" a familiar voice had called behind her.

The young Karen stopped and turned to see her beautiful mother standing behind her. Her long, blonde hair rested across the front of her shoulders. She wore a pink dress and that familiar, tender smile.

"Mom!" Karen cried out.

Then she was jolted out of the dream by the sound of the motel alarm clock.

Karen pushed thoughts of the dream out of her mind. Dreams of her mother were nothing new. She used to write the dreams down and spend days trying to understand them. It was a hopeless obsession. She could never make sense of them because her dreams never made sense. *Why was Joe young? Why the playground? Why did Mom show up like that?* Karen knew that her questions would only be a waste of time and thought.

She finished braiding her golden hair back and grabbed another of Aunt Val's borrowed items, a purse. Outside her hotel room, a burst of warm, late morning air hit her face. The wind was unusually strong that day, and it nearly blew the purse out of her grasp. The summer sun beamed hot on her face. She was grateful that she never had to walk far in it.

Karen hurried down the walkway along the motel doors to the small office at the end. Inside, she met the smiling gaze of a black man who sat behind a glass window at the front counter. She guessed the large man was about her father's age.

"Good morning," he greeted in a deep, baritone voice, sliding the glass window open.

"Morning," Karen said with a smile. "I need to pay for the next four nights."

The man opened a notebook on the desk and started flipping through it. "Your room number?"

"Eighteen."

She examined the clerk's desk. It was oak covered with papers and writing utensils. An old model mini-television sat on one end, flashing images of a game show. Beside the old television, something in particular caught Karen's eye.

She leaned into the window to get a better look. "Is that *The Mercy Gazette*?"

"Yes, mam. My parents live in Mercy. I like to keep up with the news, so I got a subscription when I left home. You from Mercy?"

"Yeah. Sort of."

The clerk told Karen her total due, and she counted it out in cash.

He accepted the money. "Thank you. Would you like the paper? I've already read it. There's a nice tribute in there to Lillian Denwood. Have you heard of her?"

"Who?" Karen asked, not believing his words.

"Lillian Denwood."

"Yes. I would love to have it."

He handed her the newspaper. "I went to grade school with her. She was such a nice girl. She really cared about people."

Karen thanked him as she took the paper and started to leave the office.

"Your change, mam," the man called after her.

She headed through the door. "You can keep it."

Outside, Karen began to scan the paper. Nothing on the front page caught her attention. On the second page, she saw that beautiful, familiar face. It was her mother's college photo. The article's title read, "Lillian Denwood: Remembering Mercy's Angel." She couldn't believe her eyes. With little concern about being late for work, she took a seat on the cement curb in front of the office and began reading.

She was a teacher who cared for, loved, and encouraged her students. She was a local who worked hard for the town of Mercy. Lillian Denwood was Mercy's angel.

Before she became this angel, though, she was spunky Lillian Hart. Old friends and colleagues remember her as joyful and always friendly.

"She could light up a playground on a rainy day," Theresa Bailey remembered. "She was always smiling. I'll never forget that smile."

As she grew, Denwood made it known to family and friends her desire to teach. After graduating from high school, she attended college and obtained her degree in teaching. Denwood returned to Mercy to begin her career.

"Her father was so relieved that she was coming home," Eva Perdy recalled. "He treasured his daughter more than anything in this world."

Sadly, Charles Hart passed away not long after Denwood returned. Despite her loss, she was able to carry on alone.

"She was so brave," Helen Aldridge said. "Her faith kept her going. She knew the Lord had a plan, so she just kept working for those children."

After five years of hard work, Denwood won the county Teacher of the Year Award two years in a row. Her students were learning at a faster pace, and their test scores were rising higher year after year.

After marrying and starting a family, Denwood continued to take education to new heights. She worked as a fourth grade teacher for ten years. She organized new educational activities, led academic support teams, and started the Student Helpers Tutoring Program. She accomplished all this in only a short fifteen-year career before her young life ended.

"She was the best teacher I ever had," former student Joseph Aldridge said. "She taught me a lot of important lessons, but the best lesson I've learned from her and her family is forgiveness."

Karen felt as if her heart had stopped. She couldn't move. Her eyes were glued to Joe's words as she felt them starting to burn. *Joe did this,* she realized. A hot tear fell down her cheek. She could move again, so she smiled.

She started flipping through the rest of the newspaper, glancing at the familiar pages. Her eyes fell on what appeared to be an ad, but what was actually an announcement bordered by flowers and bells.

"Congratulations to Joseph Aldridge and Emily Bailey of Mercy on their recent engagement. They plan to set the wedding date for late fall."

Karen's mouth dropped wide as she stared at the printed words. She read them over and over, hoping that they weren't real, praying that she was only imagining them. She sat frozen there on the curb again, her eyes burning with anger and hurt, her gut cramped as if she had endured a boxer's punch. Realizing that her hopes and prayers were not coming true, she released the pages from her grasp and watched the wind carry the paper across the sunny parking lot.

Chapter Seventeen

"This was your doing, wasn't it?" a familiar voice asked over Joe's telephone.

Joe sat up in his office desk chair. "Miss Valerie?"

"Yes, sir."

"My doing?"

"The tribute to my sister-in-law in the same issue as your engagement announcement."

Joe was completely lost. "Engagement announcement?"

"You planned to lift her up and knock her down all in the same issue?"

"What are you talking about?"

"You and Emily!"

Joe's jaw dropped. "What?"

"Well, guess what, *Doctor*? I'm not sending Karen a copy!"

The sarcasm in the way she said "doctor" made his stomach flip. Joe heard a click, and the receiver went dead. He dropped the phone back on its cradle and grabbed his copy of the Wednesday newspaper. He flipped through, scanning the pages, not even sure what he was looking for. Then his eyes stopped on the second page and grew wide in horror.

* * *

"Maybe you should go through with it," Joe's father said at dinner on Thursday night. "Emily is a nice girl."

Joe pushed his peas around his plate with his fork, trying to tame his tongue.

"I cannot believe Naomi did that. It was not funny at all," his mother said.

Eric growled. "Yeah, that was *really* cruel. When I saw that, I couldn't believe it. I was so mad!"

"Why were you mad, Eric?" his mother asked with a knowing grin.

Eric stuttered for a moment. "It was a lie. She lied."

Joe rolled his eyes. He wanted to tell his brother to quit dreaming and ask Emily out, but he decided to spare him the embarrassment. There had been enough of it for the past two days. The next person to congratulate Joe on his engagement was going to regret it.

Joe's father wiped his mouth with his napkin. "I've given it a little thought, and I won't be bringing up a restraining order at the town council meeting."

Joe nearly dropped his fork. "Restraining order?"

"I thought it might be necessary. Denwood *was* a prisoner."

Joe could feel the anger burning in his throat. "That's ridiculous!"

"You better watch your tone, son," his father warned. "I said I was gonna drop that."

"She's innocent. The whole trial was unfair!"

Joe's father dropped his fork and rose from his chair. "You don't know anything about that trial. You were just a kid!"

"Enough!" Joe's mother cried. "I will not have any more arguing at my—"

The telephone rang, and the room instantly fell silent.

She tossed her napkin on the table and hopped up from her seat. "Not another word from either of you until I get back."

As she left the room, Joe glared at his father who returned to his seat.

Joe's mother reentered the room. "Joe, it's for you. Make it quick."

Joe rose and hurried to the phone, not sure who it could be. "Hello?"

"Joe," a tender, familiar voice said.

"Karen?" he whispered, gripping the phone with both hands as if he might be pulling her closer.

"I wanted to let you know that I'm okay." She sounded just the opposite.

"I'm glad, but I wish you hadn't left."

"I'm sorry things didn't work out and that I ran off like that."

"It's okay. I understand."

She was silent for a moment. "I read the newspaper."

He froze. "You did?"

"Your article meant the world to me. My mother would have been honored."

"Listen, the engagement—"

"Yeah. Congratulations," she said flatly.

"No, it was—"

The line went dead. Joe turned around to look at the phone cradle on the wall. His father stood holding the button down.

Joe let the phone drop from his hand. "I was talking!"

"No one in my house talks to that delinquent."

"She's not a delinquent!"

His father scowled. "You don't know what she is! You were just a kid when it all happened!"

"I'm always just a kid to you!" Joe fumed. "I can't do anything right. I go to college. I graduate at the top of my class. I even open up my own clinic, and you aren't satisfied."

His father stepped closer to him. "You need to cool it, Joseph."

"I stand up for a practically innocent woman. I forgive her and try to help her. I do everything in my heart that I know is right, and you never approve!"

His father narrowed his eyes sharply, his lips tightening. Joe swallowed. He could feel himself shaking.

Joe's mother came in between them. "That's enough! Rich, go sit down. Joe, you too."

"I'm not hungry anymore," Joe said, heading out of the kitchen.

He went upstairs to his bedroom and collapsed on the bed. The pain had festered into bitterness over the years. It felt good to finally release some of it, to tell his dad how he felt. Yet, his words seemed to fall on deaf ears. When would his father ever acknowledge his accomplishments? When would he respect Joe for following his convictions?

Joe couldn't dwell on such questions for too long unless he planned to end up in a psych ward. He stared at the telephone at his bedside, wondering if Karen would call back, but knowing that she wouldn't.

Suddenly, an idea came to mind. He snatched the phone from his nightstand and dialed to find out the last number that called the house. He jotted it down and then dialed the operator.

"What place does this number belong to?" he asked the operator and read the number off to her.

"Sunlight Motel, Raleigh."

* * *

On Friday morning, Joe sat at his desk, fumbling through files. He found himself frequently tapping his pen or glancing away from the desk. The past two days had been pure torture for him. He could do little with Karen on his mind. He had to tell her about the fake engagement announcement, but no one answered at the motel.

Joe's mother poked her head into his office. "Joe, your next appointment is here."

"Thanks, Mom," he muttered.

"You gonna be okay?"

He rubbed his forehead. "I think so."

His mother frowned but said nothing. He assumed she didn't speak because she knew she couldn't provide the comfort he needed.

She disappeared from the doorway as Joe summoned up the energy to head to the front behind her.

He approached the reception desk where little Mrs. Perdy waited with Choo-choo in her arms.

"Choo-choo is ready for his shots," she said.

"Great," Joe said with little enthusiasm.

She smiled up at him. "I'm so glad that Denwood girl is gone. That was a wise decision you made firing her. She was no good."

As Mrs. Perdy spoke, Joe jotted down the date on Choo-choo's new chart. Then he remembered what day it was. A feeling of deep regret overcame him. It was Karen's birthday.

Without a word, he set his clipboard on the counter, removed his lab coat, and snatched his mother's car keys from the desk. Then he headed for the door.

"Joe?" his mother called.

Joe flew through the clinic door. "Cancel my appointments." Then he popped his head back in. "I'm taking your car."

* * *

Karen lay on the hard, motel bed after a long, sleepless night. She had gotten up already to shower and dress, but she only ended up lying back down again.

The rain pounded steadily on the cement outside her room. Lightning flashed through the cheap, blue mini-blinds and thunder roared. She could feel it moving through the bed as it shook the little room. She remembered once loving summer storms, how they came and went so quickly. She loved how they cooled the air, how they seemed to put the summer to sleep for a brief time. Her mother had loved to nap during those mid-day, summer storms. Karen would nap with her some times, but now she couldn't anymore. She couldn't break away from the memories long enough to fall sleep.

It was her twenty-third birthday, and she couldn't have been more miserable if she were starting her prison sentence all over again. If she wasn't missing her mother and her childhood in Mercy, she was missing Joe. He was the best man to ever enter her life, and she'd lost him before she could even completely gain him. She wanted to cry. Every part of her said she should be crying, but she was beyond that.

The phone rang out, snapping Karen out of her trance.

"Hello?"

"Happy Birthday, kitten!" her aunt's familiar voice chimed in.

"Thanks," Karen said.

"Geez, don't act like you're already over the hill."

"I wish I was buried *in* the hill."

"What's wrong? Is that Mal making you work today?"

"No."

"What's got you down?"

She hesitated, not sure if she wanted to relive her feelings again. "I read the Wednesday *Mercy Gazette*."

"Oh, no. How did you even get a copy?"

"The motel office," she said. Her energy left her. "I don't want to talk about it, okay?"

"If it makes you feel any better, I gave that boy the tongue lashing of his life for it. He will never see my Muffins in his clinic again!"

"What did you say to him?"

"It doesn't matter, kitten. He's a fool for wanting that Emily girl over you. He's not worth pouting over."

Karen had nothing to say to that. She wanted to argue Aunt Val's theory, but she knew her aunt was mostly right. She had to forget about Joe and move on with her life even if she didn't want to.

"I'm on my way over there," Aunt Val said. "We'll go anywhere you want, birthday girl."

"Okay."

There was a knock at the motel room door.

"Housekeeping's here. I'll see you soon."

Karen hung up the phone and hurried to gather her dirty towels for the maid. She opened the door with an arm full of towels. They fell to the floor when her eyes met with an unexpected face.

"Ricky?"

Ricky grinned at her, putting his arms out. "Hey, Karen. Miss me?"

He didn't wear his gothic get-up this time. Instead, he wore khaki pants and button-down blue dress shirt. His hair was combed down. Ricky looked more like the guy in the photo Karen used to fawn over. Despite his more normal and much more attractive appearance, Karen wanted to slam the door in his face.

She didn't hide her disgust. "What are you doing here?"

He put his hands up in surrender. "I wanted to apologize for last time."

Karen gathered up the towels at her feet. "How did you find me?"

"I stopped off at your aunt's house yesterday to pay you back the money I borrowed and to repay your aunt the money I borrowed from her." He reached into his pocket and offered Karen several crumpled twenty-dollar bills.

She snatched the money from his hand. "You *stole* that money!"

"I'm really sorry." He looked away as if ashamed. "I was almost out of gas, and I was embarrassed to ask for it. I'm still getting used to being out of jail. Back in prison, you took what you wanted when you got the chance."

Karen nodded. "I accept your apology, and I'm sorry if I was rude to you before."

"Look, I know you didn't want to see me again, but I wanted to try and start over. Third time's a charm." He put his arms out, offering a hug. "Maybe I could take you out for lunch."

Guilt washed over Karen, and she bit her lip. "My aunt is on the way. We're going out."

He dropped his hands into his pockets. "That's cool."

Karen could see the disappointment in his sparkling, blue eyes. The guilt tugged at her heart. She had no right to judge Ricky. All she ever wanted was to be accepted after leaving prison. What right did she have to reject Ricky, to treat him like the people of Mercy had treated her? Besides, Ricky could be a healthy distraction from Joe.

"Well, you could go with us."

He grinned. "Really? Are you sure?"

She smiled. "Yeah. I want to start over again too."

Ricky hugged her. "Awesome!"

His embrace felt like just the cure for her woes. She felt herself wanting to remain in his arms, smelling his spicy cologne. It didn't remind her at all of Joe, and that brought Karen great relief.

"You can hang out and watch TV while I dry my hair. My aunt should be here in about an hour."

He released Karen from his bear hug and followed her into the tiny room.

He dropped down on the edge of her bed. "So how long do you have to live in this dump?"

Karen headed for the bathroom. "Just a couple more weeks. I'm saving up for an apartment."

"The TV remote is by the phone. I'll be right out." She grabbed her hair dryer from a hook on the wall and headed into the bathroom, shutting the door behind her.

In the mirror, Karen once again met with a pale and worn face not unlike the one she'd encountered in jail. She frowned at her reflection and ran the brush through her wet hair. The sound of a television studio audience laughing crept through the door. Ricky was watching some sitcom rerun. After fighting her way through a few knots, Karen grabbed the blow dryer and flipped it on.

She began to wonder why Ricky was so persistent with her. The only thing they shared in common was jail time. Physically, Karen found him attractive, but his tastes didn't match her own at all. He also had no sense of direction in life. In jail, he had told Karen that he just wanted to make money. He wasn't sure what he wanted to do. Karen mentioned college, and Ricky laughed. To him, school was boring and pointless.

Ricky was on the opposite end compared to Joe. Joe was incredibly smart. He planned things out. His faith matched Karen's. He was polite, well-groomed, confident, and strong. Ricky seemed confident but also shady. She began to wonder if she was too trusting when it came to Ricky's apologies.

Karen turned off the dryer and tried to shake her suspicions of Ricky and her comparisons between him and Joe. Without the sound of the dryer, she realized that she didn't hear the TV any longer.

She reached for the door knob. "Ricky?"

The door knob turned, but it wouldn't open. She tugged at it with all of her strength, but some force kept it shut.

"A hundred dollars?" Ricky said from outside the door.

Her heart began to pound in her ears. "Ricky, what are you doing?"

"Where's the rest of the money, Karen?"

Karen's jaw dropped as she stepped back from the door. The anger in his tone sent chills down her spine.

She heard something crash to the floor. "You're saving up for an apartment so where's the money?"

Karen swallowed. "I trusted you."

"You're too gullible, Karen. You'll never make it on the outside."

Karen searched the bathroom for something to defend herself and grabbed the blow dryer. She stepped into the bathtub, pressing her back against the shower wall.

"Please don't hurt me."

"Come on, I'm not like that. Tell me where you're hiding your stash."

"My money is in the bank, Ricky."

She could hear him tearing the room apart, pulling drawers out, and turning over furniture. He slammed something heavy against the wall.

"My neighbor will hear you, Ricky." She stepped out of the bathtub and approached the door. "Let me out. You don't need to do this."

"You don't know what I need, church lady."

The noises outside of the bathroom faded. She could only hear the sound of Ricky panting.

"Ricky, we should talk this over." She turned the door knob again and pulled it with all her strength. It wouldn't budge.

"You've wasted enough of my time, Karen."

The door to her room creaked open.

Panic swept over Karen. She slammed her fist against the door. "No! Ricky, let me out!"

The motel room door slammed shut, and the room fell silent.

Chapter Eighteen

Joe pulled his mother's Mustang into the parking lot of the Sunlight Motel. It sat on a gravel lot on the outskirts of the city. The building was probably thirty years old and painted many times over. The wooden siding was currently an ugly shade of yellow. The motel room doors were faded blue and unprotected from rain or harsh sunlight.

The whole appearance of the motel plagued Joe with guilt. Karen didn't deserve to live in such a lonely, worn place. Because of his family, she had to resort to this lifestyle.

He spotted the office at the end of the building and parked in front of it. His heart knocked against his rib cage. He wondered why he was so nervous. Perhaps he feared Karen's reaction. She might be angry at him for showing up unexpectedly. He cut off the engine and thought about this possibility. She had mentioned not liking surprises.

From the corner of Joe's eye, he caught movement. Through the rain, he saw a familiar figure stepping out of a motel room. Joe squinted.

He gasped, gripping the steering wheel. "Ricky?"

His eyes weren't deceiving him. Anger swelled up in Joe as

he watched Ricky climb into a black hatchback. The car pulled out of the parking space and ripped out of the lot. *She lied to me,* he thought. *How could she do that to me? After all I did for her, she lied to me about him.*

Joe took a deep breath. It didn't seem like her to do that. Why would she? But why was Ricky here? Of all people, how could Ricky know where Karen was, and Joe had to find out from a telephone operator? Joe cut the car's engine back on, preparing to leave. Maybe it was time to let go of Karen. She apparently had other plans for her life that didn't include him.

He felt foolish for driving so far. *What am I doing here? Did I really think I was going to waltz in and make her day?*

Joe pulled the gear shift into reverse and slowly pulled out of his parking space. He punched the brake and looked at Karen's motel door. He couldn't shake the feeling that she hadn't lied to him.

He thought about Ricky again. He had looked angry, and he had peeled out of the parking lot in a hurry. Joe's gut tightened. Was something wrong?

Joe pulled the car into the parking space in front of Karen's motel room. The once steady rain now pounded down on the car in sheets. He could hardly see as he slipped out of the car and ran to Karen's door.

He knocked furiously. "Karen? It's Joe!"

The door remained closed. Joe could feel the rain seeping through his clothes. It drenched his brown hair and dripped down his face.

He called for her again, now banging on the door. Putting his ear against it, he listened for her. The pounding rain was too loud.

What if she was hurt . . . or worse? Fear gripped him as he tried to open the door. He searched desperately for someone, anyone to help him get in. No one was in sight. His eyes met the red glow of a sign of hope, the word "Office." Joe broke out into a full run down the row of motel room doors toward it.

"I need to get into room number eighteen now!" he said, bursting into the office.

A tall, black man rose from behind the desk. "Excuse me?"

Joe put his wet hands on the counter in front of the desk window. "Please. She may be hurt."

The motel clerk grabbed a spare room key from the back wall. "All right. I'll let you in, but this better be for real. I'm in the middle of my show."

Joe nodded. "She's not answering the door, and this creep just left. I saw him."

The motel clerk grabbed an umbrella by the door and followed Joe across the row of motel doors back to room number eighteen.

Joe's heart raced. "Hurry, please."

The man unlocked the door and slowly pushed it open. "Hello?"

"I'm in the bathroom!" a voice cried from the back of the room.

Joe rushed through the door. The small, dark room was torn apart. "Karen?"

"Joe?"

After climbing across an overturned mattress, Joe made it to the bathroom door. A shoestring was tied around the door knob at one end. The other end of the string was wrapped around a towel rack on the wall. This was obviously keeping Karen trapped in the room.

Joe pulled at the shoestring, trying to unravel the knot. "Are you okay?"

"Yeah." Her voice sounded shaky and weak.

The motel clerk offered Joe his Swiss Army knife. "Here. This should do the trick."

Joe cut the shoe string and pushed the door open. Karen stood before him, her face flushed.

"Did he steal anything?" the motel clerk asked.

Karen stepped out of the bathroom. "Probably just the cash in my purse."

He headed for the door. "I'll go call the cops."

Karen caught her breath. "No."

Joe clenched his fists. "This guy locked you in a bathroom and robbed you, Karen."

She began to pick up her clothes, which were scattered on the dingy carpet. "I don't want to deal with the police."

Joe realized that any encounter with the cops would probably stir up unpleasant memories. He was sure she didn't want to relive those.

The motel clerk shrugged and headed for the door. "All right then, but you had better call me if you see that thief around here again."

"I will," she said. "Thank you."

Joe watched Karen pick up the scattered mess that was her life as the clerk closed the door. "Are you sure you're okay?"

"How did you find me?" Her sharp tone startled him.

"That's not important. You were just robbed."

She stuffed her clothes into one of the drawers on the floor and tried to lift it back into the dresser. Joe took the other end, and it slid easily back into place.

She glared at him, jaw tight. "I can do this by myself."

Joe felt wounded by her words. It was bad enough that she had lied to him about never planning to see Ricky again.

He headed for the door. "Fine. I don't even know why I came here."

He heard the sound of a drawer dropping to the floor and turned. Karen stood with her palms open amidst all that she owned. He could see tears forming in her eyes.

Her voice quivered. "I don't know why I believed him."

Joe could feel a knot forming in his throat as he watched her crumple on the floor.

"I'm such a fool," she said, bringing her knees to her chest and hugging them.

Joe returned to Karen's side and dropped to his knees on the floor. He put a gentle hand on her shoulder. A single tear fell down her cheek.

Joe swallowed his sympathy. "You said you broke things off with him."

"I did, but Ricky found me. He pretended to apologize for everything."

He could feel the knot in his throat loosen. The knot was replaced with burning, part jealousy and part anger.

Karen straightened up suddenly and wiped her eyes. She pushed herself up from the floor and returned to her mess. "I appreciate you coming to my rescue, but you'd better get back to your fiancé."

Joe once again felt a blow. He rose to his feet and gently tugged her arm, demanding her attention. "Karen, the engagement announcement was a fake. Naomi Parrish, Emily's best friend, works at the paper. She put it in there as a joke."

Her expression softened as she pulled out of his grasp. "Well, it wasn't very funny."

"I think she really did it for Emily and to make you think . . . I guess Emily thinks that we have something between us."

Her cheeks became a warm pink as she replaced the over-turned lamp back on the nightstand. "You need to get out of those wet clothes. There's a laundry room around the corner. I can dry your clothes, but all I've got for you to wear is a bathrobe."

Joe had completely forgotten about the time he'd spent running in the pouring rain. "I'm fine."

She glared at him again, reminding him of his mother's disapproval.

He nodded and headed for the bathroom.

When he emerged and met eyes again with Karen, she burst into a fit of laughter. He wore her Aunt Val's lace-trimmed, red bathrobe.

Joe crossed his arms. "It's really not that funny."

"You're cheeks are starting to match the robe!"

Karen still giggled as she took the wet pants and shirt from him and hurried out of the room. Joe lifted the mattress from the floor and set it back in place on the old box spring. He dropped down on the bed, looking around the room. It was hard to imagine that Karen could make a home out of such a space, even when it wasn't disheveled. The door opened, and an empty-handed Karen stepped back in.

"You're really not engaged to Emily?"

He sighed. "No. Thank God."

She gave him a puzzled look as she sat down beside him.

"She's not *that* bad," he admitted, "but she's not my type."

"I thought you were high school sweethearts?"

He shook his head. "She's pretty and nice, but we have nothing in common."

Her shoulders relaxed a little as if some weight lifted from her. "You came all the way here just to tell me this?"

"It's your birthday. I promised you driving lessons."

She laughed. "You remembered?"

"Of course, I'm a man of my word, but I don't think you'll want to learn how to drive in a storm."

They were both quiet for a moment. The rain was starting to die down outside. He stole glances at Karen when she looked around her room. In the glow of the nightstand lamp, her features were even smoother and softer than usual. Yet, in her eyes, he could see the evidence of loneliness and even misery.

"I want you to come back to Mercy, Karen."

She frowned, looking away from him. "I can't do that, Joe."

"Just for the Fourth of July picnic. You can be my date."

He thought he saw her crack a smile but only for a second. "I'm not welcomed there, and you know it."

He took her hand in his. "Please, for me."

Karen looked down at his fingers entwined in hers. He feared that this bold gesture made her uncomfortable, but so far, so good. She looked into his eyes, and he thought he saw a hint of longing. Perhaps it was only his own. He wanted so much to be with her in another place and another time.

Karen abruptly pulled her hand from his. "I'll have to think it over."

He was getting too close to her again. His common sense told him that their relationship would never be acceptable to his family. On the other hand, his heart told him that there is always hope. People can change. Her sudden reaction to his affection made him wonder if she had completely given up.

Joe sighed. "I'm sorry about our phone conversation. My father hung up the phone."

"I guessed that."

He felt his fists tighten as he recalled his father's actions. "He won't listen to anything I say. He still treats me like a child."

Karen rose from the bed and began collecting more of her belongings from the floor. "He has every right to be angry. He lost his father."

"I'm not giving up our friendship because of my dad, Karen. He has to learn how to forgive."

Karen sighed loudly. She sounded emotionally exhausted.

"Come to the picnic, Karen. I think your mother's tribute may have cleared the air a little."

"I'll think it over," she said again, stuffing one of the dresser drawers with clothes and slamming it shut. "I'm going to check on your clothes."

* * *

Karen turned the corner a couple of doors down from her motel room and entered the motel laundry room. The cement block room contained only two pairs of washers and dryers. She opened up one of the ten-year-old dryers and gathered Joe's clothes into her arms.

As she folded his khaki pants, she couldn't help but regret being rude to him. She was so hurt and angry about the engagement that she had never stopped to even consider it being false. When he told her that it was, she had felt a hundred pounds lighter.

He couldn't possibly have a romantic interest in her, though. She was obviously head over heels. Yet, he did take her hand. His touch gave her goose bumps. She wanted him to keep holding her hand, but she couldn't decipher his intentions. One minute, he seemed to show her deep affection. The next, he was talking about their "friendship."

Karen shook her head as if to shake away all of her silly thoughts. Joe only came to see her as a friend. He would think she was crazy if he knew that she was thinking of a deeper relationship between them.

She sighed, grabbing his stack of folded clothes from the top of the dryer. She was more confused, as her aunt would say, than a chicken with its head cut off. Clearly, she would have to leave her destiny with Joseph Aldridge in God's hands and hope for the best.

As Karen approached her motel room door, she heard a familiar voice.

"What in the name of chunky chocolate is goin' on here?"

Karen stepped into the room. Aunt Val stood with her back to Karen, looking at Joe who sat on the bed. He was tongue-tied. He grabbed a pillow from the bed and hid himself behind it.

Karen laughed. "Hey, Aunt Val."

Her aunt turned to her. "You had better have a good explanation for this!"

Karen closed the motel room door behind her. "He was soaked from the rain. I had to dry his clothes."

She gave Joe the clothes, and he scurried into the bathroom to put them on.

Aunt Val sighed with relief. "Oh my word, Karen! You two really ruffled my feathers."

"Aunt Val, you didn't think . . . ?"

"I thought!"

Karen shook her head. "He needed dry clothes. That was all I had for him to wear."

"Well, what on earth is he doing here and what happened to your room?"

Karen recapped everything from Ricky's robbery to the fake engagement announcement. In rare form, an awed Aunt Val stood silent through the whole story.

Joe emerged from the bathroom fully dressed, catching the tail end of Karen's tale. "It was Naomi Parrish."

Her aunt shook her head in disapproval. "That girl has always been a troublemaker."

Joe shrugged. "Well, it was all a joke to her. Her dad suspended her without pay from the newspaper office for a week."

Aunt Val dropped her hands on Karen's shoulders. "I am so sorry about Ricky, kitten. He came waltzin' over to the house in a three-piece suit."

Karen's jaw dropped. "He was wearing a tie?"

She nodded. "Yeah. He's a real conman. He even gave me back my money. Thank the Lord I didn't let him in the house, but boy, was I a fool for ever telling him your whereabouts."

Karen embraced her aunt. "I'm fine, and he's gone now."

Aunt Val slowly pulled out of the hug and smiled at Joe and Karen. "Well, don't let me intrude on your day together. I think I'll go get some shopping done."

Karen watched her aunt exit the room, and she hurried outside after her. "You're leaving?"

Her aunt turned to her with a mischievous smile. "He didn't drive all the way out here just to tell you about a fake engagement. Happy Birthday, kitten." She gave her niece a gentle kiss on the forehead. "Have fun."

Karen watched her aunt get into the car and drive away.

Joe sidled up to her. "Everything okay?"

Karen nodded, watching her aunt's car leave the parking lot.

"Can I take you to lunch?"

Karen turned to Joe and swallowed. "Sure, but no pancake houses."

Chapter Nineteen

Twenty minutes later, they were seated in a booth at a dimly-lit, Italian restaurant. A mini-chandelier glowed above their table. Karen looked around at the people, the smell of garlic floating in the air. She couldn't remember the last time she ate in such a beautiful place. Looking at the menu, she was floored.

"It's so expensive, Joe."

His eyes loomed over the menu. "It's your birthday."

The waiter came and took their orders after Karen played twenty questions with him about the meals. She was finally satisfied with her order of chicken parmesan.

Joe sipped his soda. "I think there is a chance you'd be fine in Mercy on July Fourth. There's always so much going on that I don't think anyone will notice you."

"I hope not."

"So you'll come?"

Karen looked away. "I didn't say that."

Joe sighed. His disappointment was hardly what Karen was used to. People actually wanting her company seemed foreign.

She smirked. "Maybe I could wear a disguise."

Joe's lips curled. "Not a bad idea."

Melissa McGovern Taylor

She remembered Mr. Aldridge's anger once again. "Your dad's going to kill you when he finds out you came to see me."

"He won't know. My mom will make up something. I take her car all the time for home appointments."

"She's doing this for my mother's sake, isn't she?"

Joe hesitated. "She knows I'm your friend, and she wants to support me."

Being in the fancy restaurant atmosphere, Karen had felt for a moment as if she might be on her first date. The word "friend" erased that feeling.

The waiter brought their food, and Karen had to force herself not to wolf it down. Not only was she hungry from skipping breakfast, she was taunted by the delicious flavors she had not experienced since her teen years.

"Karen, if you don't mind me asking, what happened to your dad? Have you heard from him since he left Mercy?"

His questions caught her off guard. She wiped her mouth with the napkin. "He travels all over the country for his job. I haven't seen him since the trial."

"He never came to visit you in jail?"

"He wouldn't come unless I asked him to. I never did."

"You're still angry?"

She sipped her drink. "Then I was. Now I don't know what I feel. He wrote me tons of letters, apologizing for abandoning me and for my mom's death. He says he's a Christian now, and he never drinks. He won't come see me until I say I forgive him."

He leaned in. "Are you afraid to trust him again?"

"Yeah. But I also don't want to be a hypocrite. I might say that I forgive him over the phone or in a letter, but what if we meet face-to-face and all of the anger returns?"

Joe nodded. "I guess you'll never know for sure unless you take a risk on forgiveness."

Karen thought about his words, not knowing how to respond. Joe had done that very thing—taken a risk on forgiveness. She wasn't sure it had been the best choice for him. She wouldn't trade anything for his forgiveness, but did Joe regret his choice?

The waiter returned to refill their drinks.

Joe sipped his drink. "Where were all of your art supplies?"

Karen gave him a puzzled look.

214

"I didn't see any of your art stuff in the motel room."

She shook her head. "I really haven't had much time for my art. I work long hours now."

Joe frowned and returned to his food. Karen followed suit. She missed her art, but life as a waitress was both demanding and exhausting. This was the life she would have to cope with, but it was better than the prison life.

After a moment, Joe returned his attention to her. "What do you want to do next?"

She shrugged.

His eyebrows perked up. "How about a movie?"

Karen's heart nearly skipped a beat. She'd forgotten the excitement of going to the movie theater to be immersed in a story. The small movie room at the prison just wasn't the same.

Joe seemed to read her expression. "I guess that's a yes?"

"Definitely."

*   *   *

During the movie, Joe couldn't help but steal glances at Karen. She looked carefree as she watched the romantic comedy on the screen. It was as if all of her troubles were washed away for two hours. She was fully involved in the story, bursting into laughter in one moment and bursting into tears the next. At the end, when the male character was about to propose, she grabbed Joe's arm and leaned forward in her seat. He could see tears shining in her eyes, and a smile curve her lips as if she were the one receiving the proposal.

Afterwards, Karen couldn't stop talking about it. Joe was relieved to finally get a few words in as they walked across the theater parking lot.

"The rain has stopped. How about that driving lesson?"

Karen's eyes grew wide. "I don't think so."

Joe opened the passenger side door for her. "We'll find an empty parking lot."

"Completely empty?"

"No cars within a square mile."

She cracked a smile. "Okay, but if I see a car, we're done."

Karen couldn't stop shaking when they sat in the car a few minutes later. She gripped the steering wheel until her knuckles turned white.

"It's okay," Joe said. "You have this whole, big parking lot. Now let off the brake and push the gas nice and easy."

Karen slowly let her foot off of the brake, and the car started to roll forward. Then she pushed the gas.

Joe jolted forward. "Whoa!"

Karen slammed on the brake. The two of them plunged full force into their seatbelts.

"It's okay, Karen. Just push gently. Not so hard."

Karen swallowed, sweat forming on her brow. "I'm really not cut out for this."

"Of course you are," he said with a chuckle. "Almost everybody drives. It just takes practice."

Karen took a deep breath and gently pushed the gas again. The car crawled forward, the engine moaning as she slowly accelerated.

He nodded. "Good. Now turn the wheel which ever way you want."

Karen turned the wheel steadily left. Her hands started to loosen their grasp as she took the car into a wide circle. She cracked a smile.

Joe relaxed back into the seat. "You're doing great."

"This isn't so bad."

"I think we've covered the basics."

Karen carefully brought the car to a stop and placed it in park. "That was fun."

Joe smiled. "Why don't you drive to your motel?"

"On the road?"

"That's where cars belong."

Two close ones and three angry drivers later, Karen pulled into the parking space in front of her motel room.

Joe's heart still pounded when she cut off the engine. "Relax. You did really well."

Karen dropped her head on the steering wheel. "I'm a terrible driver."

"That was your first time! My first time driving I crashed into the garage!"

Karen gawked at him. "Really?"

"My dad grounded me for a month."

Karen laughed.

They both slipped out of the car and walked up to her door. She pulled the key out of her pocket. He wondered what to say or do. Should he kiss her? That was silly. Was this even a real date? They were just friends . . . right?

Joe shifted in his stance. The words finally came to mind. "Happy Birthday."

"Thank you."

"I'm really glad I came. I'm sorry if I intruded. I know you didn't want me to come here."

"I called you because I hoped that, by some chance, you would."

He had to catch his breath. "I really don't feel right about only giving you lunch and lessons for your birthday." Joe felt his pockets. Then he remembered his wrist watch. "Here. It's collateral until July Fourth when I'll give you a real gift."

He thought he saw tears shining in her eyes. "Joe, you don't have to give me this."

"Please. Here, I'll put it on you."

Karen hesitated, then extended her wrist to him. Joe moved closer to her and slipped the large watch on her slender wrist. He thought he caught the scent of her perfume. It brought back memories of their kiss.

She met eyes with him. "Thank you."

"My pleasure."

Every part of him wanted to lean in and kiss her, but he was unsure as he remembered her discomfort earlier when he'd taken her hand. Their time together had been so unforgettable. It felt right to end it with a kiss.

Karen suddenly opened her arms and embraced Joe. Stunned, it took him a moment to put his own arms around her. When he did, he felt a wholeness that he'd never felt before. She felt small and fragile, but she seemed to belong in his arms. Karen slowly pulled away and looked up at him.

She smiled, stepping back. "I can't thank you enough."

"Thank me by coming back home."

She sighed.

"Karen, I promise you won't regret it."

She narrowed her eyes at him. "You are as persistent as they come, Joseph Aldridge."

"Please."

A look of surrender came across her face. "I'll see you then."

He grinned at her. "I can't wait."

Chapter Twenty

The Saturday afternoon sun smiled down on Mercy Pond as it did every July Fourth weekend. The light touched the water, drying up dew drops on the leaves and heating the surrounding pines. Nothing could be a finer sight to Joe as he trekked along the shore with his arms loaded down. Every July Fourth was not only an opportunity to celebrate Independence Day, but a chance for local shopkeepers to bring in more profit. The July Fourth Fair consisted of not only a spectacular fireworks show but a town picnic, game booths, and sales booths.

Joe planned to set up a special booth for free rabies vaccinations. It wouldn't be the most exciting booth on the edge of the pond, but at least a few family pets would benefit from the celebration. Setting down his box of pamphlets and other pet owner freebies, he took in a breath and looked around at the busy locals.

Mercy Pond was usually a quiet setting, a place where people were guaranteed to find a few moments of peace among the croaking toads and singing birds. The day before the big event was quite different from that, though. The natural sounds were drowned out by the sounds of hammers and chit-chat. All around the water's edge, people whom Joe recognized from different memories were walking about, carrying boxes, building booths and busily checking off their to-do lists. Red, white and blue balloons and ribbons were beginning to take over the view of the skyline. In a nearby clearing, others decorated a dozen wooden picnic tables with festive tablecloths.

Eric furrowed his brow at Joe. "So?"

The surrounding activities had distracted Joe from the task at hand.

"It looks great," Joe said, nodding at the well-built booth before them.

Eric had fashioned together a special booth for Joe's free vaccinations. The pet owner could simply help their pet on to a table about three feet from the ground. This would be where the animal would accept a shot from an angle that would be more manageable for Joe. Eric combined the special table and booth together exactly as Joe had pictured it in his mind.

"This is perfect, Eric."

"Do you want some money or something?"

"Huh?"

His brother grinned. "You're only this nice to me when you want something."

Joe laughed. "Yeah, a free booth! What else am I gonna get out of you, Farmer Aldridge?"

Eric snickered at his brother, playfully punching his shoulder. "For your information, farming pays pretty good. Mom and Dad give me a nice cut of the profits."

Joe's expression suddenly turned serious as a question popped into his mind. "Are you going to take over the farm someday?"

Eric shrugged. "I'm thinking about it."

Joe watched his brother turn back to the booth with hammer in hand. His eyes fell on a nail that was not completely hammered in. He finished the job.

Joe missed these moments with Eric, the goofing off and the sometimes unexpectedly intense conversations. They had a good relationship, and he hated how things had gone sour over Karen.

"Eric?"

His brother turned to him, slipping the hammer back into his tool belt. "Yeah?"

"You've got to forgive Karen."

Eric's expression immediately became defensive. He opened his mouth to respond.

"Hear me out, Eric."

Eric shook his head. "You and Mom."

"Mom's been talking to you about Karen too?"

"Only every hour of the day! She won't get off of me and Dad about it." His brother crossed his arms and cocked his head. "Well, let's hear it."

"You believe in Jesus. We were saved together," Joe reminded him. "God has forgiven us of every bad thing we've ever done and will do. The least we can do is forgive one person for one horrible mistake she made as a kid."

Eric grimaced. "Grandpa was that one horrible mistake, Joe. How can you say that him being killed was just some mistake, anyway? How do you know she didn't do it on purpose?"

"Because she told me that she didn't, and I know she's telling the truth."

Joe's brother looked away, bitterness masking his usually carefree face.

"Eric, you know Grandpa's with Jesus now. He's not angry at Karen. He's happy and at peace. If he had survived that gunshot, don't you think he would've forgiven Karen for what happened? You remember how forgiving he was. Remember the time you broke the vase that Grandma made for him?"

Eric's stiff expression changed to one of shame. Their grandmother's favorite hobby was making pottery. She had made a vase for their grandfather when they were dating. He treasured that hand-painted, blue vase like it was the Holy Grail, especially after his wife's death. One day, Eric had been playing with his toy gun, whirling like a tornado through every room of the house. A foam bullet knocked the vase off of the top shelf of their grandfather's bookcase. Joe remembered hearing the pottery shatter on the hardwood floor. He raced up the stairs just in time to see his grandfather's face turn white at the sight of the vase in pieces on his bedroom floor. Eric, in his fear and shame, cried and begged for forgiveness.

"It was only a thing, Eric," Grandpa had said. "We can't take those things to Heaven with us, can we?"

To Eric's great relief, news of the vase's demise never reached his parents. Their grandfather granted mercy, and it was as if the incident had never happened.

Eric's expression revealed to Joe that his brother had relived that whole incident in his mind.

Eric sighed, avoiding Joe's gaze. "I remember."

"That vase meant everything to him, and he completely forgave you."

"Why does it matter so much to you now, Joe? Karen is gone."

"I asked her to come back for the celebration tomorrow."

Eric shook his head and narrowed his eyes at Joe. "You're just asking for trouble."

"It doesn't have to be this way, Eric!" All of the anger and frustration rose up inside of Joe. He took a deep breath. "Be merciful. Leave her alone tomorrow. Please."

Eric gritted his teeth. "What is with you and her? Why can't you just let her go?"

Joe balled up his fists. "Because I love her!"

The words spilled out of him like water over Niagara Falls. He blinked, not sure if he had really said the words aloud. Eric's expression assured him that he had.

A disbelieving grin crossed Eric's face. "What?"

Joe closed his eyes. He couldn't have said that. *I love Karen? I love Karen.* The realization was comforting. It was true. Joe was completely and utterly in love with Karen Denwood. It was her gentle eyes, her smile that could melt an iceberg and her rock-solid faith. He loved the way she looked at him, the way she talked to him, her kiss. He couldn't ignore the passion those tender lips stirred up in him. This beautiful, once caged bird had set him free. He now understood what it meant to truly forgive someone.

When Joe managed to open his eyes again, his brother was smacking him on the shoulder playfully. "You're kidding me, man!"

"No. I'm in love with her, Eric."

Eric's grin faded and twisted into a disgusted frown. "I'm out of here."

Joe watched his brother head for the tiny but packed parking lot. He disappeared among the cars without looking back.

* * *

"I hope you'll be home to stay, sweetie," Aunt Val said, beaming at the sight of her niece sitting beside her in the car.

Karen was relieved to be going back to Mercy. The old motel room and her job at the pancake house were far from any hopes or dreams of freedom she'd had in jail. She only hoped that she wouldn't have to go back to that awful life in the city.

"It's only the holiday," she reminded her aunt, looking through the passenger side window at the pink horizon as they passed the Aldridges' house. "If all goes well tomorrow, maybe I'll bring my stuff back."

"I wish you would. I've missed having you around."

Karen sunk down into her seat, wondering if she would make it into town without meeting an angry mob. "I've missed being around."

Aunt Val cracked a smile. "How in the world did Joe convince you to come back?"

Karen remained silent.

"I guess we both know the answer to that question."

"I can't stop thinking about him," Karen said boldly. The embarrassment that she'd expected to envelope her didn't. Perhaps her relationship with Aunt Val was closer than she thought. Perhaps years of communicating across a visiting room table hadn't hindered their almost mother-daughter bond.

"Tell me something I don't know, kitten."

Karen shook her head. "He's such a great guy. I can't understand why he's pulling so hard for me after all that I did to him and his family."

"God has laid it on his heart. Be grateful," her aunt said. "And wear something pretty tomorrow."

Karen rolled her eyes and grinned. She had her outfit picked out, but she wasn't about to let that information slip out of her mouth.

Aunt Val pulled the car onto her street. "I think you should try going back to church tomorrow."

Karen cringed. "What's the point?"

"Persistence. There's nothing wrong with a healthy dose."

Karen watched her aunt's expression of proud wisdom fade into confusion as she looked ahead of them. She slowed the car's pace dramatically. "Does that car belong to who I think it belongs to?"

She followed her aunt's line of sight to that familiar hatchback parked in front of Aunt Val's house.

"Ricky," Karen murmured, gripped with fear.

Aunt Val pulled her car behind his. It appeared empty. Karen slipped out of the car before Aunt Val could even put it in Park. The house was dark with no sign of Ricky anywhere.

Her aunt cut off the engine and stepped up onto the street. "Where is he?"

"I don't know."

The street was normally quiet. Karen could fall asleep on the rooftop watching the stars, it was so quiet. Yet, right then, the unusual sound of a dog barking frantically caught her ears. She followed the sound.

"Is that Choo-choo? He almost never barks," Aunt Val said, following her niece. "Something's wrong."

The two women stopped at the line of bushes separating Mrs. Perdy's property from Aunt Val's. Choo-choo stood on the lawn, shaking and barking at the front door. He didn't notice them spying on him.

"Let's go call Sheriff Wilson," Aunt Val said, taking Karen by the arm.

Karen bit her lip. *Mrs. Perdy could be in danger because of me, because I brought Ricky to Mercy.* "You go."

"Karen," her aunt protested as Karen pulled from her grasp and passed through the bushes.

"Shhh! He's probably in there," Karen whispered. "Call for help."

Her last glimpse of her aunt, reaching out to her with a pained look and dropped jaw, didn't phase Karen as she tip-toed across the lawn past Choo-choo. The dog wouldn't give up his angry alarm, not when his loving owner was in trouble.

Karen climbed the steps to the house and the sight of the door turned her stomach. The screen in the old, wooden door was ripped near the handle. The main door to the house was wide open, a dim light filtering across the porch outside it. Karen's heart raced a mile a minute as she squatted down beside the door. She could hear crying—Mrs. Perdy's crying—and rustling sounds.

"Where's all your cash, old lady?" a familiar voice screamed.

Karen swallowed, peering through the door to see Mrs. Perdy lying on her living room floor. The old woman cried tears as heavy as the guilt on Karen's heart. A small amount of blood trickled from her mouth. Ricky had obviously struck her and knocked her down. This realization enraged Karen, and she boldly stood up to sneak in the door. Ricky stood in the far corner of the living room, his back turned as he dug through Mrs. Perdy's purse.

The screen door allowed Karen to slip in without even the slightest creak or groan. Mrs. Perdy met eyes with Karen and immediately stopped crying. She signaled at the old woman with one finger over her lips. Mrs. Perdy appeared confused, perhaps she'd originally thought Karen would be joining Ricky's crime spree. She then resumed her sobbing as Karen carefully picked up a large, glass candle jar from the entertainment center beside her. She could only hope that the smelly candle would be heavy enough to knock Ricky out.

She took a deep breath and nearly lost her concentration when Ricky started to turn around. Karen hoisted the candle above her and forced it down on Ricky's head as hard as she could. It smacked his forehead hard, knocking him to the floor. He cried out but didn't lose consciousness. Her attack only angered him more.

"You!" he screamed, gripping his head.

Karen backed up, trying to catch her breath. "Ricky, my aunt has the sheriff on the phone. He's on the way."

Her words didn't affect him. With gritted teeth and rage in his eyes, Ricky pushed himself up from the carpeted floor. He reached for something shiny on the coffee table. When Karen recognized it, she panicked.

With a switchblade in hand, Ricky darted toward Karen. Her first instinct was to run for the door, but she could only think of Mrs. Perdy. She couldn't leave her alone with him, not even if help was coming.

Karen turned and nearly tripped over Mrs. Perdy as she ran into the next room. She found herself in a pansy-decorated kitchen. Her eyes met a block of knives on the counter by the stove. As she snatched the largest one from the bunch, she heard a loud noise. Turning, Karen saw that Ricky was on the floor in the doorway. Mrs. Perdy had her little hand gripping his ankle. His switchblade skidded across the kitchen floor and stop before Karen's feet. She picked it up as Ricky struggled from Mrs. Perdy's grip.

Karen pointed the switchblade and the kitchen knife at Ricky. "Stay down!"

He narrowed his eyes at her. "Tell her to let go of me."

"It's okay, Mrs. Perdy," Karen assured the old woman.

With some hesitation, the old woman released her grip.

"Are you okay?" Karen asked her.

Mrs. Perdy nodded, looking dazed. She managed to pull herself up to a seated position.

Just when Karen began to wonder where the sheriff was, the sound of his car's siren hit her ears.

* * *

Joe followed his parents and brother into the chapel, anxiously scanning the crowded room for the face that hadn't left his mind all morning. He feared that Karen decided against returning. Through the sea of familiar faces, he couldn't yet find her, but there was plenty of time for her to arrive. Near the front of the chapel, the sight of a large crowd around Mrs. Perdy sparked his curiosity.

A hand touched his shoulder from behind. "Joseph."

He turned.

Emily Bailey looked up at him with sorrowful eyes. "Hey, how are you?"

He shrugged. "Good, I guess."

"I'm so sorry about that announcement in the paper. I had no idea that Naomi was going to do that. It was so childish."

"Yes, it was."

The two were quiet for a moment, making the air between them heavy with discomfort.

Eric inched up beside Joe. "Hi, Emily."

"Hi, Eric," she said, seeming relieved by his interruption.

A goofy grin formed on Eric's face. "So you're not getting married, huh?"

Joe wanted to laugh at his brother's strange demeanor. He never was a ladies' man.

Emily forced a smile. "No."

"Well, that's good. You don't want to marry a nerd like Joe, anyway."

Emily laughed. It was genuine. Joe continued to watch her expressions as the two chatted about nerds and jocks. A look in her eyes told Joe that the two were connecting. It was almost like Emily was seeing his brother for the first time. Relief swept over Joe. Emily was over him.

"Well, I'd better find my parents," Emily said, concluding their conversation. "I guess you guys are going to the July Fourth celebration, right?"

Eric nodded eagerly, the goofy grin still plastered on his face.

"Well, see you there."

Joe watched his brother follow the pretty brunette with his love-struck eyes.

Joe patted Eric on the back. "I think she's into you, bro."

"Really?" He asked the question like a child who was just promised a trip to Disney World.

"I'd say so."

Yet another hand landed on Joe's shoulder right then. Before he turned, Aunt Connie came around to greet him.

A very stern expression tightened her face. "Can we talk for a quick minute?"

Joe froze. "Sure."

He followed his aunt through the crowded chapel and into the church's empty sanctuary. It was a smaller room, meant for early morning service and baptisms. The cross over the altar was creamy marble and decorated more ornately than the larger wooden one in the chapel. Red velvet drapes covered the tall windows on both sides of the cherry pews. The pair stopped inside the door in the center aisle. Aunt Connie pulled the door shut, muffling the chatter in the chapel beside them.

His aunt was dressed very patriotically in a white sun dress decorated with miniature, waving American flags. She was a pastor's wife through and through, caring and always helpful to the community. Her only flaw seemed to be the grudge that she held against Karen.

"Joe, I've been praying a lot about this whole issue with Karen Denwood."

Joe nodded, encouraging her to continue.

"I love the Lord, and I believe in forgiveness, but you must know how much I loved my daddy."

"I do, of course."

"I've talked with your mother, and I know you have feelings for this girl."

Joe looked away, not knowing how to respond. "Well, huh." It was bad enough that Eric knew.

"You don't have to affirm or deny it right now, Joe. Your mother has told me all you've done for her," his aunt said, her expression softening. "I heard about what she did last night for Mrs. Perdy. It was very brave."

Joe's brow furrowed. "What are you talking about?"

"You didn't hear about the robbery?" Aunt Connie asked, stunned.

Joe shook his head. "What happened? Is she okay?"

"This young man broke into Mrs. Perdy's house, and Karen Denwood went in and rescued her. She caught the robber too."

Joe grinned, unable to hide how impressed he was with Karen's actions. "This is news to me."

"I didn't think she had changed since what happened to Dad. I thought once a criminal, always a criminal, but she really showed her true colors last night."

"She was never a criminal, Aunt Connie. You know grandpa's death was an accident."

"She tried to rob him, Joe."

Joe lowered his eyes to the floor, nodding.

"Since Karen Denwood returned to Mercy, I've seen a change in the people of this town." Aunt Connie's eyes began to shine with tears. "They've either shown how unforgiving they can be, or they've shown how forgiving they can be. It's really touched my heart to see how you're willing to let go of the past. God has really been working on me through those in the town who can forgive, people like your granddaddy. The Lord's calling me to step up to the plate and be one of them."

He braced himself. "Are you willing?"

She smiled. "Yes. Can you take me to her?"

* * *

A feeling of dread washed over Karen as she stepped through the chapel doors with Aunt Val. The memory of the last time she had attended worship haunted her during the whole walk over. It amazed her to think that was the first time Joe saw who she really was, and he still sided with her. They had come a long way from that day, despite having only known each other for a couple of months. Could someone fall in love in such a short time?

Love? The word felt foreign to Karen. Sure, she cared for Joe. She was attracted to Joe. But did she *love* him? These new thoughts made her uneasy. Falling in love with Joseph Aldridge was a ridiculous notion. Practically his whole family hated her. They would have to run off to another state and elope. *Elope? Marriage?* Karen couldn't believe her thoughts. *Who said anything about marriage?* Her head was spinning as she followed her aunt through the crowded chapel. Even if she did love Joe, why would he love her back? She was a former prisoner, hardly a candidate for the position of Mrs. Joseph Aldridge.

Karen had to clear her head. She began to scan the room for him. A few faces in the room scowled at her or purposely avoided her eyes. She decided it would be best to lay low and wait for Joe to find her.

"There she is!" a familiar voice cried from the front of the room.

Karen looked up to see Mrs. Perdy forcing her way through the crowd. She grinned widely at Karen, pointing at her.

"This is my hero! Karen Denwood saved my life last night!"

The whole congregation watched Mrs. Perdy walk up to Karen with outstretched arms.

Karen froze where she stood.

Mrs. Perdy hugged her. "She's not a criminal. I was wrong about her. You're all wrong about her!"

Karen returned the hug, glancing around the room to see the looks on the faces of the congregation. Most of them looked surprised. Then one of them clapped. Another joined in. Then another. Aunt Val clapped proudly with them, showing her pearly whites. Finally, the whole congregation clapped. Most of the people smiled at her. Karen found herself smiling back.

As the applause faded and Mrs. Perdy ended her embrace, the organ music started a powerful performance of "Amazing Grace." The song was one of Karen's favorites. On many lonely nights in prison, she would hum it until she fell asleep.

"Thank you," Mrs. Perdy said with tears in her eyes.

Karen bit her lip. "You needed help."

Aunt Val suddenly gripped Karen by the wrist, almost grabbing Joe's watch. "Oh dear."

Karen saw that her aunt spotted someone at the front of the room. Joe entered the chapel from the sanctuary. He met eyes with her and smiled, heading in her direction. Frank Aldridge's daughter followed him.

Karen turned toward the door. "We have to leave."

Aunt Val gently pulled her arm. "Now hold your horses. She doesn't look angry."

Karen could feel her palms growing cold and sweaty as Joe and his aunt approached. They moved in slow motion toward her. She noticed that a few of the congregation members watched the pastor's wife. Karen thought she even heard someone whisper, "Uh, oh. Here we go again."

Joe grinned. "Karen, this is my Aunt Connie."

"Hi," Karen uttered, meeting eyes with the woman who was her greatest threat. She put out her open hand, a peace offering, although she feared it might be bitten off.

"Hi, Karen," Connie said with an unexpected smile.

Instead of shaking Karen's hand, she gave her a hug, much like a mother embracing a child she hadn't seen in years. Karen couldn't believe it. Baffled, she stood with her hand still out. Then the reality of the moment hit her, and she returned the embrace.

"It's okay," Connie whispered in her ear. "I forgive you."

Joy like none she had ever felt before engulfed Karen. She could feel tears burning her eyes. Connie Bell's words replayed over and over in her head, even as she pulled away from her. She took Karen's hands into her own.

Karen shook from the emotional power of the moment. "Thank you."

The whole room watched them now, "Amazing Grace" still carrying across the pews. The words echoed in Karen's mind as tears streamed down her cheeks. Tears also stained Connie's face.

"Hallelujah!" a booming voice cried from the altar. It was Pastor Bell. More voices in the room echoed praise.

Something happened right then. A feeling, a mood swept across the room. A woman that Karen didn't recognize walked up and hugged her. Then an elderly man did the same. Soon, it seemed like everyone in the room took turns embracing her. Karen then realized that it wasn't a mood or a feeling in that chapel. It was the Holy Spirit. The tears kept coming as more and more congregation members, old and young, male and female, lovingly embraced her.

Then Joe's brother appeared before her through the crowd. "I'm sorry, Karen."

"Sorry?"

Eric's eyes dropped to the floor. "I was the one who ruined your sign."

This news didn't surprise her. Eric was possibly the boldest of all of her enemies.

He met eyes with her again. "Can you forgive me?"

"Of course, Eric. Can you forgive me?"

He nodded and hugged her tightly.

Over Eric's shoulder, Karen could see Joe's expression. He too looked emotional and joyful. Mrs. Aldridge stood beside him, smiling and wiping her eyes with a pink handkerchief. Mr. Aldridge was nowhere in sight, and Karen's heart sank.

As the organist began to play the final verse, Pastor Bell started to sing it.

"When we've been there ten thousand years bright shining as the sun," he sang as the whole chapel joined in. "We've no less days to sing God's praise than when we first begun."

* * *

"That was unbelievable in there," Joe said to Karen, still overwhelmed by the church service.

Karen walked down the steps of Mercy Church with him. "That was the work of the Holy Spirit."

"It was amazing! Not in a million years would I have expected that!"

Even in his wildest dreams, Joe didn't think the town's forgiveness would happen in such a miraculous way.

At the bottom of the steps, Karen stopped and turned to him. "Thank you. I know you had a part in your aunt's forgiveness."

Joe shook his head, stopping beside her. "That was all God. I promise. I did what I knew was right, what He called me to do. Besides, my aunt heard about what you did last night. What were you thinking?" Joe's voice went a little shrill with the question.

Karen's eyes dropped to the ground like a child caught red-handed. "It was my fault that Ricky was in town. I was responsible for Mrs. Perdy."

Joe frowned. This point hadn't occurred to him before. "But he could've hurt you . . . or worse."

"I'm okay, Joe." She looked around, seeing eager to change the subject. "Your dad left, didn't he?"

Joe felt his anger rising. In that miraculous moment, he saw his father duck out of the chapel, scowling the whole way. How could he be so stubborn? How could he see his own sister offer such forgiveness and brush it off?

Joe apologized. "The Lord is working on him, but at least the rest of the town has forgiven you."

The mix of concern and sorrow didn't leave her face. "Don't you remember what Jesus said about the one sheep? How he'd leave behind the whole flock just to find that one lost sheep?"

Immediately, Joe understood. She would always bear the burden of his father's rejection. This angered him even more. She didn't deserve to be treated this way.

"I'm going to find him."

"No, Joe. He has to work this out on his own. You've done everything you could do. Leave it to God."

He looked into her eyes. They shimmered in the sunlight. Something had changed in them. They didn't hold so much pain anymore. The weariness that had once burdened her gentle face had been wiped away. Her joy had returned.

Joe smiled. "Are you coming back to the clinic tomorrow?

Karen's eyes sparkled. "Absolutely."

It took all of his energy not to break out into a cartwheel. "It'll be great to have you back."

"I'll just be happy to get away from pancakes for a while."

They walked a block along Main Street to Mercy Pond with a large crowd from the church. Aunt Val had promised to meet them at the celebration, saying she had to change out of her outfit first.

The celebration looked exactly as Joe had expected. On the shore of the pond, various booths were completed now and decorated with balloons. Three giant gas grills released the tempting aroma of grilled hot dogs and hamburgers. Children, still in their Sunday best, chased each other around with water guns as their parents scolded them. An excited, little girl carried a pink ball of cotton candy larger than her head.

A brass band played "You're a Grand, Old Flag" near the water's edge. Picnic tables were decorated with red, white, and blue striped, vinyl tablecloths. The wind attempted to carry them way, but the weight of balloon-adorned, ceramic Uncle Sam centerpieces kept them at bay. A line was already forming at the food tables which were set up buffet style with baked beans, potato salad, coleslaw and other delicious Southern side dishes.

Karen grinned. "It hasn't changed a bit."

The new peace and joy in her heart showed through. He could tell that memories were flooding into her mind.

She frowned. "I wish my dad were here."

"Have you heard from him?"

"He called Aunt Val about a week ago, saying he would be in town. He was vague about when."

Joe didn't know what to say or how to comfort her. He couldn't imagine how much she must miss her father.

"Why don't you get us a table, and I'll stand in line?" Joe said.

The two split up, and Joe found a place at the back of the line. In the parking lot, his mother waved to him. He waved back. Eric and Emily stood nearby, talking. This brought a smile to Joe's face. Then his expression faded. His father appeared among the cars, his face stiff and emotionless as usual. Joe's mother took his arm as they approached the nearest vendor booth. The vendor, Mr. Gorman, greeted his dad and struck up a conversation with him.

Joe looked away, still bitter about his father's retreat from the church. He returned his attention to Karen who had found an empty table several yards from him under a large oak. She took a seat on the bench, catching her dress from the warm wind's grasp. He could hardly believe a former prisoner could be so beautiful. Her yellow and pink, flower dress matched her golden hair which flowed in gentle waves to her shoulders. The wind picked up her locks, revealing more of her creamy, flawless face. She looked almost exactly as he'd imagined the first time they met at the prison Bible study.

Once again, Joe faced the reality of his feelings for Karen. What was next for them? Could he ever tell her how he felt? What if she didn't feel the same way? He would feel like a fool. The memory of their kiss on the rooftop broke into his thoughts. He longed desperately to relive that moment, to recreate it—a lifetime of that moment.

I'm in love, he realized silently. *I want to spend every minute of my life with Karen.*

As the line moved forward, Joe turned to get one more look at the woman of his dreams. He made a double take. She wasn't alone at the table now. Tommy Parrish was shaking her hand and taking a seat in front of her. Joe's gut began to tighten along with his jaw as Karen smiled and the two shared a laugh. Was he flirting with her? That feeling returned, the one he had when he saw Ricky put his arm around Karen. Right then, Joe knew what he had to do, and he had to do it today.

Chapter Twenty-One

"So you and Joe are an item?" Tommy Parrish asked Karen, leaning over the picnic table.

She couldn't help but think that more than curiosity prompted his question as she gazed into Tommy's hazel eyes. It was a good question, though. It was clear how she felt about Joe, but how he felt about her was a mystery. She knew that he wanted her friendship. She glanced at Joe in the line as if he would have the answer for her. Joe met eyes with her for a split second, then he turned away.

"He's a good friend."

Tommy nodded. "Hey, you should come by my office sometime. I have some interviews on tape about your mom. People shared their memories. I couldn't fit it all in the paper."

"I might take you up on that."

Joe arrived at the table with a full plate of food in each hand. "Who's hungry?"

"Yum!" Karen cried, more out of relief than hunger. Tommy was certainly handsome and seemed like a nice guy, but she wasn't interested in creating a love triangle. Things were complicated enough already.

Joe seemed to be forcing a smile. "Hey, Tommy."

Tommy rose from his seat. "Hey, I was just about to get in line. It was a pleasure meeting you, Karen—again."

"You too, Tommy."

"Again?" Joe asked as Tommy left them alone with their food.

"We actually used to go to the same summer camp together." Joe nodded his head. "Oh."

Do I sense a hint of jealousy? Karen wondered.

Joe clasped his hands together over his food. "Do you want me to say the blessing?"

"Sure."

Eric walked up to Joe with an overflowing plate of food. "Mind if we join you?"

Emily Bailey stood beside him, beaming. Karen felt like she'd been pushed off of a cliff.

Joe smiled at them. "Yeah. There's plenty of room."

Emily took a seat beside her while Eric sat beside his brother across from them. Karen looked at Joe and then at Emily. She suddenly lost her appetite.

Joe said a blessing, and soon they began gobbling down their food.

"Karen," Emily said, "I'm so glad that everyone has been able to let go of the past."

"Everyone except for Dad," Eric said.

Joe frowned. Everyone at the table followed his glance a few tables over where Joe's parents shared their meal with Pastor Bell and Connie. Joe's father was in a better mood now, even laughing, much to Karen's relief.

"Karen!" a familiar voice called in the distance behind her.

Karen turned. In the parking lot, Aunt Val jumped up and down, waving her arms like a mad woman.

Joe rose from his seat. "What's going on?"

Karen saw a man walking alongside her aunt. "I don't know."

Her heartbeat quickened. Was it him? Karen jumped up from the table and hurried to meet them at the edge of the parking lot.

She could feel Joe following behind her. "Who's that?"

Karen could see the man's features more clearly as she got closer. Those eyes looked familiar. He was a tall, stocky man. His hair was salt and pepper now, no longer brown. He didn't have the mustache that she remembered. That smile. She recognized that smile in a second.

She broke into a jog. "It's my dad!"

Her father grinned, jogging to meet her. "Karen!"

"Dad!"

They embraced. She hadn't felt those strong arms around her in years. His smell of musky cologne hadn't changed. Karen could hardly contain the mixture of emotions inside. She began to sob on his shoulder uncontrollably.

"I missed you so much, honey," he said in an older and wiser voice.

"I missed you too, Daddy."

He sobbed. "I'm so sorry."

She could hardly breathe now, but she managed to collect the words that she'd wanted to say for nine years. "I forgive you."

* * *

Joe spent the rest of the Fourth as a third wheel with his brother and Emily. He decided it was best to back off and give Karen and her father some time to get reacquainted. She'd been waiting many years for this reunion, and he was glad to see her so happy. The profession of his love would have to wait for another day.

He did keep a vigilant eye on the chatting pair, though. Occasionally, Karen would catch him, and they would exchange smiles. Her father would glance over his shoulder and offer a wave. Joe would politely wave back.

Karen and her dad talked until sunset. By then, Joe was exhausted and not sure about staying for the fireworks. He decided to head home with his parents.

On the way to the parking lot, Joe watched his mother and father walk arm in arm in the fading sunlight. His hibernating bitterness emerged from its slumber. His father had avoided him all day. He showed no signs of surrendering his grudge with

Karen. Every bone in Joe's body begged for a heavy confrontation right then, but he had to respect Karen's wishes and trust God.

Just then, he heard Karen call him through the growing symphony of crickets. She ran up to meet him as his parents disappeared among the cars. The smell of her sweet perfume fell upon his nose like a soft blanket.

He stopped in his tracks. "Hey, I was just heading in for the night. Where's your dad?"

"He left with Aunt Val. I was hoping I didn't miss you. I wanted to talk."

A knot formed in Joe's throat. *It's now or never.*

"Me too," he said. "The fireworks are starting soon. Let's find a place to sit."

Along the shoreline, most vendors had packed up their booths and made room for locals to spread out blankets. Families and couples set up camp to await the spectacular fireworks show, one of only three per year in Mercy. Zigzagging among the spectators, Joe and Karen found a secluded picnic table at the edge of the pines.

Joe could feel his palms growing sweaty as the words replayed in his head. He had rehearsed them carefully in his mind for most of the day, fearing the moment when the curtain would open and he would have to bear his soul to Karen. Her almost angelic appearance under the light of the moon made this approaching task seem all the more daunting. If only he could know for sure how she would respond.

"I've been—" Joe's words tumbled into Karen's. They both stopped speaking. Karen smiled. His throat closed up.

She giggled. "You go ahead."

"No. You first."

She bit her lip, an adorable sign of her excitement. "I can't believe how amazing this day has been. I forgave him. I really did, and it felt so wonderful."

Tears began to well up in her eyes as a smile crossed her soft face. "Joe, I can't tell you how happy I am. I haven't been this happy in years."

Would his confession make her happier? He nodded, smiling and waiting for her to continue.

"He says he got a permanent job in Maryland. He wants me to come live with him."

Joe could feel his smile starting to fade. He tried to maintain what was left of it.

"Live with him?" Joe repeated as if he imagined hearing her words.

"He's going to pay for me to attend art school, Joe!" she said in a tone of excitement he didn't recognize. "I can't believe it. Art school! I'll *really* be an artist."

"But you're already an artist," Joe protested gently.

She sighed, still smiling. "I know you think I'm talented, Joe, but I don't have a leg to stand on in the art world. With some classes, I could get better. Maybe one day I could teach or even open my own studio."

Joe had to remind himself that this was Karen's dream. It had taken up residence in her heart way before he came along. And who was to say that there was any room for him in there?

"That sounds great, Karen," he finally said, forcing enthusiasm. Karen's dream would come true. He had to be happy for her.

"He's leaving on Tuesday evening to catch an early Wednesday morning flight, and he wants me to come with him."

"On Tuesday?"

This new revelation completely swept the smile from Joe's face. He couldn't ignore his sudden loss of breath.

She looked up at the moon with a thoughtful gaze. "I know it's really sudden. I need to sleep on it, but I feel like God's giving me a great opportunity. I could still come into work at the clinic tomorrow."

"I thought classes didn't start again until the fall," Joe said, hoping that this fact would stall her transition.

"Dad says he could get me a part-time office job at his work. I could start this week."

Joe's rollercoaster of hope took a plunge.

"What should I do, Joe?"

She might as well have asked Joe, "Are you going to be selfish or let me have my dream?" The silence between them grew. He had to respond and fast.

"Go for it, Karen. This is your dream. You deserve to have this."

For a moment, Joe thought he saw a spark fade from Karen's eyes.

"Really?" Her tone was indistinguishable between surprise and hopefulness.

Joe nodded, gazing up at the moon as if it would offer relief for his aching heart.

"Did you need to tell me something?"

The words he'd memorized in his head replayed yet again. Why would he waste his breath on them now? Karen's dream wasn't to be stuck in Mercy as Mrs. Joseph Aldridge, the vet clinic secretary. Who was he to encroach on the one chance she had at art school and the professional title of artist? Joe reached into his pocket and pulled out a wrapped box.

He handed her the gift. "Happy Belated Birthday."

She smiled, taking it from his hand.

Inside, she found a gold cross on a matching herringbone chain. An oval cut diamond sparkled in the center of the little cross.

"It's beautiful," Karen whispered.

She removed the oversized watch from her wrist.

Handing it back to him, she leaned forward to embrace Joe. "Thank you."

Joe returned her hug, holding her close as if to tell her with his touch how he felt. He wished it would last forever.

He gently pulled away. "I'll put it on you."

She gave the tiny necklace to him, and he took his time clasping it around her gracefully carved neck. The smell of her perfume enticed him once again. This time, the aroma left him feeling down rather than up.

In that moment, the band began to play "Stars and Stripes Forever." Mercy locals applauded, eager for the celebration of explosions to begin. Whistling rockets flew into the sky one after another. Deafening explosions and the smell of burning wicks overwhelmed the night air. Joe hardly noticed. All he could do was stare at Karen's perfect silhouette in the flashing, artificial light. Her eyes lit up from the spectacle as she smiled. She never looked happier.

The fireworks exploded in blasts of dazzling red, white and blue, crackling and shimmering like so many of Joe's fantasies of life with Karen. For a moment, both were so grand, and in the next, they faded into a ghostly grey.

Chapter Twenty-Two

The morning sunlight submerged the attic bedroom in a golden glow. The light touched every painting, scaring away the shadows of night and reviving the acrylic colors. Karen stared at the pair of windows at the other end of her room. They looked like entry ways to Heaven, overwhelmed by pure light and warmth. She blinked a few times. The memory of yesterday's life-changing events hit her like calm ocean waves as she sat up in bed. However, the memory of Joe's words smacked her like a bad odor.

"Go for it, Karen."

His reaction to her news was hardly what she had hoped for. He could've said, "No, don't go, Karen. I want you to stay with me. I want us to be together." But he didn't. He told her to go. That could only mean one thing.

She sighed, rubbing her sleep-sprinkled eyes. Most of the night consisted of tossing and turning. Instead of agonizing over an unforgiving town, she was tortured by moments with Joe, misleading words and signals. Her experience with men and dating was limited. She must have misread him completely, misinterpreting his every action and living in a fantasy world.

What a fool she was to kiss him! Regret and humiliation overtook her disappointment. How could she face him today now knowing for sure that his feelings weren't mutual?

A knock at Karen's door yanked her from her thoughts. "Karen?"

"Come in, Dad."

Her father entered the attic wearing blue jeans and flannel. Despite the passing years, his taste in clothing hadn't changed. She had been relieved the day before to find that many other things about him had remained the same as well. The most important of all, though, had changed. He was no longer a slave to alcohol.

He smiled. "Good morning."

She still couldn't accept those new age lines on his face. Seeing him so much older felt surreal to her.

"Good morning." She cracked a smile, all she could muster up at the moment.

She watched her father glance across the walls of paintings.

"They're beautiful," he whispered.

A look of pride crossed his face as he examined the works. At the pond, he had told her how Aunt Val had showed him the paintings before the two came to the pond. He said her talent clearly stemmed from her mother and that she would be proud. His words had warmed Karen's heart.

He took a seat on the edge of her bed, concern changing his wise face.

"You look like you had a rough night, dear."

She drew her blanket-covered knees up in front of her. "I have a lot on my mind."

"I'm sorry. I didn't mean to complicate things for you."

"No, Dad. You didn't do anything wrong. I guess I always pictured myself living in Mercy."

He nodded in understanding. "I don't want to put any pressure on you, Karen. If you choose to stay, I understand."

She shook her head more vigorously than she had intended to. "There's no reason to stick around here. I don't want to be a vet clinic receptionist for the rest of my life."

"What about Joseph Aldridge?"

"What about him?" Her lack of interest didn't sound very convincing.

"Well, you two seemed to have hit it off very well. Your aunt says you have feelings for him."

Karen's jaw dropped. "She had no right to tell you that."

"Honey, I could tell by the way you talked about him yesterday that he's certainly found a special place in your heart."

Karen hadn't meant to bare her soul, but it had been an emotional day.

"Well, apparently he doesn't feel the same way, so I'm not going to wait around here for him to fall in love with me. I have dreams and ambitions, Dad."

He nodded, smiling. "Are you sure he doesn't already love you?"

She lowered her eyes. "Yes, one hundred and ten percent."

* * *

The front porch at the Aldridge house usually buzzed with life, whether it was gossiping ladies or two rambunctious boys playing tag. Now it was still and quiet in the warm, dusk air. This place brought back many memories for Joe, but at the moment, he couldn't concentrate on them. He could only relive what had so far been the saddest day of his life. Certainly the day his grandfather died was sad, but it was a different kind all together. That grief couldn't be prevented. Today's sadness was clearly preventable, yet Joe couldn't bring himself to take a chance, to try and turn the good-bye into the beginning of a new relationship. The fear of rejection and the overwhelming possibility of it were too great.

His horrible day had consisted of avoiding Karen at the front desk by appearing busy and even prolonging appointments. He supposed that he could have talked with her on her last day there. They could have flirted in their subtle way, shared a laugh or two. He could have tried to make a few more memories with her, but he didn't. Why bother making memories when that's all you'll have left?

He had spent the day counting down to her departure, hiding his disappointment. About half an hour ago, she called to say she would be a little early leaving town. She and her father had to stop off at the Sunlight Motel and gather her other things before finding a place to stay near the airport. He knew she would be glad to leave that dirty, old motel room far behind. Now he glanced at his wristwatch every ten seconds, waiting for her to drive up with her father and say good-bye to him forever.

Maybe she would go to art school and meet some fellow artist and fall in love with him. Perhaps they would have a grand wedding and two or three creative children. They would run a gallery together in New York City and paint together every day. They would be the famous, painting couple.

Along with these thoughts, nausea overcame him. The most sickening part was feeling like he could've done something. He could've been kinder to her. He could've been more charming, brought her roses when he drove to her motel, kissed her the first time he had sensed the urge. He could've worked harder to make Karen fall for him.

Joe shook his head in frustration. He had to remember that God had a perfect plan. Sometimes that plan included disappointments, misunderstandings, and rejections. Karen's future as an artist was God's plan, and Joe had no right to complain about it. No matter what he did or didn't do, this was how it was meant to be. In the end, the most important thing was Karen's happiness.

Lord, help me to accept Your will and not be selfish, Joe prayed.

He watched the edge of a fiery sun disappear behind the pines on the horizon. An otherwise delicious dinner sat in his stomach like a marble slab. Down the street, the sound of an approaching car silenced the various bird songs in the air.

Joe's stomach did a cartwheel, not an easy task for a slab of marble. He rose from his seat on the brown wicker chair. A red BMW came into his view. In the remaining daylight, Joe could see that Mrs. Thornton, the town attorney's wife, was the driver. He sighed in a gust of relief as he gave her a friendly wave. She returned the greeting.

Joe sank back into the chair, unsure if he would prefer sitting a little longer with his thoughts or getting the whole awful farewell over with. The past two days had been nothing but thoughts of what ifs, could haves and should haves. He tossed and turned at night, thinking of her face, her sweet perfume, and her gentle touch. The memory of her kiss tortured him into restless sleep. He couldn't shake the feeling that he was about to say good-bye to his whole future.

Another vehicle hummed its way up the street. This one was a green SUV. It slowed its approach and, much to Joe's dread, it turned into the Aldridge driveway. A rental car company plate on the front bumper confirmed Joe's fears.

Karen waved at him from the front passenger seat. Her father smiled as the car came to a stop in front of the separate double garage. She slipped out of the car, wearing a pair of dark blue jeans and a red t-shirt that clung to her torso. Her blonde hair was pulled up in a ponytail. After saying something to her father, she pushed the door closed.

Joe had planned on meeting her at the steps, but he sat frozen in the wicker chair unable to move. She walked in slow motion toward the porch, her ponytail gently tossing about in the light, summer breeze. Her smile, which typically raised his spirits and caused a flutter in his belly, now felt like a dagger in his heart. He forced a smile in return, finally rising from the chair. As he descended the steps, Joe rubbed the back of his neck. His father shared the same mannerism in awkward moments.

Karen's smile faded as she met Joe at the bottom of the steps. "You know I'll be back to visit."

Joe nodded, rubbing his neck raw. "I know."

"And it's a quick flight." Sadness saturated her tone.

He nodded, dropping his fists into his khaki pockets.

"Joe, you've been such a blessing to me," she said, her voice cracking. She looked away. "If it weren't for you, I'd never feel the freedom that I feel now. I don't have to live with the guilt anymore. I mean, I know that your father—"

"He doesn't count," Joe interrupted rather curtly. He didn't mean to sound harsh, but he was hiding so many feelings that something had to give.

Karen shrugged. "Maybe someday."

She took in a deep breath, forcing back a mixture of emotions that Joe couldn't quite separate.

"Let's just say 'See you later'," Karen murmured, glancing back at her father.

He appeared to have his attention on the car radio dial.

"Well, I hope you'll call me from time to time."

She nodded. "Of course. I want to know how the clinic picks up."

"I think it'll struggle without you," he said, really referring to himself.

She smiled again, a full grin. He loved that grin so much.

"See you later, Joe."

He nodded, expecting her to step forward and embrace him. Instead, she turned back to the SUV. His heart shattered into a hundred pieces as he watched her climb back into the vehicle. Her father waved and smiled with a nod. Joe forced himself to return the same gesture. Karen waved again as the Explorer backed out of the long driveway.

Joe could feel his legs buckling underneath him. He turned and grabbed the stair railing as casually as he could. His face felt hot, yet he knew that it must have looked ghostly white right then. He stood as still as death, watching the love of his life disappear down the road.

* * *

Karen stared through the passenger window, her stomach tight and throat dry as an old canvas. Pines climbed the grey horizon along the narrow road that led out of Mercy. She had seen this path a thousand times before. Yet, it had never looked depressing. The sunlight was completely gone now, and night enveloped the road, forcing her father to flip on the headlights. Neither of them had said a word since they left the Aldridge house. She didn't speak because she feared what she would say. The words on her mind, aching to dive from her mouth, would cause a downpour of emotions that she was trying to ignore.

The hardest part of the good-bye was saying it without even a hug. She had planned on embracing Joe originally. A blueprint of the whole farewell had been sketched in her head. However, when she saw him sitting on the front porch, an avalanche of memories buried her. She wanted to cry. She wanted to scream at him in anger. How could he be so sweet to her? How could he flirt with her and give her a beautiful necklace, only to encourage her to move hundreds of miles away from him? Standing before him, she had feared that an embrace would spark a chain reaction within her. She couldn't allow that to happen.

"Honey, are you okay?"

"I'm fine," she whispered.

"Don't despair. You're young, and there are plenty of fish in the sea."

She remained silent, staring down at the white line on the road beside them. She knew what kind of fish were in that sea, fish like Ricky. *Maybe there are a few others like Joseph Aldridge.* Yet, this thought weighed heavy on her heart. She didn't want a man *like* Joe. She wanted Joe.

Karen wondered when her heart would stop aching. Perhaps the distance between them would help her move on. Even though she had promised to visit, she dreaded it. Seeing Joe again might only lock her back into the same emotional rollercoaster.

She deeply regretted not hugging Joe, though. Where was the closure? Now she would forever wish she had said good-bye the right way. Years from now, she might still be in turmoil over him because of it.

She sank back in her seat and closed her eyes. Thoughts of Emily Bailey returned. Maybe her interest in Eric was a diversion. It was possible that she still had a crush on Joe. Perhaps in a few years, Karen would return to Mercy to find Mrs. Emily Aldridge and her happy husband blessed with a beautiful home and two lovely children. The thought caused Karen's eyes to snap open. Her stomach turned.

Lord, forgive me, she prayed, bowing her head. *I know you will never give me more than I can handle, but I'm almost at my breaking point.*

When Karen opened her eyes, light from a passing car bounced off of the gold cross around her neck. It shimmered for a second, then disappeared in the dim light of the vehicle's interior. She took the charm between her thumb and forefinger, remembering the strong but enticing scent of Joe's cologne as he had placed it around her neck. Remembering their one sweet kiss, she closed her eyes and drifted off to sleep.

Chapter Twenty-Three

A full moon peaked into the open window like the shiny end of some gigantic, distant telescope. An orchestra of crickets played an unrelenting melody in the thick night air, drifting through the screen into Joe's bedroom. He had hoped that the sounds of nature would give him a pattern to fall asleep by. Staring at the digital clock on his nightstand, he realized that any hope of a restful night was long gone. It was now almost five in the morning. Karen's plane would be leaving in nearly two hours.

The sound of footsteps in the hallway and then movement on the stairs caused Joe to rise from his millionth position on the bed. All in all, he probably got about two hours of sleep. Suspecting that he looked like death warmed over, he turned on his bedroom light and glanced at himself in the dresser mirror. His suspicions were instantly confirmed. His hair was disheveled, eyes heavy with sadness and lack of sleep. The last time he looked this bad was when he stayed up until four in the morning cramming for a college exam. That was the first and last time he would procrastinate on something so important.

The sounds of clinking glasses and closing cabinets drifted up through the ceiling from the kitchen. His father was awake at the usual time. As long as Joe could remember, his father was up by five. That was the life of a farmer, rise before the sun and rest after sunset. He would have a cup of coffee, then do a couple of hours of work. By that time, Joe's mom and brother would be up. His father would venture back inside for breakfast, then return to the fields with Eric to do whatever work the current season required.

Joe didn't attempt to fix his hair. He merely rubbed his eyes for a moment, yawning unexpectedly. Perhaps a cup of coffee with his father would keep his mind preoccupied while the distance between he and Karen grew. Naturally, he was still angry and bitter with his dad. His father probably felt the same but for different reasons. As Joe threw on his bathrobe, his brow furrowed at the realization that his father was most likely pleased about Karen's more permanent departure from Mercy. He shook his head, remembering his prayers. It was time to let God handle his father. Passing judgments and holding on to his anger would only worsen a tender situation. It was time to let bygones be bygones.

Joe tip-toed out of his bedroom, but clambered down the stairs unintentionally. His legs were heavy with exhaustion after a full night of tossing and turning. He only hoped that his noisy gait hadn't disturbed his mother and brother's peaceful sleep. At least most of the occupants of the Aldridge house were getting enough shut-eye. Joe wouldn't wish such a restless night on his worst enemy.

Downstairs, Joe's father read the Raleigh newspaper at the kitchen table. The *Mercy Gazette* delivery hadn't yet reached their home. The coffeemaker on the counter gurgled, the pot almost full. His father looked up from the paper and nodded at Joe who took a seat at the table across from him.

Joe dropped his arms on the table. "Any good news?"

His father's eyes still scanned the Business section. "You look like you could use some."

"Who doesn't like a little good news from time to time?"

"You look like you were up dancing with the devil all night, son."

Joe shrugged. "I couldn't sleep."

"Well, you should've counted sheep. You've got a busy day at the clinic today, don't you?"

"Yeah. My schedule's been filling up since church on Sunday." Joe was grateful for the opportunity to remind his father of that unusual service.

"Is your mother helping you out today?"

Joe nodded. "Just until I get a new receptionist."

"Good luck."

The coffeemaker bubbled one last time, topping off the pot with several drops. Joe was relieved to have an excuse to pull away from the conversation. He rose from the table and eagerly grabbed a coffee cup from the cabinet.

"Bring me a cup, would you?" His father's tone was a polite one unlike those Joe had recently endured.

Joe poured them each a full cup and carried them over to the table where cream and sugar in dainty white porcelain sat as centerpieces. He could find nothing to say as he watched his father gently stir cream into his morning brew. Joe merely sipped his coffee, recalling the morning at the clinic when Karen told him that she didn't drink coffee.

"Why don't you drink coffee? Everyone drinks coffee."

She had looked away in shame. "I've had it thrown on me a few times in prison."

Joe couldn't believe her words at the time. How could anyone treat such a sweet, beautiful woman in such a horrific way?

"Some of the gangs in prison would do awful things to assert their dominance," she had said. "I guess I got too cocky when I first moved from juvenile corrections."

The sound of his father accidentally dropping his stirring spoon on the table snapped Joe back into the present. The depression that had kept him tossing like a ship on stormy waves all night returned with full force. He had once felt like Karen's rescuer, a new facet to her life that could wipe away the pain of years of imprisonment by creating new, happier memories for her.

"Have you ever had coffee thrown on you, Dad?" Joe asked, overcome by a sea of emotions.

"No. Sounds like it would hurt." His expression grew defensive. "Why would you ask me that?"

Joe rolled his eyes like a sassy twelve-year-old. "I'm not gonna throw coffee on you."

"Well, you've done crazier things lately."

"Karen told me that women in the prison threw coffee on her, and that's why she doesn't drink it," Joe explained.

His father smirked. "That would turn me off of coffee too."

"It's not a joke, Dad," Joe snapped, feeling his anger start to boil.

"Is this what you came down here for? To talk about that Denwood girl?"

"Her name is Karen, and she's not a girl anymore," Joe said, trying to keep his tone as calm as possible. "She's a beautiful, Christian woman."

Joe froze, waiting for his father to slam down the newspaper and put him out of the house for good.

Instead, his father folded the paper and gently placed it on the table beside his half empty coffee cup.

"What are you doing here, Joseph?" he asked, concern lacing his every word and covering his face.

Joe was silent, unsure of what he meant.

His father shook his head. "You may be smart as a whip. You may have gone out there and conquered the veterinary world, but you don't have a lick of common sense."

Joe felt his muscles tense up as he prepared to defend himself.

His father pointed an accusing finger at him. "You never listen to a word I say. Not since you were about thirteen did you ever listen to me. Instead of using your good sense, you had to leave the farm and go to college. You had to graduate at the top of the class. You had to come home and open up your own clinic."

"I—" Joe couldn't get more than a single word in.

"Now you're moping around town like a lost orphan over a woman who *you* let get away because you have *no* common sense."

Joe was stunned. This was hardly what he expected to hear from his father's mouth. Was he actually approving of Karen?

"Are you—" Joe couldn't finish.

"So again, I ask you, what are you doing here?" He emphasized each word of the question slowly as if talking to the hearing impaired.

"But you hate her."

"Son, you're wasting time. It takes a good hour and a half to get to the airport."

Joe rose from the table, not sure if he was actually awake at all. Perhaps he had drifted into some strange dream many hours ago, and he was actually resting peacefully in his bed.

"Joe, has God set this woman apart for you?"

The question was one that he hadn't thought about. Yet, he knew the answer right away.

"Yes."

"Then let no man put asunder." His father pointed to the key hooks on the wall. "Take my truck. It's got a full tank."

Joe had to catch his breath. "Thank you, Dad."

An hour later, Joe's mind was still reeling from their conversation. He found himself switching from gas to brake along the interstate in his father's big Chevy. The drive to the airport seemed endless, with an array of turtle-paced drivers and bumper-to-bumper early morning traffic.

Frustration and impatience weighed heavily on Joe as he glanced at the clock. Karen's flight left in twenty minutes. He could see his exit up ahead, but the traffic was at a standstill now. He tapped his hands on the wheel. Taking a deep breath, he tried to think of the words he would say. Karen's dreams of art school returned to his mind. He had a solution, though. She could attend the community college about half an hour from Mercy and get her associate's. Then she could attend the university which was also half an hour from Mercy to get an undergraduate degree in art. Sure, neither establishment was a fancy art school, but it was a good alternative.

What was he thinking? How could he be sure that his sudden confession just minutes before her flight would be well received? Certainly, if Karen truly loved him, even the best art school in the world wouldn't keep her away. This was a random art school, and Karen was leaving. Joe could feel his heart sinking.

Perhaps he ran into traffic for a reason. Maybe God wanted to prevent him from making a fool of himself.

More debate continued in Joe's mind as he recalled Karen's kiss. She had to have initiated it for a reason. Why would she kiss him if she didn't have feelings for him?

Movement on the road began to pick up again as did Joe's spirits. He knew he was doing the right thing. He even had his father's blessing, something that seemed impossible only a few hours earlier. He just had to arrive in time.

The traffic finally let up, and Joe pulled off on his exit eagerly. Much to his dismay, the parking at the airport was a nightmare. He wasted about ten minutes, finally finding a space on the top level of one of the parking decks. His hope was shattered as he looked at his wristwatch. She would leave in eight minutes.

Joe entered the crowded airport, dodging travelers and their rolling luggage in the corridor. A glowing LED board posted Karen's flight number and the words "ON SCHEDULE." Remembering the terminal number, Joe rushed down the busy throughway. He picked up his pace, jogging steadily.

Three minutes. There was still a chance. He broke out into a full run, nearly knocking over an elderly couple.

"I'm sorry!" he cried, not looking back. His tone was high-pitched, breathless.

When he finally saw Karen's terminal, his legs felt like gelatin. It had been a long time since he'd ran like that. As the waiting area came into full view, Joe saw nothing but empty chairs. All over again, he felt the deep, stunning disappointment he had felt when Karen denied him a farewell embrace. He blew it. She was gone.

* * *

The Aldridge house, in all of its Victorian grandeur, hadn't changed much in the past ten years. Karen remembered how she admired the house as a girl. One day she hoped to raise a family in a home just like it. As she walked along its driveway, she recalled the social events she had attended on the front lawn in her younger years. All of the elementary school children in town were invited there every year for an Easter egg hunt. Every Christmas, the Aldridge family hung lights and displayed elaborate lawn ornaments, including a nativity scene. She had so many fond memories of the home and its inviting front lawn. Yet, she had never set foot inside.

Now she found herself knocking on its heavy wooden door with butterflies in her stomach. She couldn't wait to surprise Joe. She only hoped that his father didn't answer. Much to her dismay, he did.

"What are *you* doin' here?" He chewed on breakfast between words. Judging from the aroma that drifted out of the house, he was having pancakes.

Karen swallowed the giant lump of fear in her throat. "I'm sorry to bother you, Mr. Aldridge. Has Joe left for the clinic yet?"

"I thought you were flying out this morning." His tone puzzled Karen since he sounded only confused, not at all offended.

"My father got a call late last night. He doesn't start his new job until Monday, so we decided to come back."

He nodded thoughtfully. "Your father is a changed man now, I hear."

She nodded. "Yes. I feel so blessed to have him back in my life."

"He was a bad drunk," Mr. Aldridge recalled aloud. "You forgave him after what happened to your mother?"

"At first, I didn't know if I ever could," she said, surprised at her willingness to open up to Joe's father. "But once you know that you're forgiven through Jesus, it's a little easier to share forgiveness with those who hurt you."

Mr. Aldridge didn't say anything for a moment, still appearing thoughtful.

"I saw that painting you did of my dad."

She held her breath, having feared his criticism the most.

He opened the front door a little wider. "Have you had breakfast?"

Karen smiled so widely that she thought perhaps her ears had been pushed to the back of her head. "Just a granola bar."

"Why don't you come in for some pancakes? Joe should be back any minute now."

Karen felt the final weight, the last one but possibly the heaviest, lift from her heart. "I would be honored, Mr. Aldridge."

The inside of the Aldridge home was even more beautiful than Karen expected with its dark, hardwood floors and muted blue and red tones throughout. Old and new family photos adorned every wall. She could hardly wait to see what lay beyond every corner. After breakfast, Eric and Mr. Aldridge headed back out to the fields while Mrs. Aldridge gave her a tour.

They were sitting down together with glasses of orange juice when Karen heard the front door open. Heavy footsteps dragged into the house slowly. Karen exchanged a smile with Mrs. Aldridge, wondering where Joe had run off to so early in the morning. Excitement rose in her as she watched the kitchen entrance.

Her first sight of Joe was startling. His polo shirt wasn't tucked in and his khakis were wrinkled as if he'd thrown on dirty clothes in a rush. She hardly recognized his pale, weary complexion, sleep-deprived eyes, and melancholy expression. However, when their eyes met, his demeanor completely changed, almost as if a lighting bolt hit him.

"Karen," he said, his eyes wide and full of life again.

Mrs. Aldridge grinned from ear to ear. "She's staying in town for a few more days, Joe. Isn't that wonderful?"

Karen couldn't stop staring at him. "Joe, are you okay? You look like the walking dead."

He smiled. "I'm great. I thought you were gone."

"My dad doesn't have to be back until Monday."

Mrs. Aldridge rose from her seat. "Well, I have some errands to run."

She hurried out of the kitchen and upstairs. Karen wondered why she rushed out so quickly, but her ponderings immediately shifted.

"I had breakfast with your family," she said, still reeling. "Your dad actually invited me!"

He nodded, one side of his lip curling. "He's forgiven you."

"I can't believe it. God's timing was sooner than I ever expected." She frowned. "Where have you been?"

"I, huh . . ."

She watched him take the chair from the head of the table and set it beside hers. He dropped down in it.

"You what?"

He was quiet, looking down at his clenched hands on the table. His eyes met hers once again, but now they held the weight of some deep emotion. She couldn't decipher it.

"I have to tell you something."

She cocked her head at him, listening intently.

"When I thought you were gone for good, I thought my life was over."

Karen lost her breath, the butterflies returning to their wild flutter in her stomach.

He swallowed. "I know you have dreams about going to art school, and I don't want to stand in the way . . ."

His voice trailed off, and his hands seemed to be shaking a little. Karen could feel her heart's pace speed up. What was he saying?

"Karen, I love you."

She drew in a gasp as the words hit her like a frigid blast of air. Did she really hear those words? The look in his eyes answered her question.

"Joe," she exhaled in a whisper.

Karen took his trembling hands into her own. Tears began to burn her eyes. "I love you too."

Her words washed away the worry and fear that was so evident on his face. Joe smiled, gripping her hands tightly.

His gentle, brown eyes held her gaze. "When we met, I just knew."

Karen reached forward and wrapped her arms around Joe's neck. He held her close. His strong arms around her made her feel safer and happier than she had ever been. She didn't want their embrace to end, but Joe slowly pulled back. She followed suit as their eyes met. He took her hands in his again.

His expression suddenly looked very serious, even fearful.

"Karen, will you marry me?"

She had fantasized about this moment for so long. Yet, she never imagined that the man asking could ever be Joseph Aldridge.

She smiled at him. "Yes."

Joe gently caressed her cheek with his hand, wiping away a stray tear. In the excitement of the moment, every word and deed was fast-paced, but right then, time slowed. They could only gaze into each other's eyes, overwhelmed by the realty of their mutual love. Finally, Joe moved in and kissed her. His warm lips felt even better than Karen remembered. She returned the kiss full force, pulling him close. Their passion for each other became evident in their long embrace.

Karen slowly pulled away from their kiss. "So where were you?"

Joe's gaze fell to the floor. "At the airport."

She shook her head at him, grinning. Caught up in the moment, she didn't know what to say. It was almost as though she were a part of one of her paintings, forever immortalized in acrylic, pastel hues. Someday she imagined painting this very scene, but for now, she would revel in it.

Joe hugged her again. "It feels so good to have you home in Mercy for good."

Karen dropped her head on his chest and closed her eyes, thinking of all the struggles God had carried her through.

Thank You, Lord, for Your mercy.

Epilogue
Two Years Later

A red, hand-painted sign graced the top of the brick building that once housed the Aldridge General Store. Now the renovated space housed the Mercy Veterinary Clinic on the first floor and The Forgiveness Art Gallery on the second. Those words, The Forgiveness Art Gallery, were painted in gold cursive across the six-foot wide new sign.

Joe stared up at it with his wife. "It looks great."

She turned to him and beamed proudly.

"Everyone's going to say 'What vet clinic?'" he joked, noting how much smaller his sign in the middle of the building's face looked under it.

Karen playfully pinched his bicep. "No one's going to forget about your clinic."

He put his arm around her waist. "They're already buying your paintings like hotcakes."

"Thank you, honey." She kissed him on the cheek.

He smiled. Each of her kisses seemed to top the last. Yet, the memory of their first kiss as man and wife floated fresh in his mind. They married in a huge, double wedding ceremony on the

Aldridge front lawn a little more than a year earlier. That day, Karen became Mrs. Joseph Aldridge, and Emily Bailey became Mrs. Eric Aldridge. It was possibly the happiest day of Joe's family history. That day was one of the greatest blessings that God could give him. Even after a year of marriage, he felt like everyday was a honeymoon, another joyful day as Karen's husband. They had so much to look forward to, including the official grand opening of her gallery on Saturday.

"I can't believe it," she whispered, looking up at the building. "It's my art gallery."

"You deserve it, Karen."

He pulled her closer to him and kissed her forehead.

"Let's go in again," she insisted like a child eager to reenter a playground.

"But we're meeting my parents for dinner in ten minutes."

Joe could see that no excuse, not even the most rational, would keep Karen away from this new embodiment of her dreams.

She tugged at his arm gently, offering puppy-dog eyes and a puckered lip. He laughed at her and surrendered with little resistance.

The pair strolled hand in hand around the building and followed an exterior brick staircase up to Karen's gallery. They passed another sign for the studio which included an angled red arrow pointing to the door at the top of the staircase. Karen planned to leave this door open during the comfortable seasons and hang a "Come On In" sign on it during the winter and summer.

She unlocked the door with her shiny, new silver key and gave it a light shove.

The gallery still smelled like fresh paint. Joe flipped the light switches beside the door, and the dark room burst to life. Overhead, studio lights popped on, shooting paths of light in every direction. The walls were the color of cocoa and lined with paintings which were alive with varying shades of the rainbow. Classical music filled the huge room at a low volume. Karen's easel, with an unfinished painting on it, sat in the middle of the gallery before a wooden stool and a small table. Their feet echoed across the brand-new hardwood floors as they examined the newly remodeled space. Karen smiled proudly, soaking in her surroundings. It had taken two years, but she knew God was going to come through for her.

She walked past an empty corner of the gallery. "We'll have to fill this space with something."

Joe put an arm around her shoulders. "There might be enough grant money left to order another desk. Who knows, you might need an assistant in here."

"I was thinking it might be a good place for a bassinet and a playpen." Karen braced herself for his reaction, unable to force back a mischievous grin.

Joe's eyes widened. "Are you—?"

He couldn't finish the question before Karen leapt into his arms, laughing. He caught her in a daze of joy and surprise.

"Can you believe it?" she squealed.

Joe's embrace tightened as he began to laugh. "We're going to be parents."

Acknowledgments

Because I have no agent, editor, or publishing staff
to thank, I would like to thank the following
hodge-podge of wonderful people:

Jesus Christ for giving me a passion for writing fiction.

My husband, Jerry, for his patience,
encouragement, and incredible cover design.

Mom and Oscar for being proud of me
when I won those writing contests as a kid.

Paul and Ty Joseph
for their friendship and prayers.

My students at Community Christian School
for being impressed when I said I wrote a book.

Anyone who has ever read my fiction
and given me positive feedback or helpful criticism.
Thank you for supporting my dream.